SURFACE TENSION

MIKE MULLIN

Tanglewood • Indianapolis

Published by Tanglewood Publishing, Inc.
© 2018 Mike Mullin

Interior Design by Amy Alick Perich

Tanglewood Publishing, Inc.
1060 N. Capitol Ave., Ste. E-395
Indianapolis, IN 46204
www.tanglewoodbooks.com

Printed in U.S.A.
10 9 8 7 6 5 4 3 2 1

ISBN 978-1-939100-16-0

Library of Congress Cataloging-in-Publication Data

Names: Mullin, Mike, author.
Title: Surface tension / Mike Mullin.
Description: Indianapolis, IN : Tanglewood, [2018] | Summary: After
  witnessing an act of domestic terrorism, Jake experiences memory loss and
  is targeted by the terrorist leader's teenage daughter, bullied by an FBI
  agent, doubted by his mother, but aided by his girlfriend, Laurissa,
  through it all.
Identifiers: LCCN 2017031728 | ISBN 9781939100160 (hardback)
Subjects: | CYAC: Terrorism--Fiction. | United States. Federal Bureau of
  Investigation--Fiction. | Memory--Fiction. | Brain--Concussion--Fiction. |
  Dating (Social customs)--Fiction. | Mothers and sons--Fiction. |
  Single-parent families--Fiction. | Mystery and detective stories.
Classification: LCC PZ7.M9196 Sur 2018 | DDC [Fic]--dc23
LC record available at https://lccn.loc.gov/2017031728

To librarians everywhere:
Lena Heck is my small homage to
the heroic work you do every day.

1

Betsy

Twenty-five minutes from now a plane will crash. I'll watch about a hundred and fifty people die. The doomed passengers have just started boarding, two gates down from where I sit, peering at them over the top of *Teen Vogue* magazine. It will take another twelve minutes to finish the boarding process. Four minutes more for the plane to push back from the gate. Seven minutes for it to taxi to the end of the runway. There's a small chance the plane will wind up behind Flight 1517 to Memphis on the taxiway—it's happened three times in the last sixty days. Add three minutes to the timeline if that happens. Ninety seconds for take-off. Another eighteen seconds until the plane reaches the perfect position in the sky.

And then Flight 117 from Indianapolis to Washington, D.C. will plummet to earth.

What will it look like? Not the fireball of a movie plane crash, I think, although the plane will be loaded with fuel. I may not see anything from my vantage point in the airport. Just a sudden descent and the sound of a low, distant thud.

The congressman closes his copy of the *Indianapolis Star* and sets it aside. He stands, entering the boarding line. He flies this route often. Sometimes he gets upgraded to first class, but today he's in coach. His frequent flier status lets him board ahead of most of the passengers. As he steps onto the jetway, I tap out a text on my phone. "Getting a bacon & egg biscuit. Want one?" The reply comes quickly, "No thx." If I'd typed sausage, it would have meant the congressman wasn't on board. If the reply had been yes, the operation would have been scrubbed.

A woman runs down the concourse, practically dragging a little girl of four or five. They're both out of breath and sweating. The little girl's hair is done up in poofy pigtails, held in place with yellow plastic barrettes that look like tiny bananas.

The barrettes remind me of my mother. She used to put my hair up like that. She used to hum or sometimes sing while she did my hair. I'd give anything to hear her sing again. I even had banana barrettes like the little girl's. What is it with banana barrettes? Does every little girl own a pair? Do they give them away at hair salons?

I sent out a silent prayer: Please don't stop at Gate 12A. The congressman deserves to die. And I've accepted the fact that there will be some collateral damage. A lot of collateral damage. But this is an early-morning flight normally frequented by businessmen, not little girls and their mothers.

They stop at Gate 12A. The mother rushes to the desk, holding out her phone. She shows it to the gate attendant, and they exchange a few words I can't hear. Then the mother shoves her phone into the outer pocket of her purse and trudges to the back of the boarding line.

I could call off the operation with a text. But later, I'd need to give a reason, and a little girl with banana barrettes isn't a reason my father will accept.

I rise from my chair, setting aside the fashion mag. There are only a few passengers waiting at this gate—14A. A few of them eye me suspiciously. A grandmotherly type gives me a kind smile. I've attracted a lot of attention, which is exactly how I want it. It's not really me they're looking at; it's my clothing. A flowing dress that covers me from wrist to ankle. A scarf wrapped tightly around my head, so nothing but the oval of my face is showing. The scarf is unfamiliar and feels confining, pressing my hair tightly against my head. I prefer to wear my hair down, free and flowing around my shoulders. My disguise probably won't help if I'm arrested, but witnesses will report that a Muslim girl was here, and the police will focus on that.

I walk slowly toward Gate 12A. I pretend I'm heading for the Starbucks just beyond the gate. The woman is clutching her little girl's hand tightly. The woman's purse is slung across her back. I pretend to trip, crashing into the woman.

"I'm so sorry, how clumsy of me," I say as I surreptitiously lift the woman's cell phone from her purse.

"Are you okay?" she asks.

"Fine. Sorry again." I clutch my hand to my stomach, bending over slightly, hiding the cell phone under the fabric that drapes off my arm. I pass her, continuing to the Starbucks.

I stand with my back to the line of passengers, shielding the cell phone with my body. I turn the phone off, wipe it with the sleeve of my dress, and then drop it into the Starbucks' trash can. I pretend to examine the cookies in the bakery case for a moment, and then make my way back to my seat at Gate 14A. I take out my boarding pass—it's a totally legit ticket for the flight to Chicago that boards an hour from now—and pretend to examine it. No matter what happens, I won't be on that flight.

A few moments later, the woman and her daughter have reached the front of the boarding line. She digs around in her purse, looking for the missing cell phone. Her movements become increasingly frantic as she searches. The gate attendant ushers her out of line, and she continues her frantic search as the other passengers board.

The gate attendant is shaking her head, trying to be sympathetic. The woman is in tears now. The gate attendant shakes her head again and shuts the door to the jetway.

I type another text into my phone. "I've got about eighteen dollars left," it says, which is perfectly true; I'm carrying eighteen bucks and some change. I don't hit send. The plane taxis out of my field of view, and I wait until I see it roar down the runway. As its wheels leave the ground, I push send. The people on that plane have a little over eighteen seconds left to live.

I rise from my chair, strolling to the women's restroom. As I reach the door, I look over my shoulder and out the huge glass windows that overlook the runways. In the distance, the plane, small enough that it looks like a toy, plummets straight down. It slowly tilts from horizontal as it falls. It disappears behind the low hill and trees past the end of the runway.

Nothing else happens. There's no noise, no shock wave, no explosion that I can detect from the airport. It's terribly anti-climactic. No one else at the airport even noticed it, as far as I can tell.

I step into a stall in the women's room and strip off my dress and headscarf. Under all that silk, I'm wearing jean shorts and a tee. I stuff the dress and scarf into my backpack and leave the restroom, sauntering down the concourse.

I reach the arrivals level outside the airport. The driver is waiting to extract me, exactly on time. As we pull away from the curb, the sirens begin to wail.

2
Jake

I'm hurting when I mount my bike. It's dark outside, about an hour before dawn. My headlight cuts a tunnel in the night, illuminating the empty pavement in front of me. I see a total of five cars on my way out of the city. I wonder who they are: drunks cast adrift by last call at the bars, overnight shift workers heading home from the FedEx hub nearby, or maybe just people like me? People driven by some compulsion to rise before dawn has even cracked its eyelids. Like I'm driven to ride. To race. To win.

There are days when cycling is pure joy, and there are days when it's nothing but molten pain. Days like today. I had to stretch for fifteen minutes before I could even swing my leg over my bike's saddle. Every muscle burns. My quads are exactly as soft and flexible as a pair of granite boulders.

I raced yesterday. Thirty laps in the Junior Division at the Indianapolis Criterium bike race. Then thirty-eight laps with the pros. Almost seventy miles with the hammer down. The juniors averaged over twenty-four miles an hour. The pros averaged almost thirty.

I won the junior race. It wasn't surprising; I won it last year, too, when I was only sixteen. Yesterday, I pulled away from the front of the pack on lap three. Zach, my teammate on the Sunday's Burgers and Fries team, cussed so loudly that the whole peloton heard him, but then he nutted up and followed me. We were half a lap ahead by the end, and placed one-two. We usually place that way in the junior races. Zach's beaten me once, in a race I let him win last season. He was so angry that he didn't speak to me for a week. I get that, respect it. He wants to beat me fair and square.

I crashed in the pro race. A hard elbow and a chuckhole sent me sliding to the pavement on lap 33. I lost some skin on my left leg—nothing serious. It probably didn't even rank in the top ten of Jake's all-time best crashes. I got back on my bike and tried to catch the pack, but it was hopeless. The race director pulled me about ten minutes after the crash, because the peloton was about to lap me. So I finished dead last. The only award I got was a cool-looking scab, where the blood on my leg had been whipped sideways by the wind and dried in a Rorschach blot of pain. Not my best race.

Today I'm riding the course I call the cornfield loop. It's an easy, mostly flat, eight-mile circuit on quiet country roads west of the Indianapolis airport. Occasionally the road dives through a wooded area—dark as fresh asphalt this early in the morning, but pleasantly shaded during the daytime. I plan to pedal three circuits today, keeping my cadence low—about seventy turns of the pedals per minute—and my speed down to a pokey twelve miles an hour or so.

On my first lap I get a surprise. One of my favorite areas on this loop is a long, tree-lined stretch. Ancient oaks, poplars, and maples tower over the road, their branches forming a leafy cathedral. It's so dark that I almost smash into the back of a parked semi-tanker truck. Half of it's on the shoulder, half protrudes onto the road. I swerve sharply, missing its back bumper by inches. It's unusual to even see a car on this tiny road. I can't recall ever seeing any kind of truck on it, let alone a parked tanker truck.

By the time I start my second lap of the cornfield loop, the kinks in my muscles have worked themselves out, and I'm feeling good. Traffic at the airport has picked up. Planes roar over my head at predictable four-and-a-half-minute intervals, so close I feel their noise in my bones, and the breath of their passage ruffles the tufts of hair that have escaped my helmet. I'm moving along smoothly, everything on automatic. I've pedaled past my pain, and I'm so much in the zone that the bike and road disappear beneath me, leaving just the wind and freedom rushing in my ears.

But mostly, I keep thinking about the pro race yesterday. The popping noise at the start of the race as sixty cyclists banged their plastic cleats against the pavement, pushing off. It sounds exactly like we're stomping on bubble wrap. I love that sound. At the beginning of a race, I'm tense, on edge, and then I hear the bubble wrap sound and I relax. I'm ready to race.

I remember Laurissa, cheering at the top of her lungs every time I shot past the start/finish line. She's been to every race I've entered since we started going out eight months ago. She usually reads between races. Not schoolwork, though—it's normally something related to politics or law. She's planning to get a political science degree and then go to law school. Yesterday she was reading *Thurgood Marshall: American Revolutionary*. She claimed it was "amazing."

Mom couldn't come to the race yesterday. It's the busy season at her job. Saturday work is mandatory, and most of the company works Sundays, too. I wish Mom could be there for me more often, but I understand.

After the race last night Laurissa took me out to Olive Garden to celebrate. Our meal—a huge plate of whole wheat pasta for me and a salad for her—was spoiled by an argument. She wants me to attend a fancy ball with her later this month, the Jack and Jill Summer Soirée, but I don't want to go. First off, her mother will be there, and her mother hates me. She's too polite to say it, but I'm pretty sure she thinks of my family as white trash. Which isn't really fair—there are lots of people way poorer than us.

Second, I don't want to spend the money to rent a tux. I'm sure Laurissa would pay for it, but . . . no.

My third problem, the real problem, is that I don't really feel comfortable with the idea that I'll probably be the only white person at the dinner. When I told Laurissa that, she flipped out. "What do you think my whole life is like?" she asked. "I'm always one of the only black people at your bike races! It wouldn't kill you to see how it feels."

She was right, I've decided. I'm going to call her later and apologize. I'll go to the dinner with her. Rent the tux. I can put up with her mother for a few hours.

I pass the wooded area and the parked tanker truck again. It's light now, and I can see four nearly identical trucks parked ahead of the first one. You'd think there'd be some activity with five tanker trucks parked, but it's eerily quiet. As I blow past them, I catch a flash of movement out of the corner of my eye. Someone moves to the far side of one of the trucks, where he's hidden from me. I shrug off the weirdness and start my last lap around the cornfield loop.

When I get back to the wooded area forty minutes later, there are tanker trucks parked on the shoulders of both sides of the road for hundreds of feet. I hear a plane approaching from behind, the roar of its engines dopplered up about an octave and growing steadily louder.

I swerve around the first parked truck, racing alongside it. I'm close enough now to see them all, eight on each side. Then something bizarre happens. The tanks split, sliding open in two halves, like monstrous clamshells. I've never seen a tanker truck open like that. It happens fast and in unison, as if all of the trucks are being controlled by one invisible hand.

I'm nearly overcome by a sulfurous odor so intense that I curl over the handlebars and retch. I don't notice the door of the tractor cab opening until it's too late. My bike's front wheel slides under the door, and I slam into it helmet first.

3

Jake

When I come to, I'm riding in the cab of a semi-truck, my body leaning against the passenger door. My head is like a five-alarm fire, and my mouth burns from stomach acid. I glance down; my bike jersey is streaked with vomit and blood.

Two men are in the cab with me, one driving and one on the bench between me and the driver. Both are white and wearing long, flowing robes and white headscarves, like you see on CNN reports from the Middle East.

"I think he's waking up," the guy sitting in the middle says to the driver. "Should I just gut him here?" He reaches into his robe and extracts a knife as long as his forearm with a hooked tip and cruel serrations along one side.

I can't move, can't even think. The blade of the knife is mesmerizing. One of the dashboard lights reflects off it—a shiny green smear.

"Don't use that," the driver says. "You want to clean this cab? Just strangle him or something."

The passenger puts the knife away, and my paralysis breaks. I lash out at the side of his head and miss completely, my fist flailing through the air in front of his nose. The sudden movement leaves me dizzy and so nauseated that I fall into the guy's lap face forward. His robes smell like cigarette smoke and whiskey.

The guy levers me up, lifting me by the back of my bike jersey. I lash out again, swinging wildly, my fist scraping the rough fabric of the seat. Most of my blows miss, and those that connect are laughably weak. But nobody in the cab of the truck is laughing.

The guy twists me around and shoves me face first into the passenger door. My forehead smacks against the window, and pieces of my broken helmet rain down around me. My vision dims to a pinpoint of light in a long, black tunnel.

Maybe I pass out briefly, because next thing I hear is the guy in the middle saying, "He's out again."

"Wait then. Easier to deal with him when we arrive," the driver says.

Arrive where? I force myself to relax, to let my eyes drift almost closed, to pretend to sleep. I'm sure the sweat pouring from my face will give me away. Why do these two want to kill me? They're dressed like foreigners, but they sound completely American. I ran into their truck door, but that's not exactly a capital offense. I can't fight them—I've proven that much. My

only hope is to fake being passed out and wait for an opportu-
nity to get away.

The passenger gives me another shove, and I try to stay
totally limp. I let my head loll to the side, coming to rest with
my right ear against the glass. "Yeah, okay." Then their conversation turns—they start talking about the Indianapolis Colts'
training camp, of all things.

I inch my right hand along the door, shielded by my body.
I can see the two men out of the corner of my left eye. I keep
it barely cracked, watching them for any reaction. I find the
door handle and clutch it. Can I jump out of the cab? The
truck is going at least sixty miles an hour. My bike helmet is
crushed, and helmet or not, falling from this truck will probably kill me. I wait.

Maybe twenty miles farther down the road, we pass an
Indiana State Trooper's patrol car parked on the shoulder,
lights flashing. I see it as we fly by, too late to even wave. Right
after we pass the car, I notice orange barrels lining the road,
and the interstate narrows to one lane. The truck shudders and
rumbles as we brake, slowing to something like twenty or
thirty miles per hour. I need to jump now, before the patrol car
is out of sight.

I yank the door handle and throw the door open. The guy
beside me shouts and reaches for me, but I'm already moving,
exploding into a leap. Too late, I notice that we're driving
alongside a temporary wall made of concrete K-rail. I barely
clear it, slam into the pavement, and pass out again.

4

Betsy

My father bought me a CPR dummy to practice committing murder. It's ironic, I suppose, but also a great idea. How're you going to know exactly how hard to press on the target's chest to kill him unless you've done it before? It's easy: about an inch to save his life, about two to snuff it out. Either way, you're going to feel and hear ribs breaking beneath your palms. It was a bit of a shock the first time the dummy made those crackling noises, but it was also a relief—I didn't know if I'd be strong enough to complete the op. It turns out that it doesn't take much strength—you just have to lean into your target and use your weight against him. Even my 125 pounds is enough.

The CPR dummy Dad bought was brand new; he said it would make the practice harder and more realistic. I've

practiced until my palms hurt and my forearms ache. Until
the motions are automatic. When it's for real, it'll be even
worse, the cracking noises even louder. My palms sweat when
I think about it—from anticipation, not fear. I'm sure of it.
I'm going to get this right. Make Dad proud.

I know Dad didn't really buy the dummy for me, at least
not with his own money. His pay wouldn't cover half our gear.
I didn't say anything, though. I decided to let him keep the lie
he tells himself—that he's the provider of all good things in
our lives. Dad doesn't remember that I've met our guardian
angel, the man who provisions my father and all his brothers-
in-arms. He came to one of the monthly pitch-ins about seven
years ago, when I was only ten. He called himself Swan,
though I doubt that's his real name.

I wipe my palms on my dress. There's a burning behind my
breastbone—my heartburn acting up again. I slide two Rolaids
out of my purse and chomp on them. They don't help. There's
no reason to be afraid. Dad and I have spent weeks fixing my
cover story. The target has been in the hospital imitating a
vegetable. Dad says he's not, though. Says he'll come around
soon. But so far, he hasn't been able to talk, giving us more
than enough time to prepare. We have a perfect set of documents, an uncrackable cover story. Even if a police officer were
to somehow walk in on me while I'm killing the target, I could
climb off him, make my excuses, and walk away scot-free.
Probably.

I'm more than ready. I've killed the dummy hundreds of
times. I can count out six minutes in my head and come
within six seconds every time. Two minutes to knock him out.
Two to kill him. Two more to be sure.

School is out, so I've been spending a lot of time online on the boards I moderate for Stormbreak. The folks on the forums are ecstatic—one less Muslim in the U.S. Congress. My best friend on the boards, Kekkek, has almost figured it out—he writes on Stormbreak that he wishes one of us had done it, had caused the crash that killed the congressman. I wish I could tell him all about it, but Dad wants it kept under wraps for now.

The National Transportation Safety Board is calling the crash "probably mechanical." They have no clue what made the plane fall so suddenly from the sky, so they're not looking for us. And we still have all the gear we used for the operation—we can do it again.

Dad says they'll figure it out, eventually. Then we'll blame the Muslim invaders. Their radical factions hate the Muslim members of Congress almost as much as we do. It's kind of like the way we feel about the moderate Republican cucks. They pretend to be conservative, but just keep voting to let more foreign hordes into the country. If we cause enough carnage, even the sheeple will rise up. Even the cucks in Congress will vote the right way. America will rally against the invaders, and we'll make our country pure again.

There's only one problem: The witness who saw our operation against Delta 117. But I've promised to solve that problem—permanently.

Dad has been spending more time with me since I agreed to do this. Maybe that's what it takes, what he has been waiting for, some sign that I'm just as committed to our cause as he is. I even got invited to the June pitch-in. I hadn't been to one in more than a year. All the guys were there, including a few new recruits I hadn't met before. Some of them brought their wives and sons. I was the only daughter. If I complete this assignment, I'll be a full member. No one, not even Dad, will ever be able to keep me away from a meeting again.

After the potato salad had spoiled in the warm June sunlight, after the guys were finished shooting the shit and staining the nearby grass with tobacco juice, about a dozen of us left the shelter at Eagle Creek Park and drove to the shooting range next door. I don't have my own gun, but Dad owns fourteen. I always borrow his old Glock 19. I love the way it feels in my hands, warm and almost alive. He upgraded to a Glock 22—it shoots forty-caliber shells—but the nine mil is enough gun for me. I grew up shooting .22 pistols; they yip like a Chihuahua, but the Glock barks like a Rottweiler.

I'm a great shot, almost as good as Dad. He won't admit it, but he knows it's true. The bull's-eyes don't lie. I wish I could use a gun for my assignment, stand eight feet away, and put a double tap into his chest, center-mass. But that would attract attention we don't want. Dad's plan is better, even though it will require me to get personal with my target. Very personal.

I snap back into the moment as the bus I'm riding pulls into sight of the hospital. My stop will be next. I stand as the door opens, holding the rail above my head. A breeze sashays through the bus, rustling the silk of the ridiculous dress I'm wearing. I can do this. I will do this. Jake Solley doesn't stand a chance.

5

Jake

There's a frog in my throat, but it's not a frog; it's a snake, and the snake is shoving itself backward into my lungs, scales rubbing and tearing until the inside of my esophagus feels raw and bloody.

A machine beside the bed wheezes, forcing air into my lungs. I exhale against it, trying to breathe out, and my entire chest erupts with pain.

A harsh beeping noise fills the air, like the fry machine at McDonald's as the potatoes go from crispy to burned black. A woman's face appears, hovering above me, her slept-on hair wreathed in harsh fluorescent light. She's old, maybe in her forties. I don't recognize her but somehow have the feeling that I should.

The thing in my throat is a plastic tube—I can see it snaking over my head. I want it out—now! I try to reach for it, grab it, rip it out, but my hands are strapped to the bedrail. I thrash but can't free myself.

The woman pushes a button on the headboard. "Calm down, honey," she says. "Relax. Help is on the way."

I want to ask who she is and why she's calling me honey, but I can't. The machine forces another breath into my lungs, and I fight it despite the pain.

The older woman reaches out, trying to take my right hand. I ball my hand up into a fist, preventing her from holding it. Her face collapses into an expression so pitifully crestfallen that I instantly feel guilty.

The pain in my chest is intense enough that my eyes tear up involuntarily, leaking down into my ears and making the room quiet and bubbly.

I need to grab onto something. I unball my fist and she seizes my right hand, gripping it like the last life ring in a drowning world. I'm struck again by the familiarity of the woman's face, the insistent thought that I should know her, know her name.

That thought leads to another one: I don't even know my own name.

A woman in red and black nurse's scrubs appears at the other side of the bed and does something to the IV bags connected to my left arm. I hadn't even noticed the IV before. Another woman in a doctor's lab coat is close on her heels.

A warmth spreads through me. I'm floating on an oversalinated ocean. My chest and throat quit hurting. Aches I hadn't been fully aware of in my head, arms, and legs fade smoothly away. The ventilator working my lungs is a breath of spring air, not an invading gust. Nothing is real—not the bed, not the tubes and machines, not even the nurse still bustling about. The only exception is the woman's hand in mine; that's solid and real.

The woman smells vaguely like caramel corn, buttery and warm. The scent calls back a memory. I see a younger version of the hand-holding woman. She was leaning against a fireplace mantel, her head turned away from me. I stepped closer and saw that she was crying quietly, her tears tracing watersheds of grief along her cheeks. Her hands clutched the mantel as though it were the only means she had to hold herself upright.

A squat urn sat on the mantel beside the woman's face, so close that it could have been a second head sprouting from her shoulders. A medal hung from the urn on a red, white, and blue ribbon. One of the woman's tears struck the brass medallion, slashing an over-bright line down its center. Beside the urn sat a small, twisted piece of white metal, one edge scorched black.

The woman ignored my approach, so engrossed in grief that she either didn't notice or couldn't acknowledge me. I stretched upward, laying one hand over the top of hers. Her fingers were icy. Her crying redoubled, and she turned her hand, clutching mine with such force her grip was almost painful.

The television at the foot of my hospital bed blares, calling me away from my memory. Half the screen shows the site of a horrific plane crash, blackened wreckage strewn throughout a partially burnt forest glade. Dozens of people in white bodysuits swarm over the wreckage, tagging pieces and loading them into a waiting semi. The other half of the screen is filled by a smiling blond. She says, "A month after the accident, investigators have still not released a statement explaining why Delta 117 crashed shortly after takeoff on June 11th. A source close to the investigation told CNN the plane likely crashed due to an as-yet-unidentified mechanical failure, rather than an act of terrorism."

The television news means nothing to me, and I'm steadily getting sleepier. As I drift back into whatever netherworld birthed me, I remember. The woman holding my hand is my mother. And I am Jake. My name is Jake.

6
Jake

The tube is gone from my throat, and I'm alone. The chair beside my bed is empty. My left arm, the one with the IV, is still strapped down, but my right arm is free.

There's a soft tapping at the closed door to the room. I try to say "come in," but my throat is raw and sore. Before I can pronounce the words, the door opens and a figure slips into the room.

My eyes feel crusty, and the light from the doorway hurts. I blink, but the figure remains fuzzy, silhouetted in the light from the hall. The door closes, and now I can tell it's a girl, maybe about my age. She's wearing a burgundy head-scarf and matching outfit. The scarf is tucked around her head, hiding her hair completely. The sleeves of her dress reach to her wrists, and her skirt brushes the floor.

"You look terrible, Jake," she says.

I manage to croak out a few words in response. "I? What? Who?"

"You don't remember me, do you?"

I think for a moment. I don't even have the flash of familiarity I had with my mother. "Should . . . I'm sorry."

"Oh, Jake, it's just terrible what happened to you." Her voice practically drips sympathy, but she doesn't come across as unhappy. She's not smiling, yet her deep brown eyes almost twinkle.

"I'm not even sure what happened. Do I know you?"

"Of course you do. I'm just devastated." She sounds anything but devastated.

"Sorry, I don't remember."

"It's okay. The nurse said you were having memory problems. It's not surprising for a guy whose skull is being held together with half a dozen stainless-steel screws."

That throws me for a loop, although it does explain the horrible headache ricocheting around my brain.

"You don't even remember my name?"

"Sorry," I say again.

"I'm Laurissa. Your girlfriend."

"Oh." I'm genuinely surprised. Her cheeks are a bronze color—deeply tanned but soft and creamy. They beg to be touched. Her lips are full and lush—I can't tear my eyes away from them. I wonder if I've kissed those lips. She said girlfriend—I must have kissed them. Why can't I remember?

"You look low, Jake." She sits on the bed and reaches for

my hand, grabbing it before I can decide whether to pull away or not. Her hand is damp and clammy, which seems strange—she doesn't look nervous.

"I'm okay," I say, although it's not really true—my head wouldn't hurt any worse if the Road Runner were running laps inside my skull, dodging anvils dropped by Wile E. Coyote.

"You want to fool around?" Laurissa scoots closer to me on the bed, her hip against mine. She's leaning down toward me, her lips hypnotic as they draw closer to my mouth.

"I don't even remember you," I say.

"So we should start getting reacquainted, right?"

I start to reply but she silences me with a kiss. Her lips are even better to kiss than I'd imagined. I must taste terrible—I can't remember the last time I brushed my teeth, can't remember ever brushing my teeth, but she either doesn't notice or doesn't care.

"We should do this right," she says when the kiss breaks. "I know what would cheer you up." She hikes her dress up to her thighs, and I see a flash of black silk. She kneels on the bed and straddles me.

Is she serious? As much as I like the idea of a gorgeous girl wanting to have sex with me, I really don't feel up to it. I point at the door with my right hand. "There's . . . are the nurses—"

"You can be quiet, right?" she whispers.

I start to reply but she kisses me again. I'm totally into it despite my headache, and my whole body stretches upward to meet hers.

She breaks the kiss and plants one hand on the center of my chest. She's frowning—maybe she did notice my undoubtedly foul breath. I try to ask what's wrong, but she's leaning on me so hard that I can't get the words out. I wait for her to let up, lean back, so I can talk. She must not realize how hard she's leaning on me. There's a muted crunching sound, and pain lances through my chest.

I reach up with my right arm to try to grab her. She bats my arm away and plants her other hand on my chest, leaning harder. Every nerve in my body is firing panicky signals. Breathe. I need to breathe.

I lash out, hitting the side of her face. She barely flinches; I'm so weak, a fly would laugh off my punch. Her face is tensed, screwed up in a mask of grim determination. I grab at her back, feel the buttons of her dress under my fingers. I grip them, trying to pull her off me. The pressure on my chest only intensifies. The edges of the room fade to gray. Soon I can see nothing but her face. Still, she doesn't let up. She's killing me. Why would my girlfriend want me dead?

Help, I try to say, but no sound emerges from my throat. Then I remember: There's a button above my head some-where. Mom pushed it to call the nurse. I reach up and grope frantically. Laurissa takes one hand off my chest and tries to grab my arm. I flail around, avoiding her.

Everything dims. The room fades toward black. I stretch— the button must be there somewhere. My fingers race along the textured wallpaper. Then, my arm bumps something—a metal box with a wire attached. I grab it, mashing the button under my palm.

Laurissa bears down harder still. I both hear and feel another rib crack. A bolt of pain strikes my chest from the inside. I'm holding the call button like a talisman. Surely someone will come?

I sag deeper into the bed, so weak that I can't even keep my grip on the button. My vision is gone. I order my hand to rise, and somehow it does, glancing off Laurissa's cheek. What I meant to be a punch turns into a gentle brush across my assassin's face.

The pressure eases from my chest, and I gasp. My chest is alight with pain, but I barely notice it next to the relief that fills me with each breath. The air tastes as sweet as cotton candy. My vision starts to clear.

Laurissa mutters, "I can't do this." I want to ask what she's talking about, but I'm still gasping too hard to speak.

Light from the hallway falls across my bed as the door opens, and another voice shouts, "What are you doing!" My head feels too heavy to move, but I manage to turn toward the voice. A burly nurse is standing opposite Laurissa, hands on her hips.

"Just, you know, improving your patient's morale," Laurissa says. She climbs off of me and stands beside the bed, smoothing her skirt down.

"He's not well enough for that kind of activity, young woman. And this is a hospital, not some sleazy motel."

I try to speak between gasps, "She . . . she—"

"Sorry," Laurissa says to the nurse. And she does sound genuinely sorry. I doubt she regrets breaking the hospital's rules, though. Laurissa flees the room while I'm still trying to gasp in enough air to explain what happened. Before I can string more than a couple of words together, the nurse does something to my IV, and I fade into la-la land.

7

Betsy

I leave the hospital at a walk, though my feet want to break into a screaming run. Why couldn't I do it? I'd killed that CPR dummy a thousand times. It wasn't lack of desire—I know exactly how badly Dad needs this guy to die. I know exactly how he's going to react to the fact that I FUBARed the mission. So why?

I stride into an alley near the hospital and jink through the back ways for a couple of blocks. My bag of normal clothes is right where I left it—tucked behind a dumpster behind a broken-down building on Illinois Street. I fumble around in the bag to find my bottle of Rolaids. I shake four tablets into my hand and toss them all into my mouth.

A couple more blocks brings me to a McDonald's. I duck inside and change in a stall in the women's bathroom. I've traded the dress and headscarf for baggy shorts and an over-sized tee. I put the high-heeled brown boots into my discard bag with a sigh—they were kicking boots, in both senses of the term. My Chuck Taylors aren't nearly as badass.

I buy a Diet Coke before I leave the McDonald's, just to make the visit look legit. I take two sips, and my stomach flops sideways. I trash the nearly full soda on my way out. A two-block walk and five-minute wait later, I'm on a bus bound for Lafayette Square Mall.

My mind returns to Jake's hospital room over and over again. I had him—he was seconds from passing out. He couldn't even fight back; he just reached up and softly ran his hand along my cheek, more of a caress than a punch. He looked bewildered and terrified. If I'd kept pushing, he probably would have died before the nurse interrupted us.

When the bus arrives, I skip the mall, walking to the nearby Goodwill Store. The sun feels great on my legs—I don't understand how Muslim girls can stand to go around covered up all the time. I don't understand why anyone would choose to be Muslim, either.

I drop off my bag of discards at the Goodwill's donation door. Obviously, I don't get a receipt. Dad told me this would be safer than dumping the clothing in a trash bin downtown. If the police get a bee in their bonnet, they'll search every dumpster in a mile-wide radius of the hospital, he said. And nobody would know better than him.

Another long bus ride with a transfer brings me to Greenwood, on the complete opposite side of the city from where Dad and I live. There's no way anyone could have followed me. If there were any pursuers, the walks, the bus rides, and the change of clothes has shaken them.

Dad's personal car—a battered white Crown Vic—is parked behind a Hardee's, exactly where he said it would be. I freeze up for a moment, standing on the sidewalk beside the restaurant and staring. But waiting here won't make anything better—won't make admitting my failure easier. I slouch across the parking lot and slide into the passenger seat beside Dad.

"You're late," he says.

"Bus was late," I reply.

Dad closes the magazine he was reading—this month's issue of *Guns and Ammo*—and tosses it into the backseat. He looks over at me, staring for a moment. "You FUBARed it, didn't you?" he asks.

Even here, with just the two of us in his own car, he's careful not to mention exactly *what* I FUBARed. The man is a machine. "I'm sorry," I say.

Dad racks the shifter into reverse and backs smoothly out of the parking space. He drives like he shoots: smooth, precise, and lethal. "What kind of shitstorm did you cause?"

"None! There won't be any blowback."

Dad signals and pulls into traffic, neatly inserting his boat of a car between a utility van and a Prius. "What happened?"

I hesitate. I should have thought of this moment, practiced for it. I want to give it to him straight, tell him I flinched at the last moment. He'd be even angrier, sure. But maybe he could help me, could diagnose the weakness that resides in my breast and cut it out. But that's not what comes out of my mouth when I finally do answer. "A nurse interrupted us."

He grunts, and we drive in silence for a few minutes.

"I want another chance," I say.

"Not going to happen," he replies. "We'll move to the backup plan."

"Dad, no! I can do this. I want to do this! Give me another chance."

"You'd screw it up again. Like you screw everything up. Besides, it's too risky. He's seen you. Keith and Joshua can take care of it."

"I just want—"

"Decision's final. Shut up."

We drive the rest of the way home in stark silence.

8

Jake

When I wake, Mom is sitting by my bedside. She's not doing anything, just staring at me, her clasped hands wringing compulsively. I'm glad to see her keeping watch, but it's also kind of creepy.

"Who was—" I'm interrupted by a coughing fit that threatens to blow off the top of my head.

Mom grabs my arm as if she's grateful for something else to do with her hands. "You're awake."

I clear my throat. "Who was that girl?"

"What girl?"

"She was here last time I was awake. Wearing a long dress and a headscarf. She climbed on top of the bed, on top of me."

Mom leans closer, concerned. "A headscarf? Like Muslim girls wear? You sure?"

"I think she might have broken my ribs."

Mom folds the bedsheet down to my waist and starts gently tugging at my hospital smock. I lift my body an inch or so to make it easier on her. My whole body hurts but it's sort of a dull, faraway pain. Muted somehow, like noises underwater. My chest doesn't feel any better or worse than the rest of me.

"She said she was my girlfriend," I say. "Said her name was Laurissa."

"Laurissa has been here almost every day," Mom says. "She's been amazing. But she's not Muslim. And she's been holding your hand and reading to you, not climbing into the bed."

"She tried to kill me."

"No. Not Laurissa. That girl loves you." Mom is minutely examining my chest. It's eggshell white, so thin that every rib is clearly visible. There's a series of yellow and green bruises all across my left side, but they're clearly old and fading. "You look okay," she says.

"I heard my ribs cracking."

Mom presses the call button. "When was this?"

"Last time I was awake."

"Laurissa was here yesterday. She told me you didn't wake up."

"I was awake."

"Zach's visited a lot, too," Mom says.

"Zach? Who's that?"

"Your best friend. And bike-racing teammate."

Someone else I have no memory of? How many strangers are going to walk into my life claiming they know me? I wish everyone would leave me alone until I'm better.

A nurse I don't recognize comes in, and Mom asks her to check my ribs. The nurse gently presses on them one by one.

"What are you doing?" I ask. "Shouldn't you scan them or something?"

"We might," she says. "Tell me what you feel."

I actually don't feel anything besides my general soreness.

The nurse calls a resident who does pretty much the exact same thing she did.

"I think you're okay, Jake," the resident says. "You're doing great. Just focus on resting and letting your body heal."

"But there was a nurse," I say. "She came in and interrupted us. She was white, kind of stocky, average height."

"That would describe about half of us," the nurse shrugs. "When was this?"

"I don't know," I say. "Last time I was awake."

"There are a lot of nurses on this ward," the nurse says. "I'll ask around."

The resident and the nurse say goodbye, and Mom rearranges my hospital gown and sheets. "Your neurosurgeon said stuff like this might happen. Your brain can do strange things after a bad injury. Create hallucinations, even. Just relax."

I stare at the ceiling tiles, trying to relax. Everything about Laurissa seemed completely real. But how would I know if she were a hallucination?

"I'm going to go down to the cafeteria and get some dinner," Mom says. "Will you be okay for a few minutes?"

I want to grab her hand and keep her here beside me. Prove that she's not a hallucination, too. But would a hallucinated mom need to eat? Maybe not. "Okay," I say.

Only a minute or two after Mom leaves, a nurse pops her head into the room. "You've got a visitor," she says.

"Who?"

She's already turning away as she answers. "Says her name's Laurissa."

9

Jake

No! I try to yell, to call the nurse back, but a croaking sound emerges from my mouth. I grab at the call button, but before I can push it, a girl steps into the doorway.

I clear my throat. "You're not..."

"Your mother said that you might not remember me," she says. I don't. She's short, curvy, and black—nothing like the girl who nearly smothered me. Her belt catches my eye—it's wide and black, and so shiny that I'm sure I could see my face in it if she were closer. She's wearing the belt high over a nearly fluorescent red dress. She's cute in a teddy-bear way— guys wouldn't follow her around with their tongues hanging out, but they might want to give her a hug. Her hair is jet-black and tightly curled. I wonder who she is. She's not the possibly-a-hallucination Laurissa, that's for sure. She's a different Laurissa? I'm confused.

I let my hand fall away from the call button. "Who?"

"I'm Laurissa, your girlfriend."

"No, you're not."

"Don't you remember *anything*?"

Can I trust her? I don't respond.

She's still standing in the doorway. "May I come in?"

The other Laurissa didn't bother to ask. "I guess."

She sits in the chair by my bed. "How are you?"

"Okay," I say. But, considering my physical state and the fact that my head is reeling from meeting another Laurissa, it's not really true. At least this Laurissa doesn't seem to want to kill me.

"You don't look so good."

"I probably look better than I feel."

"You haven't seen yourself?" She lays a hand on the bed, palm up. Her fingers brush mine, and I move my hand away. "No."

She fishes a compact out of her purse. She snaps the compact open, holds it up, and I peer into the small mirror. My hair has been mown down to a stubble. My forehead and right temple are criss-crossed with rows of stitches, Frankenstein's monster style. My face sports the faded yellow shadows of several old bruises.

"No wonder I feel so crappy," I say.

"You really don't remember me?" she asks.

"Who was that girl who came in here before?"

"What girl?"

"She said she was Laurissa." I ball the sheet up in my hands, clenching it.

"I told you, *I'm* Laurissa."

"But then who was she?"

"I don't know who you're talking about." She's taken her hand off the bed, and she's gripping the armrests of her chair.

"She dressed different from you. In a headscarf and long dress."

"Like a Muslim girl?"

"Mom said that, too. I guess so."

"I'm not Muslim."

"Yeah, Mom told me. Are you going to try to screw me to death, too?"

"Screw you?"

"Yeah, the other Laurissa—"

"I don't know any other Laurissa."

"She climbed on the bed like we were going to do it right here."

"So you don't even remember me, and you've been cheating on me?" The new Laurissa shoves herself upright. "You know I planned to apologize to you, but I'm not sure I need to."

"She almost suffocated me."

"You sure you weren't just dreaming?"

"No."

The new Laurissa starts pacing back and forth alongside the bed. "That must be it. You had some kind of wet dream or something."

I'm still not sure. My whole body hurts, and the pain makes it difficult to think. But maybe that's some after-effect of whatever put me in the hospital? What *did* put me in the hospital? I realize I still don't know. "Being suffocated wasn't really all that exciting."

"Fine. It was a nightmare, then."

Maybe she's right. "How do I know you're really Laurissa?"

"I am."

"The other Laurissa said she was, too. Said she was my girlfriend, just like you."

"I wouldn't climb on top of your hospital bed and try to have sex with you. And I don't think a Muslim girl would, either."

"That part wasn't so bad," I admit. "At least at first."

"Your wet-dream girl is a complete skank."

"Well, yeah, girls in wet dreams are skanky by definition." I can't believe I'm talking about this with a girl I don't even know. "That has nothing to do with whether you're really my girlfriend or not."

The new Laurissa stops pacing suddenly. She bends over and pulls a wallet out of her purse, sliding a driver's license free. She hands it to me. It slips through my fingers, landing by my hip. I pick it up and examine it: DAVIS, LAURISSA N. Sex F, Height 5'4", Weight 145, Eyes BRO, Hair BLA.

"So you're really Laurissa. But that doesn't mean you were my girlfriend."

She takes back her license and offers me her phone, showing me a selfie. I see an unmarked version of my own face pressed close to hers. My hair is shaggy and unkempt. We're smiling, and in the background, there are trees and grass—a park, maybe. She swipes through at least a dozen more selfies of us standing in a bookstore, eating ice-cream cones, drinking from Starbucks cups, lying in the grass, and smiling up at the sun. There's a whole series of them sitting in front of a bronze statue I don't recognize. In the first couple of pictures we're just sitting together, then hugging sideways, then laughing uproariously at God-knows-what. The last one in the series is blurry and crazily off-center, the frame containing about as much sky as it does the statue and us. Laurissa starts to swipe past it and I stop her. In the picture, my arms are wrapped around her. Her head is bent slightly back and sideways, and we're kissing in a way that ought to melt the Gorilla Glass screen right off her iPhone. One thing is clear: I loved this girl. And now I don't even know her.

After a long silence, I say, "You said something about apologizing?"

"Oh. That. It was nothing." Laurissa says.

It didn't sound like nothing when she mentioned it earlier. "I want to know."

"We had a huge fight the night before your accident. I just didn't want that to be the last..." Her voice cracks and she's silent for a moment. I kind of want to take her hand, but I don't. "You know, I was afraid you'd never wake up. That I'd never get the chance to say I'm sorry."

She's staring at me in a way that makes me uncomfortable. Am I supposed to say I'm sorry, too? When I can't even remember her? "I don't remember the argument," I say.

"I figured. It really was nothing. I wanted you to come to a fancy scholarship dinner with me, but you didn't want to go. It's over now. The dinner was last week."

"How was it?"

"I didn't go. I was here. With you."

"Mom said you've been here almost every day. Guess I slept through it."

"You know, getting your head bashed in was a ridiculously

extreme way to get out of the dinner." She grins at me, but her eyes are sad.

"Yeah. Sorry about that. I'd rather be pretty much anywhere than this hospital."

"I'm just grateful you survived."

There's another long silence. Her fingers brush my hand again, and instead of moving away, I rest my fingertips against hers. Her fingers are freezing. I clasp her hand in mine, trying to lend her some of my warmth. A question keeps ricocheting through my brain. Without really meaning to, I say it out loud. "So who was the other Laurissa?"

"A figment of your perverted imagination," this Laurissa responds.

"I guess you're right."

Later that night, as I drift off to sleep, I worry. What if the new Laurissa is right, and the Fake Laurissa was just a fever dream? It felt so real. Can a guy who has had his head bashed in trust anything he remembers?

10

Jake

Mom is sitting by my bed when I wake. She's holding a closed book, her finger in the middle to keep her place.

"What're you reading?" I ask.

"A book about brain injuries." She holds the book so I can see the cover. The letters on the cover swim around fuzzily.

"I . . . I can't—"

"I'm sorry, honey. Dr. Malhotra said you might have trouble reading for a while. Don't worry, it'll come back." She flips the book around and reads the title. "*Cracked: Recovering After Traumatic Brain Injury.*"

"So am I going to recover or stay cracked?" I ask, but I'm not sure I want to hear the answer.

"Most people recover. It can take some time, but we've got plenty."

Mom's wearing a silver necklace with a captain's wheel pendant. It looks kind of like a bicycle wheel, and as soon as I start thinking about bikes, another memory returns.

When I was in fourth grade, I attended a crazy Montessori school where we could plan "special projects"—basically do whatever we wanted so long as it was remotely educational. Mom loved this old movie about bicycle racing—*Breaking Away*—and after we watched it together, I decided to organize a race of my own.

The school was in a huge old mansion nestled in a wood. The driveway looped through the trees and past the school. It was poorly maintained, full of chuck holes and patches.

I tried to talk Mrs. Rittman, my teacher, into a 500-lap race in honor of the Indy 500, but she thought that would take too long and insisted that ten laps would be enough. We compromised at twenty.

Five teams of four kids entered the race. I badgered the kids on my team into practicing after school every day. Mostly we practiced the hand-offs—jumping off the bike and running alongside while passing it to the next rider.

It turned out that the hand-offs were the most difficult part of the bike race. Every other team bungled at least one of the them—bikes flew away, riderless, and some teams had to come to a complete stop to trade, wasting all kinds of time.

Well, avoiding the massive chuck-hole just past turn two was important, too. One girl hit it so hard that she crashed. She wasn't hurt, but the front wheel of her team's bike was mangled, and they had to drop out.

We lapped every other team—some of them more than once. As I rode through the finish line, a gaggle of girls cheered.

Just the memory of it makes me happy.

Mom's voice breaks into my reverie, "You zoned out again."

"Oh. Sorry."

"Don't worry about it. It's normal." Mom gestures with her brain injury book and then sets it down on the side table.

"It's frustrating. I don't even know who I am! How old am I? What was I like?" I grip the rail of the bed as if I could crush it.

"Calm down, Jake. Where do I start? You're seventeen. You go to Ben Davis, a high school not far from our home. You're a good student, at least when you bother to make an effort." Mom puts her hand over mine.

"I want to know. Want to remember. Everything." I grab her hand, holding on as if it were the key to all my lost memories.

"Give it time. It'll come back."

"I did remember something. Or imagined it. I don't know for sure."

"You were smiling. Something good?"

"A bike race at my elementary school."

Mom smiles. "You practiced for that crazy race for weeks. Not that you needed to—you were the only one who took it seriously."

"I wanted to be a Cutter so bad."

Mom laughs and sits down in her chair by my bedside. "I haven't seen that movie in forever. And I hope you'll go to college, not cut blocks in a limestone quarry."

There's a long silence before I speak again. "What happened? Why am I here?"

"You may never remember that part. The traumatic episode is usually the last memory to return and often never comes back."

She sounds like she's quoting her book, which annoys me somehow. "But what happened to me?"

Mom moves her book and sits down, still clenching my hand. "A construction worker found you. Near Cloverdale on I-70, lying inside a low wall made of concrete k-rail. He thought you were dead at first. Nobody knows how you got there, and your bike still hasn't been found."

"I don't think I'd ride on the interstate."

"You wouldn't."

"So what was I doing on I-70?"

"Nobody knows. Even the FBI doesn't know."

"The FBI? What do they have to do with it?"

"There was a plane crash the same day as your accident. An agent came by while you were still out of it. He said he was checking on people admitted to the hospital that day."

"An FBI agent?" My life continues to get weirder and weirder.

"Yeah, Agent Soufan—he gave me his card. He didn't think your accident was related to the crash. He was a really nice guy, though. Told me about his kids. He's got a son about your age. He said he'd pray for your recovery."

"You said something about my bike?" I say. "I remember the cheap Huffy I rode in the race at school."

"I dug your dad's bike out of the back of the garage and gave it to you not long after that race. It was way too big for you back then."

"I don't remember Dad's bike." I don't even remember Dad. Why isn't he here?

"I gave you a box of his old training logs and race results, too. You used to spend hours poring over those things."

"He raced?"

"He'd quit by the time you were born. He was an airline pilot. He wanted to spend the time he wasn't flying with us, not out on his bike."

"I don't remember him at all," I say.

"You were only six when he died," Mom says. "I'm not surprised you don't remember."

"I remembered something else yesterday: You were standing by a fireplace crying, resting your head beside an urn."

Mom looks away briefly. "Yes. That happens sometimes. I feel close to him in our living room. Like he's watching me."

I wish I could remember him, but then I realize I do, vaguely. I remember a man in a white, short-sleeved shirt, a pilot's uniform, picking me up and swinging me around and around while I cackled with glee. He was a lot older than Mom, his hair shot with gray.

"What happened?" I ask.

"Plane crash." Mom looks away.

"You don't have to talk about it. It's okay," I say.

"Your dad was on a Seattle-Seoul route, over Alaska. He flew into an ash cloud. Some obscure volcano in the Aleutians had erupted earlier that day."

"Why'd he fly into the cloud?"

"He couldn't see it. Up high, the ash can be almost invisible at night. Geologists have been telling the airlines to install ash detectors on their planes forever. But they don't. It would cost too much, they say.

"He lost all four engines. Somehow, he got the plane

turned around and dead-sticked it out of the ash cloud. Only one engine came back up. He crashed on a little road outside of Dillingham, Alaska—slid into a cliff nearly head-on. Almost everyone in coach survived. The pilots and first class weren't so lucky."

My dad was a hero? Somehow it feels right, like something I'd known all along. When I picture him, it brings up a sense of longing, a dull ache of loss, but also intense pride. "So that urn on the mantel...?"

"Some of the ashes from the crash. Maybe his."

"And that bent piece of metal?"

"Part of the plane."

"That's kind of macabre, Mom."

"Maybe so," she says, dropping my hand. "But I like the reminder. Your father was the best man I ever knew."

11

Betsy

When I'm feeling down, I think about my mother. Why did she leave? Where is she now? Why doesn't she ever try to contact me? I've asked Dad to try to find her—with his resources, it'd be easy—but he won't. He says Mom made up her own mind, and she'll get in touch with us if anything changes. When he's in a bad mood, he says she left because of me, and I'm lucky he doesn't leave, too.

I don't even remember Mom's face clearly. I only have a vague impression of a dark-haired woman with brown eyes so large you could get lost in them. Her hugs, however, I remember as clearly now as the last time I got one, about seven years ago.

Some boy in my fifth-grade class decided that the best way to tease the quiet girl who sat in front of him was to press his gum into her hair. So I turned around and slugged him. It was a perfect right cross—he fell out of his chair, clutching a bloody ear. I was a bit surprised he wasn't knocked unconscious. When Dad taught me to punch, we practiced aiming for the knock-out-spot, right at the hinge of the jaw, where it meets the ear. I thought I'd hit it perfectly.

Of course, I wound up visiting the assistant principal. Apparently, there are rules about punching asshats in school. Mom had to pick me up—my three-day suspension began *immediately*.

Dad laughed when he heard the story—one of the few times I remember him smiling. Mom hugged me, saying, "Oh, honey, violence isn't the answer." I clung to her, eyes closed. Wrapped up in her hugs, I always felt profoundly safe, even when she was upset with me. When I opened my eyes that day, though, the feeling of safety vanished. Mom and Dad were glowering at each other over my shoulder. She left about two weeks later.

I've looked for Mom on my own, but I only have access to the public Internet databases. As far as those are concerned, she may as well have leaped into a hole in the ground seven years ago. There's nothing. Dad says it's not hard to disappear, that people do it all the time. I just wish Mom would write me a note, maybe open a throw-away messaging account and send me a text. It's not easy growing up with a memory instead of a mother.

I told Kekkek about it once, in a WhatsApp chat. He said that might be why I'm such a good moderator on Stormbreak, because I'm trying to be a mother to all the forum members. Maybe he's right.

Today, I know exactly why I'm feeling down. Dad assigned me to help Keith and Joshua practice the op he planned. As if my failure weren't punishment enough, now I have to work with the idiots who'll replace me. At least Dad believes my excuse—that the nurse walked in on us. If I told him the truth, I'm sure I'd be shut out of the group forever. Some part of me still wants to tell Dad the truth, to tell him that I had Jake Solley's life under my palms, but I couldn't keep pushing. Wanting to tell Dad is like standing on the shoulder of a busy road and listening to the tiny voice inside that encourages you to step into the rushing traffic, to test God and see how much He values your life. But I know I'd really only be demonstrating how little I value my own life.

Keith and Joshua are dumbasses, and they're taking the job that's rightfully mine. The job that—if I finished it—would earn me full membership in The Sons of Paine. They'd have to change the name. The Sons and Daughter of Paine has a nice ring to it.

I'm pretending to be Jake. We've got the hospital room mocked up in a hunting cabin outside Richmond, Indiana. Others have scouted the hospital and secured the blueprints that are currently scattered across the table on one side of the cabin. We know exactly how many nurses, security guards, doctors, and other staff members can be expected at each point of the route in and out of the hospital at any given time of day or night. Dozens of people have been working nonstop for the last twenty-four hours getting this set up. Someone else will light the fire that sets our plan in motion, but Dad chose Dumb and Dumber to actually pull the trigger.

I get why he chose them—Jake's already seen them. They plucked him off the road and threw him in their truck on the day of the operation, and they let him escape. If they fail or something goes wrong, no one else in the organization is exposed. Of course, Jake's seen me, too; the same logic would apply to having me do the job. And maybe I could stand off with a pistol and shoot him. Surely that would be easier than crushing the air out of him while his body squirms beneath me, between my legs. While his hand brushes gently across my cheek.

I'm lying in our mock-up hospital bed wearing a chest protector and helmet. Keith and Joshua are using Airsoft guns, but those pellets *hurt* at close range. I can feel the welts rising on my chest, rows of them between my breasts, and we're less than halfway through our planned day-long practice session.

My attackers insist on shooting me from far too close. Time after time, they march right up to the bed, aim, and fire point-blank. If I've told them once, I've told them a thousand times: Shoot from about eight feet. Any closer and Jake might be able to knock their guns away. Any farther and these slug brains will miss. I suspect they enjoy seeing me wince in pain as the Airsoft pellets slap into my chest protector. Joshua in particular has his reasons for being angry at me, but that's no excuse for his sadism.

They approach again, shoulder to shoulder. They stop, too close again, holding out their guns. I've had enough of this crap. I grab Joshua's gun and swivel, lifting my left leg off the bed and wrapping it around his arm. I twist so that I've got him in an arm bar and tighten down. It's a simple self-defense move—Dad taught it to me for the first time when I was a kindergartner, and we've practiced it from time to time since. There's a crack, and Joshua's hand goes slack. I half hope that I've broken his elbow. I grab the gun and reverse it, putting a double tap into Keith's chest. Even though he's wearing a heavy firefighter's overcoat, he yelps. I kick Joshua in the chest, knocking him on his ass. Instead of launching some kind of counterattack, he sits on the floor rubbing his arm. I put a double tap on his center-mass too. Maybe that'll teach him something, though I doubt it.

"This," I yell, shooting Keith again, "is why," I shoot Joshua, "you should always," I shoot Keith, "stay at least eight feet away from your target." I continue shooting them until the magazine runs dry. They scramble around the room, trying to dodge and reach the door at the same time, but they only succeeded in running into each other. Keith, instead of returning fire, has dropped his pistol. Like I mentioned before, when God was handing out brains, these guys were last in line.

They want to quit for the day. I tell them to quit being wusses and get back to work. For some reason they agree, although they grumble about it plenty. I run them through the drill six more times. They never come closer than eight feet again. The pellets don't hurt nearly as much from that range. Joshua complains incessantly about his sore elbow, but he's managing to shoot just fine, so I don't care. Once I'm satisfied that they've got it, I suggest that they spend some time studying with their Berlitz Arabic tapes. It's part of their cover. If something goes wrong—say, the fire gets out of control and dozens die—we'll see that the Muslims get the blame. There's a war coming between us and them, and anything we can do to wake the sheeple is worth it.

But I'd prefer it if everything went according to plan. We need an easier, less obvious way to kill Jake. I spend some time searching the Internet on my phone and come up with something that might work. It's so simple that even Keith and Joshua might be able to handle it. If it fails, they'll still have their guns for backup. I call them over to try to sell them on my idea. They agree right away. They seem a little bit scared of me now; I don't mind that in the least.

I wish I could say that I'm confident, that Jake is a goner. But honestly, if we get through this op without a massive screw-up, I'll be shocked.

12

Jake

The next time I wake, Mom is sitting on my bed, next to me. She's saying something softly, but I can't make it out and have to ask her to repeat it.

"Zach's here," she says. "You feel up to seeing him?"

"You told me I rode with him?"

"He's your best friend. And racing buddy. You train together on weekends, sometimes, and go to all the same races."

I don't feel great, but I'm curious to "meet" this Zach. "Sure. Send him in."

Mom leaves briefly and ushers in a short, rail-thin guy with a frizz of reddish hair curled atop his head.

"Dude," he says as he approaches the bed, "you look like shit."

57

Mom glares at him.

"Well, let's crack your head open and see what you look like when we're done," I shoot back.

Zach holds out his hand and I grab it, clasping thumbs. "Maybe we could skip that. You know, just say we did. You don't want to see my butt-ugly brain anyway, do you?"

"Not in the least."

"Is it true? That you can't remember shit?"

Mom sighs and rolls her eyes at Zach.

"Yeah, it's true," I say.

"So you can't even remember how I've smoked your ass in every race this season?"

I glance at Mom. She's shaking her head.

"My brain is so scrambled that I can't remember stuff that never happened," I say.

"Hope you're out of here soon. I want another chance to try to beat you."

"Me, too. I mean, I want to get out of here. Beating me? That's just crazy talk." I don't really believe what I'm saying—I'm pretty sure I couldn't even ride a bike right now, let alone race one. But the banter seems to come naturally with Zach. Maybe at some level, I remember more than I think I do.

"Hey," Zach says, "I tried to cancel your race entries for the rest of the season, you know, to get the entry money back, but none of the a-hole directors will give refunds."

I shrug. It hadn't even occurred to me.

"So would you be okay if Bulb raced on the team, used your entry fees?"

I'm not sure who he's talking about. I hope Bulb is just a nickname—surely no one has parents who'd pick a name that ridiculous. If so, they ought to be sued for parental malpractice. In any case, I don't care about a racing season that I can't remember. "Sure."

"Cool. It's a shame, man. You were tearing it up. You might have made Cat 2 this year."

I wonder what Cat 2 means and decide I don't care. "Maybe next year."

We talk for a few more minutes before Zach says he has to go. "I almost forgot. Brought you a present." He pulls an air freshener out of his pocket—one of the stupid Christmas tree shaped chunks of cardboard people hang from their rearview mirrors.

"Um, thanks?"

"Sure thing. It's so it won't smell like hospital in here. I hate that smell." Zach leaves, and I sag back into the pillow, exhausted from the effort of talking to him.

The air freshener reeks of chemicals, like Pine-Sol. It reminds me of the Christmas after my fourth-grade bike race. I'd read on the Internet about a bike computer that would track your speed, display your power output in watts, and record training rides. I wanted one for my Dad's bike. It was the only thing I asked for that Christmas. I got one, too. I started riding everywhere. My mother set strict rules—I was supposed to stay in the neighborhood. About the time I turned twelve, I started ignoring her rules, biking all over Indianapolis. By the time I turned thirteen, she'd given up trying to enforce the rules. On weekends, I'd often ride a hundred miles or more, visiting nearby towns—Lebanon, Muncie, Danville, and others.

I started riding my bike to school nearly every day, too. I wore a rain slicker with a hood when I had to. I mean, I didn't exactly like riding when conditions were terrible. But the harder the training, the easier the race. And road cyclists don't get some kind of air-conditioned stadium to compete in. We ride no matter how bad the weather is.

Another memory returns. I was riding my bike to school—I must have been a freshman. The rain was pelting down. I had cinched the hood of my yellow rain poncho tight around my face, but I was still drenched.

I realized that I'd missed the stop sign after I was already in the middle of the intersection. Something struck my right leg, and suddenly I was on top of a car hood, arms splayed, staring at the startled driver through the windshield. The car was maroon, and the hood felt massive, as if there were a whole acre of sheet metal around me. The driver slammed on the brakes and I flew off, the pavement rushing to meet me.

"Shh, honey, it's okay," Mom says. "You're okay." She's next to my bed now, holding my hand. Zach's gone, and the hospital room is dark except for a reading light above Mom's chair. Her book is open and face down at the edge of the bed. She's almost finished with it. Her eyes look droopy and dark.

"Sorry," I say as my panicked breathing and hammering heart start to return to something like normal. "Just a bad memory. Or dream, or something."

"It's okay. Your brain uses dreams to process memory. You can tell me about it if you want."

I tell her about my memory of the bike wreck.

"That did happen. You weren't hurt badly—a bunch of bruises and scrapes on your legs and hands. Your bike was a mess—it took you two days to fix it. By day three you were out riding again, never mind that your poor mother was scared out of her wits."

"Sorry," I say, although it occurs to me that it's kind of ridiculous to apologize for something that I did years ago and barely remember.

"The worst part was getting the call from the police saying that you'd been in an accident. I thought about banning you from riding, but I knew I wouldn't be able to stop you. You loved it too much to quit. But now, I wish I had."

"You're right. I wouldn't have quit. Half the stuff I'm remembering is about my bike. It's in my blood."

"I know."

"What was that stuff Zach was saying?" I ask. "About racing and Cat 2?"

"You're a Category 3 rider. Which means you can race with the pros in some of the small races. You almost had enough points to move up to Category 2. Probably would have made it this year if you hadn't—"

"What does it matter?"

"If you kept racing well, you might have gotten some attention from USA Cycling. Maybe gotten a scholarship to train at their training camp in Belgium. That's what you wanted. I was hoping you'd get a college scholarship. And you were thinking about a couple of college cycling programs— Brevard in North Carolina and Marian here in town."

"Maybe next year," I say. But I'm wondering if I'll ever make it. If I'll ever recover enough to compete again.

"I hoped you'd pick Marian. Hoped they'd give you a scholarship. Belgium seems impossibly far away. If I were a better mother, I guess I'd wish for you to get your top choice, to get chosen for the USA Cycling Development Team."

"Mom! Of all my mothers, I'm pretty sure you're the best."

"Thanks . . . I think. I love you, Jake. Never doubt that, problems or not. I'll always be here for you."

"I love you too, Mom."

13

Jake

When Mom wakes me, it's early in the afternoon. I can tell from the window in my room—it faces east, so it's always in shadow around that time. "I've got to go to work for a while, honey," she says. "I'm afraid I'll get fired if I get much further behind."

"Uh, okay." Her job must be pretty crappy if she might get fired for taking care of her brain-damaged son.

"Laurissa's going to sit with you while I'm gone."

I'm instantly on alert. "Which one?" I ask.

"What do you mean?"

Mom has pretty much forgotten about Fake Laurissa. She's convinced that I hallucinated the whole thing. Anyway, she's already got her purse on her shoulder, and she's headed for the door. Maybe now's not the best time. "Never mind," I say.

"Love you," she says as she hurries out.

I'm relieved to see real Laurissa appear in the doorway. "Hey," she says. "Can I come in?"

"Sure." I gesture at the chair beside my bed.

"Your mom was sure in a hurry," she says as she sits down.

"She's afraid she's going to get fired. I can't even remember what she does."

"Production planning for Spectrum Insecticides," Laurissa says.

"Must be a completely crappy job," I say.

"I guess. If she does get fired, I'll talk my dad into giving her an interview."

"What's your dad do?" I ask.

"Owns a couple of restaurants. I brought you something." Laurissa reaches into her shiny black purse and pulls out an iPod, a charging cord, and a set of earbuds.

"What's that for?"

"Your mom told me you were having trouble reading, so I loaded my old iPod with some audiobooks for you. You've got the whole *Beka Cooper* trilogy—it's set in the same world as the *Trickster* books, but two hundred years earlier. You loved the *Trickster* books."

"Wow. Thanks. I don't remember them."

"They're by Tamora Pierce. I bought you *Trickster's Choice* on our first date."

"You could have given me that again; I wouldn't have known the difference." I laugh. "If my brain never gets better, I'll be able to listen to all my favorite books for the first time again."

"It'll get better. Give it time."

"I'm sorry I don't remember . . . more."

"The important thing is that you're okay," she says. "What do you remember?"

"Every now and then, I get a bit more back. I just . . . don't have any memories of you."

"Hey, it's all right," Laurissa grabs my hand. "It will come back."

Her hand is warm and soft. I want to grab onto it with both hands, to touch the back of her hand, her wrist, her arm. But I'm afraid that might seem creepy. "When did we meet? And how?"

"At a basketball game. About nine months ago. Your school was completely creaming mine."

"Where do you go?"

"Park Tudor." Laurissa's nose wrinkles. "Do you smell smoke?"

Now that she mentions it, I do. While I'm sniffing the air, an alarm sounds. A voice comes over the loudspeaker, "Code Red, Code Red. Evacuate Annex B immediately."

"Is that us? What do we do?" I say.

"I have no idea."

I reach up and push the call button. We wait for a moment, but nobody comes.

"I'll go see if I can find someone," Laurissa says.

As she gets up, two firefighters tromp into the room. They're in full gear: boots, pants, coats, and helmets adorned with reflectorized yellow tape. "We're here to prep you for transport, Mr. Solley."

How does he know my name? He didn't even look at my chart. "I think I can walk." I start to sit up, but the IV tugs painfully at my arm.

"Just lay back and relax. This'll only take a moment," the closest firefighter says.

"What's going on?" Laurissa asks.

"Fire at the other end of the hall. We're evacuating this wing as a precaution." The firefighter extracts a massive syringe from the pocket of his fire coat and tries to slide the needle into my IV tube. He misses, nicks his own finger, and curses as a drop of blood wells.

"What are you injecting me with?" I say.

"Just a sedative." He stabs at the IV line again.

"No," I say. "I want to be alert."

The firefighter finally gets the needle inserted into the IV tube.

Laurissa grabs the syringe, preventing him from pushing down the plunger. "Didn't you hear him? He doesn't want a sedative. And did I just see you using a needle contaminated with your own blood? That's disgusting. And unsafe."

The smell of smoke is getting stronger. The second firefighter, who's been silent until now, says something fast in a foreign language. It sounds vaguely Middle Eastern.

"What are you saying?" Laurissa asks. The first firefighter lets go of the syringe, and Laurissa pulls it out of my IV line. "This is empty! What are you trying to do, kill him?" Laurissa is in his face, yelling at him, even though she's almost a foot shorter than he is. She doesn't see the guy behind her, who reaches into his firefighter's jacket, withdraws a ridiculously long pistol, and aims it at the back of Laurissa's head.

14

Jake

I grab Laurissa's arm and yank as hard as I can. She falls on top of me in the bed. The gun fires twice in quick succession, making a pair of surprisingly soft pops. A puff of smoke or steam fills the space Laurissa's head had just vacated. The other firefighter was standing in front of Laurissa—he stumbles back a half step as if someone had just punched him in the shoulder.

"Jesus's teeth, Keith, what'd you do that for?" The first firefighter yells. He's clutching his arm and blood is welling around his fingers.

"OPSEC," the guy with the gun, Keith, growls.

"Hell with OPSEC, you freaking shot me!"

"I'm sorry! What more do you want? I can't unshoot you. Can we finish the job?" Keith says.

The first guy inspects his arm, pulling at the bloody rubberized material of the sleeve. I glance around wildly—there's nowhere to run. They're between us and the door. I mash the call button under my hand, but I don't hold out much hope.

"It's just a graze," the first firefighter says.

"So we can get on with it?" Keith asks.

The first guy shrugs with one shoulder and reaches into his jacket, pulling out a pistol that's a clone of Keith's. I realize that it's a small gun with a silencer attached, not some kind of weapon with an insanely long barrel. They swivel toward us. I grab Laurissa and roll, throwing us both off the far side of the bed. My IV rips out, but I barely have time to notice the pain before I hit the floor and my chest and head spike with agony so intense I nearly pass out.

I hear four quick pops as both firefighters shoot at us. I can see their legs, spread wide in shooting stances, through the metal framework of the bed. Tufts of shredded mattress float through the air above me. I try to shove the bed into them, but the wheels are locked. They start to walk around.

I feel like vomiting. We're trapped—I can't get under the bed and the window doesn't open.

I reach upward and grab some wires and tubes connected to the back of one of the machines by my bed. I yank as hard as I can. The wires rip free, and a loud alarm starts wailing.

A pair of shiny black boots and blue trousers appear in the doorway. "Thought you guys cleared this floor already?" a new voice says.

The firefighters had just rounded the corner of the bed. Now they tuck their guns out of sight under their jackets and rush to the doorway.

Laurissa clambers off me, and I pull myself up to peek over the bed. There's a police officer standing in the doorway. Keith says, "We're just clearing the last patients now," while the first firefighter, shielded by Keith's body, raises his gun. A trickle of blood drips from his arm, splattering against the floor.

Laurissa runs *toward* the door, which seems insanely brave to me. I'm terrified, and all I'm doing is peeking over the top of the bed. Laurissa yells, "They've got guns!"

The first firefighter levels his pistol, aiming over Keith's shoulder, and pulls the trigger twice. The policeman lurches backward as two bloody dots bloom on his forehead. Laurissa bowls into the back of the shooter, and he stumbles into Keith, driving them both into the hallway. Laurissa slams the door on them.

"Son of a Balrog!" she yells. "There's no lock!"

I get up and start working my way around the bed to grab the chair. Maybe we can wedge that under the doorknob. But Laurissa has already figured out something better. She takes off one of her shoes—some kind of fancy leather things with pointed toes—and shoves it under the door. Someone slams into the door from outside, and it opens an inch or so before it jams on the heel of her shoe. She slips her other shoe off and kicks it into place alongside the first.

I hear the pops of more silenced shots and a series of thunks as bullets hit the outside of the door. It's a solid oak door, though—nothing gets through.

I feel like a balloon stretched to the point of bursting. One puff of air is all it would take for me to explode. "Why are they shooting at us?"

"We've got to get out of here," Laurissa says.

"How? We're trapped, and the hospital is on fire."

"Stand back." Laurissa picks up the chair and hurls it, two-handed, over the bed and directly at the window. The glass explodes outward, shattering into hundreds of tinkling shards, and the chair flies out into the street below us. The noise from outside instantly redoubles; I hear sirens and men shouting.

Laurissa tosses me a pillow. "Use this to protect your hand. Clear the glass." Something thuds against the door so hard that the whole wall rattles. Laurissa starts stripping the sheets off the bed.

I wrap the thin pillow around my hand, clutching it to keep it in place. I punch at one of the jagged shards of glass still clinging to the window frame. It snaps off, flying into the street two stories below me. There are firefighters and trucks everywhere. A couple of the firefighters are pointing at me and yelling.

I realize I'm almost naked—wearing a blue hospital smock that inevitably leaves my butt hanging out in the breeze. My arm is bleeding where the IV ripped out; blood runs down my forearm, leaving livid red streaks on the pillow. As I finish clearing the glass, several of the fire trucks start moving. "It looks like they're trying to bring a ladder truck over here."

"Crap!" Laurissa has tied all the sheets together, forming a long rope. She's tying one end of the rope to the bed.

"A ladder will be way easier than that rope."

"The guys outside the door, trying to kill us?" Laurissa says. "They're firefighters."

There must be fifty or more firefighters running around beneath us. They can't all want to kill us, can they? Laurissa tosses the other end of her makeshift rope through the window. It doesn't quite reach the ground.

"Come on!" Laurissa is straddling the window, one leg dangling outside. Her purse is slung across her back like a messenger bag. She gets me to sit in her lap, which protects my butt from the fragments of glass littering the window frame. We both clutch the bedsheet, Laurissa's arms wrapped around my body.

We swing our legs through the window and fall together.

15
Jake

The makeshift rope snaps taut. My knuckles scrape painfully against the brick wall. We're still falling, but slowly. I hear the hospital bed above us dragging across the floor. It hits the window, and we slam to a sudden stop, dangling halfway between the window and the ground.

Both of us are clutching the rope. Laurissa has her legs wrapped up in it somehow, so she's supporting most of our weight—I'm still more or less sitting in her lap. We move slowly down the rope, hand over hand. I glance down—the rope reaches the ground now. There's a firefighter waiting for us at the bottom, his arms outstretched. Paramedics are running toward us, carrying a stretcher.

We work our way down the last few feet of the rope into the arms of the waiting firefighter. "Might have been safer to wait for the ladder truck," he says.

Laurissa swivels and knees him in the groin.

He doubles over, moaning in pain. Laurissa takes my hand, and we run. We dart across the street, leaping over hoses that seem to be strung everywhere. The paramedics are yelling at us, and a couple of police officers are running our way. Something stabs into my bare foot. I grit my teeth and keep running. My head swims and I stumble. The only thing keeping me going in a straight line, keeping me running at all, is Laurissa's hand clutched in mine.

We duck into a narrow alley between a parking garage and a medical building. We're halfway down the alley before I hear footsteps behind us. My foot hurts, but I barely feel it. Zach told me that part of the reason I was a good bike racer was my capacity for suffering. Maybe he was right, although I doubt I ever got splinters of glass shoved into my bare feet while bike racing.

We turn twice, sticking to alleyways, trying to lose our pursuers. Laurissa is faster than I am, despite her shorter legs. She's towing me along, urging me to run faster. We duck into another alley and then into an alcove that shelters a door. Laurissa tries it—locked, of course. We flatten ourselves against the door and listen while our pursuers rush past the mouth of the alley.

After a minute or two, my breathing starts to calm and the sounds of pursuit fade. I check my foot—it's bleeding, but the cut doesn't look deep.

"My car's in that garage we passed," Laurissa says. "Wait here—I'll go get it."

"Why don't I come with you?"

"A guy running around with his butt hanging out of a hospital smock is kind of obvious, don't you think?"

"Oh. Yeah."

"Not that I mind. You're not exactly hard on the eyes."

"Thanks?" I shrug. I still don't have any memories of her. I wish I did. What she did—saving both our lives—was nothing short of amazing. I try to tell her so. "You're . . . that was—"

"Never mind. We can talk about it later. I'll pull up at the mouth of the alley. Blue Prius. Five minutes. Okay?"

I nod. She stretches onto her tiptoes and kisses me. And then she's gone, running down the alley away from me.

I want to call her back, to hold on to her and kiss her again, but this isn't the best time. Instead, I wait anxiously, keeping my weight on my good foot and leaning against the metal door. Why would I be a target?

My head reels, and I lean more heavily against the door. My hands tremble at my sides, jangly nerves from the aftermath of my adrenaline-fueled flight from the hospital. I want to slump to the asphalt and close my eyes.

A blue Prius pulls up at the end of the alley. The passenger door pops open. Laurissa whispers just loud enough to carry, "Get in. Let's go. Go, go, go!" I look both ways—the alley is empty. I limp to the car and slide in next to her. "I'll take you to my house," she says. "Dad will be able to help. Help us figure this out."

"No," I say. "Home. I want to go home." I barely remember my home, but I still want to go there. Wherever it is.

Laurissa guns the engine, and the Prius responds sluggishly, the fuel efficiency numbers on the dash plummeting into single digits. "We need to get help. Tell someone. Report it."

"I want to go home," I say again. I don't want to talk about it, don't even want to think about it. I turn my head toward the window and try to watch the buildings pass, but they blur and swim. A wave of nausea crests in my gut, and I close my eyes and put my head down, hoping it will pass.

"I mean, we saw a guy get murdered. A cop!"

I'm still afraid I'm going to vomit, so I open my eyes long enough to hit the button on the window, cracking it about an inch. I arch my neck, lift my lips upward, and breathe the warm outside air. But it smells like diesel fumes and only makes the urge to vomit worse. "Let's just get home. Then we'll figure it out."

"Okay." Laurissa drives in silence for a while, pulling onto the I-70 ramp.

"What did that guy say? Before the shooting started. One of them jabbered in another language."

"I don't know," Laurissa says. "I couldn't even tell what language it was."

We lapse into silence for a moment, both trying to digest the insanity that has engulfed us. "That was crazy," I say, finally. "Were you always that brave? What you did back there—"

"I just did what I had to do."

"If I'd been alone, I'd be dead now." I feel the car lurch as Laurissa taps the brakes, and I open my eyes. There's a Honda Civic poking along ahead of us. "I don't get how that syringe would have killed me—there was nothing in it."

"Air embolism." Laurissa guns the engine, trying—and failing—to overtake the Civic. "The air bubble gets into your bloodstream and when it hits your brain or heart—poof, that's it for you."

"Oh."

"I saw someone get killed that way on a *Law and Order* rerun."

I'm not sure what to say to that, and we ride in silence for a few minutes through the turns to my house.

"I left the iPod you gave me at the hospital."

"It doesn't matter," Laurissa says. "I'll get another one if you want."

"It was an amazing gift." Not only have I lost all my memories of her, to add insult to injury, I've lost the one concrete thing she's given me.

"I just don't see why anyone would want to kill you," Laurissa says as we pull up to my house. It looks different from the little-kid memories I have of it. There's more peeling paint now and more bare wood. It's on a quiet road north of the airport, about twenty minutes from the hospital. I realize I'm going to be mooning the world on my way from the driveway to the front door. Luckily, none of the neighbors seem to be around.

"I don't understand it either," I say.

Laurissa steps up onto the front porch. She picks up a rock, which turns out to be fake, and pulls a key out of it. As soon as she gets the front door open, I dart into the house.

It's dingier than I remember it. There's a short entry hall that leads directly to the living room. The off-white paint on the walls is even more off-white than I remember. And the carpet in the living room has deep flattened tracks connecting the entryway to the kitchen and to the hall that leads to our bedrooms.

My foot still hurts, but it has mostly quit bleeding. I limp to my bedroom. The SpongeBob posters on the wall have been replaced by pictures of high-end bicycles and Tour-de-France podium girls—but the dresser and desk are the same. I strip off the hospital smock and pull on boxers and shorts.

Laurissa has followed me. I grab a T-shirt from the basket on the floor and stretch into it. Blood from the scrape on my knuckles smears the sleeve.

"Is there a first aid kit around here anywhere?" Laurissa asks.

"Under the bathroom sink," I say. "Or at least that's where it used to be."

I hobble out to the living room. I'm so tired I can barely stand. Everything hurts. I flop face-down onto the couch with my arm stretched out and the sole of my injured foot facing up. Laurissa comes back holding several washcloths, a bottle of rubbing alcohol, and a plastic case marked FIRST AID in big red letters. Laurissa pours some alcohol onto a washcloth and starts cleaning the wound on my foot.

After a while, I'm vaguely aware of Laurissa making a phone call, but I can't pay attention. It's all I can do not to pass out.

16

Jake

Laurissa's foot-washing has been over for a few minutes when I hear a police siren in the distance. It grows steadily louder and cuts off as I hear the crunch of a car in our gravel driveway.

"Wha-why? Why are they here?" I open my eyes, but the light is so bright, I close them again immediately.

"I called them," Laurissa says. "People were shooting at us, remember? There's an ambulance coming, too."

"I'm not going back to the hospital."

"You had brain surgery, Jake!"

"Call my mom, would you? Tell her I'm okay, and she doesn't need to leave work."

"She's on her way home."

"What? No. She—"

A knock at the door interrupts. Laurissa goes to answer it. I hear her asking the cops for ID—which seems funny to me. Isn't it usually the cops who ask for ID?

"Mr. Solley?" a deep voice says. "I'm Captain Beaner."

I squint at the source of the voice. He's standing at the foot of the couch. He's tall and blond, with pool-water blue eyes and a hooked nose.

"This is Detective Morris." The guy with him—squat and blocky, with a thick black mustache—nods a greeting. "May we sit down?" They're wearing suits, not uniforms.

"Sure," I say.

Beaner takes the plush armchair. Morris drags a chair over from the breakfast nook, sits, and removes a pen and small notebook from his pocket. Laurissa perches on the edge of the couch by my feet.

"You were both at Methodist Hospital this afternoon?"

"Yes," Laurissa and I say almost in unison.

"Name, please?" Morris says.

"Jacob Solley," I say.

"Laurissa Davis," Laurissa says.

Morris's pen glides across his notebook. "Social security numbers and birthdates, please?"

We give them to Morris—except for my social security number, which I can't remember—and then Beaner takes over, asking me, "You were a patient at Methodist Hospital?"

"Yeah." I gesture at my stitched-up head.

"They're both seventeen, Al," Morris says.

Beaner frowns. "Where are your parents?"

"His mother is on her way here," Laurissa says. "My folks are at work."

"And your father?" Beaner asks me.

"Dead," I reply.

"Do you want to wait until your mother is here to continue this discussion?" Beaner asks.

"No, it's okay," I say. Laurissa nods.

"Okay," Beaner says. "When were you admitted to the hospital?"

"I don't remember."

"June 11th," Laurissa says. "It was the first week of summer break."

Morris scribbles furiously.

"What time were you admitted?" Beaner asks.

"I don't remember," I say.

Beaner glances at Laurissa.

"I'm not sure," she says. "Late morning? Jake's mom called me while I was finishing my lunch."

The front door opens, and Mom rushes into the room. "Why is there a police car outside? Who are these people? Why aren't you at the hospital? And what happened to your foot?"

I reach out and take her hand while I try to answer, "The hospital was on fire and the firefighters started shooting at us and we climbed out the window on my bedsheets and—"

"Wait, shooting at you?" Mom grips my hand so hard it hurts.

"Yeah. But I'm okay."

"I'm calling an ambulance." Mom twists her hand free and takes her cell phone out of her purse.

"I already did," Laurissa says. "They're on their way."

I hear a siren in the distance. This whole thing is turning into a three-ring circus.

"Let's get back to what happened today," Beaner says. "So you'd been in the hospital for what, five weeks?"

"I guess so," I say.

"Being treated for a head injury?"

"Traumatic brain injury," Mom says.

"And how did that happen?" Beaner asks.

"We don't know," Mom says. "He was found in a construction zone on I-70 west of Cloverdale. His bike helmet was crushed, and his bike still hasn't been found."

"That's a long way on a bike. You rode out there?" Beaner asks.

"I could have," I say. "But I don't remember ever riding on the interstate."

"Were you carrying a phone that day?" Beaner asks.

"I don't remember," I say.

"His phone was in his shirt pocket when he was found." Mom says.

"May I see it?" Beaner asks.

Mom steps into the kitchen for a moment and returns with an older-model phone. As she passes it to Beaner, I see that it has a thumb-sized spiderweb of cracks in the upper right corner. "I'll be back in a few minutes," Beaner says. He unfolds himself from the chair and strides toward the front door.

"My phone . . ." I say, as Beaner leaves the house.

"He'll bring it back," Morris says. "Now, tell me about what happened at the hospital today."

I start explaining the insanity at the hospital, but I'm interrupted almost immediately by the doorbell. Mom answers the door, and two paramedics come in.

"I'm not going back to the hospital," I say.

Mom and I argue about it while the paramedics examine me. They take my temperature and blood pressure, check my pulse, and examine my wounds.

The paramedics can't find anything but the obvious stuff wrong with me. My balance is shot, my vision sometimes blurs unpredictably, and I am constantly nauseated. It was a miracle I managed to run away from the hospital. Adrenaline, I guess. The paramedics want to take me back. It doesn't have to be Methodist Hospital, they say. They'll take me to any hospital I want. Mom's on their side.

"Mom, please," I say. "I can't . . . I wouldn't feel safe after what happened today."

"I'll be a nervous wreck if you don't go," she says.

"I swear I'll call the ambulance myself if anything seems even slightly wrong." This is a complete lie. The truth is, lots of stuff feels way more than slightly wrong. I have a killer headache and it hurts to breathe, not to mention the new scrapes and cuts.

"I'll keep an eye on him, too," Laurissa says.

Mom's phone chirps, and she takes it out of her purse and glances at it. She deflates and a tear leaks from her eye. She looks like a week-old Mylar balloon.

I take her hand and gently turn it until I can see the face of her phone. There's a text on the screen, but the words dance and blur together. Laurissa gasps next to me. "What?" I ask.

"Your mom just got fired," she whispers. "By text message." She's clearly disgusted. I'm just worried about my mother.

Mom pulls the phone away from me. "I've got to beg for my job back," she says.

"I'd talk to my folks," Laurissa says. "You know, if you wanted. Or just introduce you, so you could talk to them. About a job or whatever."

Mom leans over and kisses Laurissa on the cheek. "I'm going to call my boss. I'll be in the hallway, watching you. You'll yell if you need me?"

"Yes," Laurissa says.

"You really are a dear, Laurissa," Mom says. "Maybe I will talk to your folks. But I'd better see about saving the job I have first."

"We need to talk to your son," Morris says.

"It's okay, Mom. I can handle it," I say, although I really wish everyone would go away and let me rest.

Mom nods at Morris and tells the paramedics that the hospital run is off, and they pack up and leave. Mom steps into the hallway to call her boss, never taking her eyes off me.

Morris takes out his notepad again. "Exactly what happened at the hospital today?"

Laurissa and I start the story while Morris takes notes. We're only halfway through when Beaner comes back in and returns my cell phone.

When we get to the part about the firefighters shooting the cop, both Beaner and Morris perk up. They fire questions at Laurissa and me rapidly. It's obvious they both knew the officer who was killed. We describe the two firefighters and their guns over and over again in exacting detail. We go through the sequence of events at least a dozen times. Finally, we move on and tell the rest of the story—how Laurissa locked the murderous firefighters out of the room and managed our escape from the hospital. By the time we're finished, it's dark outside. I can't stop yawning.

"Jake needs rest," Laurissa says.

"Just a couple more questions," Beaner replies. "Where were you the morning of June 11th?"

The question makes no sense. "Why do you care where I was a month ago?"

"Answer the question, please." Despite the "please," Beaner makes it sound like a command.

"We already told you. He was in the hospital," Laurissa says. "With a brain injury."

"I don't remember much of the last year at all," I say.

"What, precisely," Beaner says, "do you remember?"

"Just some old stuff. About my mom. Nothing from the last few years."

"Hmm," Beaner says. An uncomfortable silence follows. The only sound is Morris's pen racing across the notepad nestled in his palm.

"It's coming back," I say. "Every day I remember more. At first, I didn't even remember my own name."

"Is there anyone who can establish your whereabouts on 6/11?" Beaner asks.

"What's the point of this?" Laurissa says.

"Your bike accident was on 6/11," Beaner says.

"That's what I'm told. I don't remember," I say.

"And you weren't far down the road from where Delta 117 crashed," Beaner says.

Morris speaks up, "Al, that's not—"

Beaner glares at him, and Morris shuts up. I look at both of them for some sign that they're joking. Beaner looks dead serious. Morris looks annoyed. "I don't know anything about Delta 117," I say. "And why are you asking me about stuff that's not even remotely relevant?"

"Mr. Solley," Beaner says, "A moment ago you claimed not to remember June 11th."

"I don't," I say. "And you didn't answer my question."

"Then how can you positively assert that you don't know anything about the crash of Delta 117?"

"I've never heard of Delta 117!" But as I say it I realize that I'm wrong—it was mentioned on TV while I was in the hospital.

"He needs sleep," Laurissa says, "and I need to check in with my parents—it's getting late."

"Just a few more questions," Beaner says.

Laurissa takes her phone from her purse. "I'm calling my parents. And they'll call a lawyer. If you want to continue—"

"Fine, fine." Beaner hands me a business card. "Call me the instant you remember anything pertaining to the plane crash on 6/11. Or the shooting at the hospital today."

"Okay," I say.

"We'll be in touch," Beaner says.

Morris fills out a slip of paper labeled Incident Report and hands it to me. It has a 13-digit case number at the top and precious little other information. I pass it to Mom, who has finally rejoined us.

When Beaner and Morris leave, I sag deeper into the couch. I'm just a normal guy—stuff like this doesn't happen to normal guys. Even though I don't remember it, I want my old life back.

17

Jake

I can't sleep that night; my mind grinds the events of the day over and over. The faces of the two firefighters and the murdered policeman haunt me in waking dreams. When I do finally sleep, sometime after seven in the morning, my dreams improve.

I remember a high school basketball game. Geena Showalter had asked me if I'd be there. Like an idiot, I said yes. I blame her cleavage—it's mesmerizing.

At the game, she said hi, and then her friends dragged her away. They probably thought they were rescuing her from the guy nobody knows. I mean, I'm not some weird loner, but given the fact that I spend all my time on my bike, I probably seem like one.

I watched the rest of the first half by myself. The game was deadly boring. My school, Ben Davis, was playing Park Tudor, a small private school on the north side of Indianapolis. Ben Davis exists for one reason only: to win at sports. You don't put four thousand students on one high school campus because you want them to learn anything.

It was our first game of the season—a warm up. The Park Tudor Panthers were a class 2A team, our Giants were in the top class, 4A. By halftime we were up 60-34, and our coach had already put in all the spindly white kids who normally sat at the end of the bench. Geena had disappeared in the direction of the snack bar, surrounded by girls wearing shirts almost as skimpy as hers and guys way better looking than me.

I decided to leave. I barreled through the doors and took a quick left, heading for the bike racks. And I ran right over a cute black girl I hadn't even noticed. She'd been walking and texting, and we hit head-on in a collision at least as violent as any I'd seen on the basketball court. Her phone flew from her hands, skidding on the concrete under the bike racks.

I caught her arm before she could fall. "Sorry," I said. "You okay?"

"I think so," she replied. Her voice was a rich and full alto, not squeaky like Geena's soprano. "You see where my phone went?"

"Yeah." I stepped over to where it had hit the pavement and picked it up. It was an iPhone—the model that had come out just two months earlier. The screen was smashed, a crazed network of cracks covering most of it. It seemed to work, though—a chain of texts was visible through the cracks. The last message was, "You there?"

"It's wrecked." I handed her the phone. "I'm really sorry."

"Wasn't your fault. I'm the one who was texting and walking."

"Yeah, but—"

"It's no big deal. I'll take it to the Apple Store tomorrow and get a new one. Won't take them long to transfer the data. I've got the replacement warranty."

"They might be able to just replace the screen."

She shrugged and did something to the phone. It must have been damaged even worse than I thought, because after a moment, she sighed and stowed it in her purse.

"You need to borrow mine?" I asked and instantly regretted the question. My phone was an ancient prepaid model I'd picked up for fifteen bucks at Walmart.

"Yeah, thanks."

I fished the phone out of my pocket and handed it over. "My other phone is a *Star Trek* communicator," I said. I touched my chest and did my best starship commander impression, "Computer: Repair this girl's phone." Now I had labeled myself a total geekazoid. Smooth, Jake, real smooth.

But she was laughing. "Laurissa's phone," she said. "My name's Laurissa."

"I'm Jake," I said.

"I'm going to call you Kirk."

She knew *Star Trek*? My kind of girl. "Darn it! I was trying for Picard. But with better hair."

"No . . . you're more of a Kirk."

I wasn't sure if she was complimenting me or calling me a player. Nothing could have been further from the truth. "How'd you become a Trekkie?"

"My parents. They love the original series. I probably saw it for the first time *in utero*."

"Mighty small screen."

She gave me a funny look.

"You know, to fit in your mother's . . ."

She laughed again, a resonant sound I felt in my gut. I loved her laugh. She thumbed a number into my phone and put it to her ear. I turned away to give her some privacy, but her voice carried.

"It's me," she said. "Yeah, I broke my phone . . . I need a ride . . . Tommy's being, well, Tommy . . . I know I should have driven, Mom, but . . . well, send one of the Brothers Grimm then. . . . It's not like I ask them to drive very often. . . . Thanks . . . Love you, too."

"Everything okay?" I asked as she handed my phone back.

"Fine," she said. "Just freaking perfect."

"Boyfriend troubles?"

"Ex-boyfriend. My troubles with Tommy are over. Forever."

"You didn't kill him, did you?"

"No, I left my phaser at home with my Enterprise uniform. I don't know that I'd set it to 'kill' anyway."

"Just stun?"

"Those phasers should have had an in-between setting. 'Wound painfully' or something like that."

"What kind of name is Tommy, anyway?" I say, and then realize that I don't really want to talk about him anymore.

"I know, right? So boyish. Not like Jake—that's masculine."

"You wouldn't think so if you knew how my parents chose it."

"Oh, really?" Her eyebrows invited me to continue.

"Well, my mother was in labor, and she and my dad were

walking around the hospital, and she got this desperate need to pee. And my dad, who was quite a bit older than her and British, sat her down on a bench and told her to wait a moment while he went to find 'the jakes.' Mom yelled, 'That's it!' and I wound up named after a hospital restroom."

Laurissa laughed. I could listen to that sound all day. "None of that's true, is it?" she said.

"Nope, I made it up just now." I wanted to ask her what she meant by "the Brothers Grimm," but I didn't want to seem like a creeper who was listening in on her conversation. We chatted about other stuff for a while, leaning against the brick wall of the school. Laurissa was easy to talk to and even easier to listen to.

Eventually, a black Mercedes-Benz sedan pulled up to the curb. A hulking guy got out and held the back door open—he looked like he had been chiseled out of a block of bone-white granite rather than birthed. He was wearing a gray suit that didn't fit him right—his shoulders were threatening to rip out the seams.

"That's my ride," Laurissa said.

"Guess you don't go to Ben Davis." Mercedes aren't exactly common in the Ben Davis parking lot.

"No. Maybe I'll see you around."

Normally, I'm a complete klutz around girls. If I tried to ask for a phone number, I was more likely to stutter gibberish than compose an intelligible question. But something about talking to Laurissa made me feel comfortable. It just felt right. "Maybe I could text you?" I asked.

Laurissa hesitated a moment, then said, "Can I see your phone again?"

"Sure." I handed it over.

She thumbed the screen for a moment. When she handed the phone back, a new contact was there: Laurissa Davis, complete with her phone number. She hurried to the front passenger door of the Mercedes, and I waved goodbye. In the black-tinted side window of the Mercedes, I watched my reflection wave back at me. What was it like to ride in a car that likely cost more than my house? Her whole world was as mysterious as the inside of the car. I knew next to nothing about her—but I wanted to learn more.

18

Jake

Mom wakes me up the next morning. I hear her whispering, "Jake, Jake, wake up," and try to ignore it as she steadily increases the volume. Eventually she's almost yelling, and I respond just so she'll stop.

"Okay. I'm awake."

"Laurissa's on her way here. I let you sleep as long as I could."

"Laurissa? What? Why?"

"You've got an appointment with Dr. Malhotra at ten. And Detective Morris wants you to meet with a sketch artist. That appointment's at three. She's taking you."

"Ugh." I just want to curl up and pull the covers over my eyes. Maybe sleep for a week. "Why is she taking me?"

"I got my job back. But I've got to go to work today."

Before the accident, I would have ridden my bike to an appointment like this one. I hate that everyone has to plan their days around me, hate being a burden to anyone. But it can't be helped. I roll toward the edge of the bed. The pillow squelches under my head—it's soaked with sweat. "I need a shower."

"You want help?"

"God, no." It was bad enough when the nurses had to help me in the hospital.

"I'll be in the kitchen. Yell if you need anything."

Mom leaves my room. She's left the door cracked, presumably so she'll be able to hear if I fall. I lever myself off the bed, gripping the edge of my desk for support. I am woozy—maybe I should have let her help me. But my head clears, and I manage to take a quick shower.

By the time I get to the kitchen, Laurissa is there. She's setting the table while Mom dishes scrambled eggs and toast onto three plates. I feel like I haven't slept at all, but Laurissa looks as perky as always. I give her a quick kiss and collapse into a chair.

Mom slides plates in front of us. We both pick at the food.

"You okay?" Mom asks me.

"Yeah."

"Really?" She clearly doesn't buy my answer.

"I saw that cop get shot again and again, a thousand times while I was trying to sleep. Two spots of red on his forehead. It's freaking me out." I realize that I'm gripping my fork like I'm about to stab someone and slowly put it down.

"I didn't sleep much, either," Laurissa says. "And my parents aren't handling it well."

"I understand," Mom says.

"My mother wanted to ban me from leaving the house completely," Laurissa says. "Dad talked her down."

Laurissa could be grounded? I have no way to visit her house. The thought of losing her now is terrifying. I force myself to eat the rest of my toast.

Laurissa, Mom, and I leave the house together. Mom climbs into our Toyota, and Laurissa and I hop into the backseat of a gleaming black Mercedes sedan. An enormous blond guy fills the driver's seat. As the car pulls away, I whisper to her, "Who's driving?"

"Oh. Sorry," Laurissa says. "Jake, meet Dieter. Dieter knows you already. From before."

"Hi, Dieter," I say. He doesn't respond, just keeps his eyes glued to the road ahead of us.

"He's one of our bodyguards. Hans is the other. I call them the Brothers Grimm."

"You need bodyguards?"

"Yeah, well, my dad does. He owns a chain of restaurants, Sunday's Burgers and Fries, and a couple of them are in pretty tough parts of town. A couple of years ago, the Crips visited two of them, demanding protection money. Dad said no, they threatened him, and ever since then we've had two utterly humorless German bodyguards living with us."

"Wow. Must be weird."

"It was at first. Now it's only annoying. They want to follow me everywhere."

I marvel at this as Dieter pulls onto the interstate. I can't imagine living with bodyguards.

The neurosurgeon's office is in a medical building attached to the back of Methodist Hospital—the same place where I nearly got killed the day before. I'm glad Dieter is coming along. We don't have to go anywhere near the front part of the hospital, where the fire was, but still, I'd rather not be here at all.

The lady who runs the front desk is friendly, cooing sympathetically about the trauma of being driven out of the hospital by a fire. I don't tell her about the people who shot at us or Laurissa's heroics with a chair and improvised rope.

Dieter stands in a corner of the waiting room with his back to the wall. His eyes scan the room unceasingly.

After a few minutes, a hospital discharge nurse shows up from next door, his arms overflowing with files and forms. He ushers me and Laurissa into a small office and starts shoveling forms at me. It seems I violated at least seventy-two hospital regulations, six federal laws, and one commandment from on high by leaving the hospital without a doctor's order. I'm further wrecking his system by having Laurissa present (she's a non-related minor, the nurse tells me in an appalled tone) and by not having my mother present (who simply must sign fourteen forms in triplicate immediately, if not sooner). He makes a call, trying to find out if he's even allowed to discuss my discharge without my mother present. Whoever's on the other end of the line gives him permission to proceed, and he continues the onslaught of forms.

After half an hour of this, the nurse leaves me with a stack of information about post-hospitalization care, a folder to give to the neurosurgeon, and another for my mother. When did I become an errand boy for the hospital, anyway? Then he herds us back to the waiting room. No part of Dieter has moved except his eyes, which apparently never stop.

I pick up a ragged, year-old copy of *National Geographic* and do my best to ignore the non-stop drug ads playing on the waiting room TV. Laurissa watches me for a moment and then cracks open the law book she brought.

I can't focus well enough to read. Yesterday's events are running through my mind like some crazy page of GIFs on Tumblr.

A different nurse calls us back to an exam room. She takes my vitals and leaves. At least back here it's private. Laurissa and I talk about the day before. Were the two firefighters really firefighters? Or just dressed perfectly to fit the part? Why'd they try to kill us? Were they after Laurissa—something to do with her family's restaurants? But that wouldn't explain Fake Laurissa. Or the syringe. Or the foreign language they were speaking. Neither of us has a clue what language it was. Real Laurissa still thinks Fake Laurissa was a hallucination created by my hormones. We have dozens of questions and zero answers.

After an hour or so, there's a knock on the door, and the neurosurgeon enters. I recognize him from my hospital stay—Dr. Malhotra. He asks me to do a zillion goofy tricks: lie on the exam table and raise one leg with the knee bent. Breathe through my nose while he holds one nostril closed with his finger. Then breathe through the other nostril. Follow a light with my eyes without moving my head. Balance on my left foot. Balance on my right foot. Touch my left index finger to my nose. Touch my right pinkie to my nose. And so on. He says I'm recovering normally, but he still wants to readmit me to the hospital for observation—just for another day or two, he says. I tell him no way. He orders an MRI—punishment for my intransigence, I assume.

The MRI machine is in the basement of the building. We have no appointment, so we wind up waiting more than two hours to get our "rush" scan done. They give me a long lecture about the dangers of metal objects in the MRI machine. Apparently, it uses magnets so powerful that metal stuff can get pulled right through flesh. I wonder if the metal screws in my head are going to kill me, but the tech says they're made of a special non-ferrous alloy.

After the scan is done, we wait another half hour for Dr. Malhotra to read it and tell us that it "looks good." I've spent six hours in this office building to find out that everything "looks good"? Finally, they allow me to leave. We've missed the appointment with the police sketch artist. Dieter and Laurissa drive me home. The day of waiting has left me exhausted—I want nothing more than to curl up in bed and hide from the world.

19

Betsy

We are well and truly screwed. At least a dozen times a day I have to bite my tongue to keep from telling Dad, "I told you so." All our group events have been canceled. The Indianapolis police are like a pack of wasps swarming a bear, except they don't realize what a big, nasty bear they're trying to take down. They're just looking for Keith and Joshua. We know every detail of their investigation—after all, we have an excellent source of intel.

A nurse, a security guard, and two hospital visitors saw Keith and Joshua, and with their descriptions, a police artist has created fairly good sketches of both of them. Dad sent them to our North Carolina branch. Their cell phones have been crushed; their cars sold for scrap. They'll live off the grid until things cool down. Neither Keith nor Joshua seem too upset about it, which doesn't make sense to me—living without Internet for even a couple of days would drive me nuts.

I spend most of my days online, talking to people on the Stormbreak forums. One of the many reasons I love summer break is all the extra time I can spend chatting. During the school year, I stay up late and sleepwalk my way through school. My favorite classes are the ones where the teachers let you nap. In the summertime, I can sleep as late as I want in the morning.

The forums are buzzing over a new bombing in Egypt and beheading in Syria. Our plane crash has almost dropped out of the news. Dad still hasn't released the statement intended to link the plane crash to Islamic terrorists, but one of their groups has claimed responsibility anyway. They want this war just as badly as we do. I want to talk to someone, especially Kekkek, about what we're doing, but I know I can't. He says America is weak—that we could kill all the terrorists, turn the deserts of the Middle East to glass, but we won't. America might be weak, but Americans aren't. The Sons of Paine are taking the action our government is too wimpy to take. We'll wake up the sheeple. But of course OPSEC dictates that I can't talk to anyone, not even him. Dad is even grumpier than usual. There's a scowl engraved across his face. If we had a cat, he'd be kicking it. I'm glad we don't have pets. I try to stay out of his way. He doesn't aim anything more hurtful than a few gruff words toward me, and I intend to keep it like that.

During the week, I spend my evenings taking night classes in accounting at Ivy Tech Community College. Dad was pissed when I signed up for summer classes. He doesn't think accounting is a "proper pursuit" for a girl. I guess he expects me to hang out at home and cook from my Betty Crocker cookbook, like some kind of fifties housewife. Screw that. When he realizes how useful I can be as an accountant, he'll come around. There must be hundreds of thousands of dollars flowing into The Sons of Paine from Swan. Maybe millions. Someone's got to track it all, disburse it, make sure the funds aren't misspent. That will be me, after I earn full membership and my accounting degree. As soon as I finish high school, I'll start taking accounting classes full-time. I'm pretty sure I can graduate in three years.

The only use I have for high school is getting through it with passing grades, so I can move on and get my accounting degree. North Central is full of libtards and sheeple, too ashamed to stand up for America. Luckily, there are 3,500 students there, so it's easy to ignore everyone and be ignored in turn.

On Sunday, my dad and I go to church—Dry Run Creek Baptist. It's about the only thing we do together every week without fail. I never feel so close to God as when we're singing in church. Dad has a rich, rumbling voice that makes me wonder why he talks so little during the week. He never sings outside of church, but during a hymn, his bass and my soprano harmonize beautifully. We're at opposite ends of the scale, but perfectly in tune.

I always feel a bit sad when I sing with Dad, though. It reminds me of the long car trips we used to take to visit my mom's parents, back before she left us. Mom and Dad would sing together, sometimes. One late night—I must have been five or six—I was napping in the back seat and woke to hear them singing "You Are My Sunshine" in harmony. It was so beautiful that even now the memory brings tears to my eyes.

I could live without the sermons at this church. Pastor Lee often veers into political subjects he knows nothing about. He preaches forgiveness, understanding, and compassion, even for heathens. He doesn't understand that there's a war being waged outside the peaceful walls of his sanctuary, a war that has gone on for more than two thousand years. Christians are under attack all around the world, and sometimes we have to fight to protect them. To kill, even. Innocents have always died in this fight—it's a necessary evil.

Today's sermon isn't bad, though. It's all fire, brimstone, and the end times. Hell doesn't scare me, because I know I'm fighting on God's team. It's strange hearing Pastor Lee roaring about preparing ourselves for judgement—he's a complete dweeb. He keeps his reading glasses perched so far down his nose that it looks like they might leap to their death at any minute. One verse he quotes sticks with me: "And he doeth great wonders, so that he maketh fire come down from heaven on the earth in the sight of men." Little does Pastor Lee know.

We used to go to a different church, Two Swords Baptist. I don't remember much about the services there. We switched when I was only ten, not long after Mom disappeared. But I do remember that I liked Pastor Hobbes. He kept a huge bowl of hard candy on the desk in his office, and he usually had more in his pockets. He'd slip me a piece now and then, even though Mom told him not to "rot my teeth."

I asked Dad once why we switched. He said, "Dry Run's closer," and that's true, but I think there's another reason, a deeper reason. Mom loved Two Swords and loved Pastor Hobbes, despite his support of my candy addiction. Maybe it was too painful for Dad to keep attending Two Swords. Too much of a reminder of Mom.

Even though we're barely speaking, Dad and I still eat dinner together when our schedules permit. About a week after the fiasco at the hospital, we're sitting at the kitchen table, eating a meal of microwaved lasagna in total silence. Dad speaks with no warning, and I just about drop my fork in shock.

"You want another shot at solving our problem?" he says.

I think for a moment. "I want to become a full member of The Sons."

"You solve our problem, then yes."

"Despite the rule that women can't be members?"

"Yes," he says.

I know what he's asking. Could I do it, even though I've failed once already? I remember Jake's hand brushing across my cheek and shudder. "You said I FUBARed the first try."

"At least you got away clean."

"What kind of op prep would I need to do?"

"It's mostly done. We can track him through his cell phone. I took care of that right after the fiasco at the hospital. He isn't moving around much."

"And my cover? Jake must know I'm not really Laurissa. But has he reported it?"

"Not as far as I can tell," he says.

I pause for a moment. I want this, even though I'm not sure I can do it. "I'm in," I say finally.

"We'll finish the recon work," Dad says. "When the police cool down a little, you'll get your shot."

I nod. This time, I'm going to do it and become a full member of The Sons of Paine. This time, Jake Solley is going to die.

20

Jake

I lie awake at night while my brain feeds me looped movies starring the murderous firefighters. When I do finally drift off, usually about the time the sun comes up, my dreams improve.

I don't go anywhere. I know I'm not totally safe—if the "firefighters" wanted to visit our house to kill me, they probably could. I find our address listed on half a dozen sites online and send requests to have it delisted, but anyone with the resources to buy a convincing firefighter outfit will be able to find me. Despite all that, I feel safer at home.

Dr. Malhotra prescribed three different kinds of painkillers, but only one of them is available in generic form, which is all our insurance covers. I told my mom that it takes care of all the pain, although it doesn't really. We visit Dr.

Malhotra's office again, and a physician's assistant takes out my stitches. My hair has grown back to about an inch and a half, so I look less and less like a pasty white Frankenstein's monster every day.

Detective Morris calls me once, wanting more details about the two firefighters who shot at us in the hospital. He's not upset that I missed the appointment with his artist—they got good sketches without me, he says. Captain Beaner calls twice, wanting to know if I've remembered anything about 6/11 or Delta 117. I haven't, and I'm tired of him asking. Neither of them will tell me anything about the investigation into the police officer's murder, which I assume means they've gotten nowhere. I tell Beaner that I'm regaining my memory, but I'm still years behind. I promise to call him as soon as I remember anything from the day of my accident.

I sleep twelve hours or more a day, never getting up before noon. I pace around the living room, and my balance steadily improves. I try to read. Every day I'm able to concentrate for a little longer. My mother works long hours most days. When she's home, she hovers, and sometimes I have to retreat to my room. I love her, but I want her to quit worrying about me. She still looks so tired.

Zach calls me a few times, but it's awkward. All he wants to talk about are bike races. The Sunday's Burgers and Fries team is doing okay in my absence. All the sponsorship money that Laurissa got from her dad was spent on jerseys and entry fees before the start of the season, so Zach and Bulb are pretty much set. I'm starting to remember a few of my races, but I don't want to talk about them. I want to race, not talk about racing. Sometimes I watch biking vids on YouTube, but even that is difficult. The more I watch, the more I want to ride. My balance is improving, and maybe I'll be able to get on a bike soon. If I'm ever going to make it to Belgium, I've got to start training again.

The best part of each day is when Laurissa visits. She comes every afternoon and sometimes stays for dinner. She doesn't hover over me like Mom, obsessing about the accident. Talking to her helps me remember, but she doesn't push, just accepts me as I am.

Either Hans or Dieter is always with Laurissa. They watch the house from outside. It's the only time of the day I feel completely safe.

I'm not sure exactly how to behave around Laurissa, though. We have all this history together that I still can't access. Like, if we're kissing and my arm accidently brushes her chest (yes, it *can* happen by accident), am I supposed to apologize or keep going? We kiss all the time, but the goodbye kisses are the good ones. We're always standing in the entry hall of my house where neither Mom nor Laurissa's body-guards can see us. Each goodbye is hotter than the last—if they get any more intense, I'm going to have to start shower-ing after she leaves.

I've discovered that Laurissa makes a little moan deep in her throat when I nibble softly on her earlobe. I love that sound. I'd sample it and play it all day on a loop like some kind of demented deejay if I could. It all feels new to me. I still don't remember much of our relationship before the accident. It's like I'm falling in love all over again.

About a week after the hospital incident, Laurissa and I are snuggled together on the couch watching a completely ridiculous action movie and munching on microwave popcorn. I'm pretty sure the director slept through high school physics, or he'd understand that stuff doesn't just randomly explode.

I don't mind the terrible movie, though. I'm focused on the warmth of Laurissa's shoulder against mine. Every now and then, I catch a faint whiff of vanilla and cinnamon under the buttery popcorn smell. I'm not sure what it is—her lotion?—but it makes me want to nibble on her instead of the popcorn. The smell triggers a memory.

I remember texting Laurissa after the basketball game where we met. I picked up my phone a dozen times the following day, opened her screen on my contacts list, but didn't press the text button. Finally, I sat down with a notebook and pen and planned out a text. Who does that—writes out what they're going to text? I guess I do, at least if I'm sending a first message to a girl I'm interested in.

After trying and discarding about a zillion ideas, I settled on a totally corny *Star Trek* message. I mean, I knew she was into that. And that was part of the reason I was interested in her.

"Scotty, beam me down to Planet Park Tudor." Okay, it's a lame joke, but it was the best I could do.

"There's nobody named Scotty here," Laurissa texted back. Before I could think of a response, she texted again. "And there's no way you'd want to visit Planet Park Tudor. The natives are deadly boring."

"There's at least one native who's not."

"You'd be violating the prime directive."

"I'm pretty sure I'd violate the prime directive for you."

"JUST like Kirk, ha!"

"Well, sort of."

"What's your last name?" Laurissa texts. "I'm adding you to my contacts."

"Solley," I text.

"Like that marine? From Avatar?"

"Yeah, but spelled different."

"Got it."

"Can I call you?"

"Yes."

I dialed her, and we talked for hours about nothing, although everything Laurissa said seemed important. We never ran out of topics: her school, my school. Her friends, my friends. Books, music, and movies. She even listened to me blather on about bike racing, although she wasn't a cyclist. She seemed interested and asked smart questions.

She told me she wanted to study political science and then law. She wanted to go to Princeton, or maybe George Washington University, but wasn't sure her grades and extra-curriculars were good enough. My dream of being invited to train at USA Cycling's development camp in Belgium seemed lame by comparison.

That talk led to more. I called her almost every night that week and texted during the day. It seemed I'd never run out of things to say to Laurissa, stuff I wanted to tell her. Finally, on Friday, I summoned the nerve to ask her out.

"Want to get lunch tomorrow?" I texted.

"Yes! Let me ask Mom," her reply read. I waited anxiously for what seemed like eons. "She said no. We have plans, I guess."

"Bummer."

"I could go to the basketball game tonight. Park Tudor at Speedway. Want to come?"

Speedway isn't far from me. "Sure."

I rode my bike to Speedway High School that night. I spotted Laurissa right off—she was one of a grand total of three black people on the visitors' side of the gym.

We sat in the stands and talked, pretty much ignoring the game. Mostly we talked about books. By the time the game was over, I'd punched ten of Laurissa's book recommendations into my phone. Not that I was going to be able to find time to read more than two or three of them. My training schedule left hardly any time to sleep, let alone read.

I asked her out again the next week, and instead got another invitation to the basketball game, this time at Beech Grove. Since my accident, I can't imagine riding that far. But back then, a trip to Beech Grove was nothing. And I loved talking to Laurissa, even when we were surrounded by a few hundred screaming fans. Toward the end of the game, I asked if she'd like to get lunch the next day. She said she had plans, and I didn't press her. When the game ended, I discovered that the temperature had dropped precipitously, and I'd only brought a lightweight jacket. The ride home was bitterly cold.

I called her Thursday night to ask her to go to lunch with me on Saturday, and she turned me down again, inviting me to a home basketball game. I decided it was time to ask her why.

"I'm just . . . I'm more comfortable taking things slowly," she said.

"It's just lunch. I'm not inviting you to a hotel or anything," I said.

She snorted, a sound more endearing than pig-like. "I know."

"Neither of us really care about basketball, anyway."

"It's okay. But you're right, I probably wouldn't be going to the away games if you weren't there."

"So, lunch?"

"I'd like to. But I don't think I can."

"Why not?"

"If we went out for lunch, I'd have to tell my mother. I couldn't just say I was going to the basketball game."

"You could tell her you're going shopping or something." I never told my mom where I was going—taking a bike ride was my all-purpose explanation for everywhere I went. I didn't lie to her, not really. After all I did bike almost everywhere I went.

"I couldn't do that."

"Why not just ask her, then? I mean, if you really do want to go."

"I do! But she'll want to meet you."

"That's okay with me." I didn't really see the point—it wasn't like I was going to propose, but whatever.

"Mom has . . . strong opinions about what kind of friends I should have. And even stronger opinions about who I should date."

"Oh." I wasn't surprised, not really. My family's annual income was probably less than what her parents paid to send her to Park Tudor. "Well, that sucks."

"I like you, Jake, but . . ."

"But I'm not really a Park Tudor-type guy." Not rich enough for her, I thought.

"No!" Laurissa said. "I don't care about that. Well, maybe my mother does, but that's not the real problem."

I'd pretty much given up hope, but I was still curious. "So what *is* the big problem?"

"The biggest fight I ever saw my older brother have with Mom was the day he brought a white girl over to the house. They—"

"So it's because I'm white!? I never thought that might be the problem."

"Look, Jake, maybe you should have thought about it."

"Why?"

"You *have* noticed that I'm black, right?"

"Yeah . . . ." I was feeling lost, like I had jumped into the middle of a conversation despite being ignorant of what had been said before.

"And I'm proud of being black. Of our culture and history. It's part of who I am."

"Yeah. That makes sense."

"And my mother is proud of being black. So when my brother brought home a white girl he was dating—"

"Your mother probably felt like he was rejecting her."

"Exactly."

"I hadn't thought about it that way before."

"I like you, Jake. I like you a lot. But if we are going to date, you need to think about it. You can't be so wrapped up in your own perspective that you can't see how much race matters in America. Or how much it matters to me."

"I like you, too. A lot. And . . . I'm sorry."

A long silence broke our conversation.

"You know what?" Laurissa said, "I'm going to go talk to Mom. Right now. I'll call you back."

"Good luck," I said.

Waiting for her to call back was unbearable. I gave up after about five minutes, threw my bike helmet on, and went for a ride.

Laurissa shifts next to me on the couch, and the point of her elbow interrupts my memory. Something is exploding on our television. "Do you remember asking your mom if we could have lunch?" I ask.

"Oh my God, yes," she says. "Worst argument I've ever had with her."

"Like, shouting and throwing things bad?"

"No, Mom's not really a shouter. It was more of a slow, simmering argument that started not long after I met you and didn't come to a boil until right before our first date."

I pull her closer. Her head fits perfectly in the hollow of my shoulder. "I'm glad you won."

"I didn't really win. Dad got involved. He's . . . a little more easygoing than Mom."

"Then I'm thankful for your dad."

"Yeah. Me, too."

I squeeze her gently. "I don't remember much of you from before the accident, but—"

"It's okay," she says. She's wrapped her arm around my chest. "It'll come back."

"But I don't need to remember it. I love you."

"I love you, too, Jake."

We watch the rest of the movie without talking. I don't need to—it's enough to feel the weight of Laurissa's head against my shoulder, the warmth of her body against mine. We're like two puzzle pieces from a chaotic jumble of thousands—we fit together perfectly.

21

Jake

Zach thinks I should be riding. He says I'm moping, and maybe he's right. I haven't left the house in more than a week. The only cure, according to Zach, is to get back on a bike.

I don't share Zach's theory with Mom. I'm pretty sure she would ricochet off the ceiling, ban him from calling me, attempt to lock me in my room, or possibly do all three.

Despite the fact that I've told him no about a dozen times, he shows up one morning in his prehistoric F-150. When I peek through the window before opening the door, he's practically bouncing with excitement.

"Dude," he says before I can even say hi, "check out what I brought."

I follow him to his pickup. There are two road bikes in the bed: a total piece of crap GMC and a decent Vilano. "What are those for?" I say.

He fakes a deep, stentorian voice, "The oracle prescribes a wind cure. Brain damaged, depressed, lay-about friend must remount the bike that threw him." The effect is totally ruined when his voice cracks.

"Neither of those pieces of crap threw me," I say.

"Hey, the junker bike is Bulb's. Mine is better than what you were riding, so don't diss it."

"If I smoked you in every race on a bike worse than that, I must be Eddy Merckx reincarnated."

"Fighting words!" Zach says gleefully. "It's on."

He gets two helmets and an extra pair of cycling shoes out of the cab of his truck. Before I can protest effectively, I'm wearing one of the helmets. I have to bat Zach's hands away to keep him from untying my shoes and shoving the cycling shoes on my feet.

I know this isn't a good idea. But I do want to ride, and I'm wondering if I can.

We line the bikes up on the road in front of my house. We're in a quiet corner of an old subdivision—there are rarely any cars to contend with. I push off, smiling at the clack of my cleats against the pavement. And then I'm rolling down the street.

I try to click my right cleat into the pedal. Normally, it's instinctive. This time, I miss. Nothing's working right. I try again and slip partway off the seat. Zach is three houses down already, looking over his shoulder at me. He pulls a U-ie.

I'm still rolling slowly. I get my right cleat snapped into the pedal. My front wheel bobbles, I hit a curb, and crash onto the sidewalk, banging my knee painfully.

Zach pulls up alongside the crash site. "Uh, dude. Maybe this wasn't such a good idea."

I throw myself to my feet so fast that the blood rushes out of my head, and I stagger.

"Let's just, like, call it a day," Zach says.

"Yeah, the hell with that," I reply. I pick the bike up, throw my leg over the saddle, and push off.

This time I get both feet clipped in before I crash. I fall on my side in the road, leaving a nasty scrape along my elbow. I'm going to have to wear long-sleeved shirts if I want to keep the morning's activities a secret from Mom.

Zach grabs the bike. I try to wrench it away from him, but either he's stronger than he used to be or I'm pathetically weak. "Come on," I say. "One more try."

"Last try, dude," he says, still gripping the bike.

"Okay." I push off, and this time Zach runs alongside. I turn to tell him to back off, and before I can say anything, I crash the bike again. Zach does catch me, so I suppose his over-protective crap was good for something. We go down in a tangle, and Zach winds up with blood from my elbow scrape smeared across his shirt.

I push myself up off the pavement. I want to kick the bike, just cock my foot back and let loose on it. I want to kick Zach, still lying at my feet.

Instead, I turn and stalk back toward the truck, leaving Zach to wrangle both the bikes. I rip off the helmet and shoes, toss them into the cab, and retreat to my house before Zach even makes it back to the truck. I lock the door behind me and head for my room.

I rip the mattress off my bed, hurling it to the floor. I grab my desk, toppling it. The edge of the desk falls on top of the mattress. Books and pens cascade everywhere, covering the floor and mattress. I give my dresser the same treatment. Something cracks as it crashes to the floor.

There's nothing else heavy in my room, so I start on the posters, tearing and ripping until there are shreds of Pinarello bikes and podium girls mounded across my floor like November leaves.

I collapse amid the rubble. The doorbell is chiming—I hadn't noticed it before. I ignore it. A few moments later, my phone rings. I ignore that, too. My phone rings twice more, and then it's quiet. I contract into a fetal curl and finally allow myself to cry.

An hour or two later, I rise from the mattress, disgusted by what I've done. I get a trashbag from the kitchen and start picking up the poster shreds. Then I pull the scraps of tape and corners of posters from my walls. I've broken one of the legs of my dresser. I kludge it back upright by substituting a stack of books for the busted leg. It takes me a couple of hours, but eventually, my room is put back to rights. It's actually way neater, although it feels sterile.

Then I call Zach. "I'm sorry," I say before he can even greet me.

"No dude, I'm sorry," he replied.

"For what?"

"I shouldn't have hassled you about riding. It was a dumb idea."

"About that? I need you to bring the bikes back tomorrow."

"Yeah, no."

"Yeah, yes."

"And if you bite the pavement and screw up your brain even worse? No, just no."

"I'm going to try to ride whether you come back or not," I say. "I'll borrow someone else's bike. Or go buy a garage-sale clunker."

"Fine. It's on you, then."

"If you come back, I'll have a helmet. And you can catch me."

"No."

"It's on you if you don't come back. What if I fall and there's no one around?"

"You're a real hardass, Jake."

"You coming?"

"I don't like you anymore," Zach says, which A) is not true and B) means he's coming back. I'm going to learn to ride again. Or kill myself trying.

22

Jake

When Laurissa visits that afternoon, I tell her about my morning's misadventure. She's worried and makes me promise to wear a helmet. Since I'm not an idiot, promising to wear a helmet isn't an issue.

I don't really want to revisit my biking fail any further, so I ask her about our first date. As we talk, it all comes back to me. I had planned the date for two weeks. I figured we'd get lunch at the Illinois Street Food Emporium. There's a bookstore and a coffee shop nearby, so it seemed like a great place to spend the afternoon. And it's way closer to Laurissa's house than mine.

I decided to ride to the restaurant—that beat asking Mom to loan me the car. Then I obsessed for a while over what to wear. Isn't that supposed to be a girl thing? Finally, I decided to wear my usual Saturday outfit: bike shorts, jersey, jacket, and helmet. Then I obsessed over whether I'd be too sweaty when I arrived, so I packed an extra shirt and a stick of deodorant in my backpack—I could hit the restrooms at the restaurant and change. Then I decided to pack a pair of jeans. Bike shorts might not be the best idea for a first date.

I got to the restaurant almost fifteen minutes early. A mom was pushing a stroller down the sidewalk, with three older kids running laps around her and screaming their heads off. At first, I thought I'd beaten Laurissa to the restaurant. There was no Mercedes parked along the street. But then I saw her get out of a little sky-blue Prius not far from me.

I pedaled over to her and dismounted my bike. "Hey, Jake," she said, smiling softly.

"Hey, you," I replied. "Where's the basketball game?"

Laurissa laughed. "Not here!"

I chained my bike to a telephone pole near her car. "No Mercedes today?" I said.

"No, thank God," Laurissa said. "I always feel weird riding in those cars. They're kind of pretentious."

Those cars? Her family had more than one Mercedes? Mom and I shared a twelve-year-old Toyota Corolla. "Yeah, I left my Pinarello Dogma at home for the same reason. Figured you'd think it's too pretentious."

"What's a Pinarello?"

I shrugged. "The Mercedes of the bike world. I don't really have one. They cost a fortune."

"I talked Mom into letting me drive myself."

"Nice car," I said.

"Thanks."

The restaurant was mobbed. It was one of those places where you wait in line to order, and the line stretched nearly out the front door. "I'm going to hit the restroom," I said.

"Want me to watch your stuff?"

"Sure," I shrugged off my backpack and handed it to her, then realized that I needed the clothes and deodorant I had stowed in my pack. Laurissa reached under my chin and clicked the release on my bike helmet's strap. I put my hand on the helmet, holding it on. "It's . . . I'll just take it off in the restroom."

"Seriously? You're worried about a bad hair day?"

"Well, you know. Helmet head."

"You are such a girl." She tugged on the helmet, and I let her pull it off. "Your helmet hair is adorable." She reached up and ruffled my damp hair, running her fingers through it. I loved the feel of her fingers against my scalp. It was somehow relaxing and exciting at the same time.

"I'm a little sweaty, sorry," I said.

Laurissa leaned closer and sniffed. "You smell great to me. Do you really need to use the bathroom?"

"No," I admitted. "I was just going to change my shirt and comb my hair. Put on some jeans."

"You're fine."

We both turned our attention to the menu board above the counter, staring at it in silence. "What are you having?" I asked.

"Not sure. I'm just glad they don't have burgers."

"You don't like burgers?"

"I love them, but . . . I haven't told you what my dad does for a living yet, have I?"

"No . . ."

"You know that chain of burger joints? Sunday's?"

"Yeah."

"He owns them."

"All of them?" There must have been fifteen or twenty just in Indianapolis. And I was pretty sure they had locations all over the Midwest.

"Yep, all of them. He opened the first one before I was born."

"Wow, that's cool."

Laurissa shrugged.

I'd eaten at Sunday's a few times. It was a rare treat for our family to eat out. "They're really good burgers. I mean, even before I knew you, I thought they were the best burgers in Indy."

"Punch Burger is pretty good, too."

"Never heard of it," I said.

"It's a little restaurant downtown. But yeah, Dad's food is amazing. Way better than any other fast food place."

I nodded my agreement—we had finally reached the register. Laurissa tried to pick up the bill, but I protested, and she let me pay. I'm not sure why it was a big deal to me, buying her lunch. After paying, I was left with eleven dollars and some change.

We found a table and as we sat down, Laurissa asked, "You have any brothers or sisters?"

"No. You?"

"Just one brother, Brand. He's away at college, UC Berkeley, studying computer science. I only see him for holidays, now."

Our conversation was interrupted by the arrival of our food—a salad for Laurissa and a turkey sandwich for me. After lunch Laurissa and I walked to the bookstore kitty-corner from the restaurant—Kids Ink. We sat on the floor in the teen section and talked about books for what seemed like hours. She asked if she could take a few pictures, and we wound up taking dozens of selfies on both of our phones.

I bought her a book she hadn't read—one of my favorites, *Graceling* by Kristin Cashore—and wrote in the front "To Laurissa, on our first date—Jake." I added the date and handed it to her. The smile on her face was worth the fact that I'd be broke for a week—the lady at the register was nice enough to give me a dime because I didn't have enough cash to cover the tax.

Laurissa bought me a book—Tamora Pierce's *Trickster's Choice*—and inscribed it, "To Jake, on our first date. The first of many, I hope—Laurissa."

"You want to hit the Starbucks?" she asked.

"Sure, but I'm broke now," I said.

"My treat. You bought lunch—it's only fair."

"Sounds good."

The Starbucks was just a few doors down. Laurissa ordered some kind of complicated drink—Chai Mocha Spice Latte Frappasomethingorother. I got a small black coffee. I don't even like coffee much, and I never drink it black, but I was always impressed with people who ordered it that way. It seemed manly or something. I took about two sips and set it aside.

We talked for the rest of the afternoon and took more selfies. It seemed like no time at all had passed when Laurissa said, "It's after five. If I'm not home for dinner, my parents will kill me. Or tell the Brothers Grimm to do it."

"Yeah, me too. Although Mom won't be home from work for a couple of hours."

"On Saturday?"

"Yep. Six days a week this time of year. Seven days a week in the spring. I wish she'd find a better job."

"My dad's like that. He just never quits."

We left the Starbucks and walked to my bike. I unchained it and wheeled it to her car. "I had a good time," I said.

"Me, too. Do something next weekend?" she asked.

"I'd like that." I would have liked to get together before then, but we both had busy school schedules, and we lived on opposite sides of the city. Texting would have to do.

Laurissa put her hand on my neck and tilted her head upward. I froze, unsure what to do. Sometimes I am completely and utterly oblivious. She tugged gently on my neck, and I finally got a clue. I bent, closed my eyes, and kissed her.

Her lips were soft and lush. The kiss lingered, setting off fireworks from my brain to my groin. My whole body warmed despite the chilly November air.

When the kiss broke, she opened her car door. "See you next week, Jake," she said softly. She wore a dreamy smile, and I grinned like a total freak.

I raced home on my bike, barely feeling the pedals beneath my feet, the seat under my butt, or even the road. My head floated above the bike, and the street vanished behind me. I could fly!

23

Jake

Laurissa goes home before Mom returns from work. Despite my long-sleeved shirt, Mom notices the road rash on my arm. Of course she does. I've never been able to hide anything from her. All it takes is a slight flinch when I bump into the refrigerator door, and she's on to me. I confess the morning's activities, and our conversation quickly devolves into a shouting match. According to her, I'm forbidden from biking until I turn thirty-two. She might as well forbid me from breathing.

Mom is not impressed by my arguments. Finally, I point out that there's nothing she can do to stop me from riding short of quitting her job to babysit me, and if she does that, we won't have any money to buy food and I'll starve. I'm dead either way, so what does it matter? I think my logic is impeccable, but Mom still isn't buying it.

Nonetheless, the next day after she leaves for work, Zach visits. It's just as bad as the day before. Zach doesn't even try to ride. He just runs alongside me like the world's youngest overprotective dad.

One of our neighbors walks around the side of his house pushing his lawnmower and stops, mouth agog, watching as I try to ride and Zach tries to prevent the inevitable crash. I ignore him and focus on falling on the grass instead of the pavement.

I crash five more times before we give up. I'm going slowly and Zach usually manages to catch me so I don't hurt myself. I make him promise to return the next day.

I've got a surprise for him when he returns. I present it right after I open the door: a pair of training wheels from my old Huffy. I still have the Huffy. I used to mess around on it occasionally, trying to do tricks, but its training wheels were gathering dust on a shelf in the garage.

"You can't be serious," Zach says.

I just nod.

"Will those even fit on a road bike?"

"One way to find out."

"Bulb is going to kill me."

"We'll take them off before you take his bike back."

We wheel Bulb's GMC into the garage and take the back wheel off. The training wheels don't fit. The rear axle on Bulb's road bike isn't long enough to accept them, and the arms on the training wheels aren't long enough to reach the ground properly on a racing bike with 700c wheels.

"Let's take it to Bil," I say.

"No way," Zach replies. "We'd never live that down. Like, never. Do you really want to be known as Training Wheels Solley for the rest of your life?"

"If it helps me relearn to ride—"

"It's not worth it, dude."

"I. Don't. Care. I'm going to relearn to ride. Are you going to help or just whine at me?"

Zach is silent for a moment, and then he helps me load Bulb's bike into the bed of his pickup.

Bil owns my favorite bike shop. He goes by Bil because his parents gifted him with the unfortunate name Bilbo—a fact he doesn't tell just anyone, and that I hope to use as blackmail to get help. Although to be fair, I think he'll help me even if I don't blackmail him for two reasons: First, he has a soft spot for broke, teenage bike racers, having been one years ago, and second, the idea of calling me "Training Wheels Solley" for the rest of my life will be irresistible.

When I walk into the bike shop, the first thing he says to me is, "I heard what happened to you. Gnarly."

"Yeah," I reply, "not the usual case of road rash. I run my fingers through the stubble on my head, pulling it apart and bending down so he can see the scars crisscrossing my skull.

"Wicked. Can I touch it?"

I shrug and say, "Sure." The scars are bumpy pinkish ridges now, and I can barely feel anything in them. It's like the nerves are messed up or something. There's only a dull pressure when Bil runs his finger along one of them.

"Whoa," he says.

Zach is standing beside us, looking at us like we're little gray space aliens.

I take a deep breath. Asking for help is not at the top of my list of favorite things to do. "So. I'm having trouble riding. My balance is worse than Golem in Mount Doom." Throwing in the *Lord of the Rings* reference is a sure way to get on Bil's good side. Despite the fact that he hates his name, he shares his parents' over-the-top passion for all things LOTR. It's complicated.

"Sucks to be you," Bil says.

"Yeah. Anyway, I need your help modifying a set of training wheels to fit on a road bike."

"Seriously?" Bil looks from me to Zach, who holds up the training wheels he carried into the bike shop with him.

"Seriously," I say.

"Can I call you Training Wheels Solley?" Bil asks, a grin dawning on his face.

"I told you he'd say that," Zach says.

"If you make this work," I say, "you can call me Training Wheels until I'm forty-five."

Bil's grin positively blazes. "Deal."

He tells Zach to man the shop counter and takes me, Bulb's bike, and the training wheels into his lair at the back of the shop. Three bikes are set up on stands in the middle of the room. Pegboard covers all the walls, and tools hang everywhere. A workbench with several large vices attached to it sits against one wall. The whole place smells like chain grease—heavenly.

Bil swaps the axle on Bulb's bike for a longer one and welds extensions onto the training wheels. It's not pretty when he's done, but it looks solid.

We take it to the shop's parking lot to test it out. The training wheels work beautifully. I can sit on the bike and take all the time in the world to clip into the pedals with no worry of tipping over or crashing. I do a couple circuits around the parking lot. Every time my balance goes wonky on me, the training wheels catch me.

I'm riding again. Exactly as well as I did when I was four years old. Go, me.

24

Jake

Zach comes over every morning, and we ride around my neighborhood together. I worry about being outside, but if the "firefighters" still want to kill me, they can do it regardless of whether I'm hiding in the house or cruising around the neighborhood. After a week on the training wheels, my balance has gotten much better. I can ride without touching either training wheel to the pavement except when I turn. Everything else is getting better, too. I can focus well enough to read, and almost all my memory has returned. I still can't remember the day of the accident, though.

The old itch has returned. An hour of poking around my neighborhood in the morning isn't enough to scratch it. I want to ride. On my own. No, I need to ride. To feel the wind rushing across my arms, the road unrolling at my feet, the flight, the freedom.

Bulb wants his bike back, and I'm pretty sure I don't need the training wheels any more. Besides, I want a bike of my own.

Mom is dead set against it. Laurissa is more sympathetic. Ever since the insanity at the hospital, her parents have insisted that one of the Brothers Grimm accompany her everywhere, so she has Dieter drive us to Mom's credit union. I have my own account, although its balance is a measly $120. I withdraw $115, the most I can take without closing the account. Then we visit the bike shop.

"Training Wheels!" Bil calls as we step through the door. Laurissa sighs heavily beside me.

"They worked perfectly," I say as we clasp hands. "You did a great job on them. Thanks again."

"Glad I could help," Bil says.

"I need my own bike. What do you have for a totally broke guy?"

"Why don't you get one of those Pinarello bikes you're always drooling over?" Laurissa asks.

"Um, because I've got $115 in my pocket?"

"My treat," Laurissa says.

Bil's eyes widen—the cheapest Pinarellos he stocks are more than a thousand dollars. A fully tricked out Dogma is over thirteen grand.

"No," I say.

Laurissa shrugs like it's no big deal. I guess spending a thousand dollars means a lot less to her than spending $115 does to me.

I bargain Bil down from the $150 price tag on an ungently used twelve-speed road bike. I accept Laurissa's offer to buy me a helmet. She grabs the most expensive one Bil has in stock and whips out a black Amex to pay for it. The helmet costs about five times what my bike did.

Then, almost as an afterthought, she asks, "What's the best bike for a beginner?"

"Road cycling?" Bil asks.

Laurissa nods, and Bil shows her a Scott Speedster. Laurissa buys it, another helmet, a bike rack that will fit on the back of her Prius, and she prepays for the installation of the rack. She makes an appointment for the next day to have the bike rack installed.

It's cool that she's taking an interest in biking. She came to my races before the accident but never showed any interest in riding herself, at least as far as I can remember. But something about this process—casually piling purchase on purchase—makes me profoundly uneasy. I go drool on the Dogma while she pays.

Then it's time for me to pay for my beat-up second-hand bike. I bargained Bil down to $115, but forgot to account for the sales tax. Laurissa has to chip in, and my humiliation is complete.

25
Jake

Dieter is appalled at Laurissa's purchase of a bicycle. "Any fool can run you down," he says. "Ist no way to protect you."

Laurissa insists that she's going to ride with me, unsafe or not. They argue for a few minutes and then agree that her father will have to decide. She winks at me and holds up her pinkie, wrapping an imaginary string around it.

The next day we're in Laurissa's Prius, returning to the bike shop. Dieter—or maybe Hans—is trailing us in one of their Mercedes sedans.

I give Bil a hand installing the bike rack; it's better than standing around watching him. And he did cut me a $35 break on my bike, so it's only fair. My used bike looks pretty pitiful on the rack next to Laurissa's brand new one, but still, I have to smile. It's *my* bike. Pitiful or not, it looks like freedom.

We go riding that same afternoon. It's thrilling, but I'm still a bit unsteady on the bike. All the practice on the training wheels has helped—I don't crash once. Laurissa is even less steady than I am. And she's slow! Wobbly or not, I want to move, to race, to fly. I match her pace, though, and ride alongside her, chatting as we meander through the neighborhood. We make an odd procession: two cyclists doing barely five miles an hour with a huge black Mercedes poking along behind us.

I get more confident on the bike over the next few days. I start sleeping less and getting up earlier, so I can ride by myself in the morning. Mom is so angry, she will barely speak to me. I hate the fact that she's upset, but I simply can't give up riding. It's as much a part of my life as working is part of hers.

Laurissa visits in the afternoons, and we tool around the neighborhood with the Mercedes in tow. Sometimes, after our ride, we hang out in the living room and make out a little—nothing more than kissing and snuggling while we watch a movie. Laurissa doesn't want to take it further, and I don't push her. I love how I feel when I'm around her and don't want to do anything to mess it up.

A few days later, I take a serious ride—my first long ride since the accident. I ride fast, trying to out-pedal all my doubts and fears. The wind rips at my ears, and I push myself, flying ever faster above the pavement. By midmorning, I'm almost twenty miles from home, racing along my favorite section of the Fall Creek Trail.

Most of the trail runs alongside a road, but for a mile or two, it diverges and runs beside the creek. Nobody's around today, and I'm pushing the pedals for all I'm worth, doing better than twenty-five miles an hour through this lonely stretch of woods.

Ahead, I see a girl on a red Schwinn. She's biking much more slowly than I am, but everyone I've seen on the trail today is slower. She's wearing horrible clothes for bike-riding—some kind of flowing pantsuit-type thing with long sleeves and a hood. No helmet, which I disapprove of on principle. And the loose fabric of her pants seems like a terrible idea—it's bound to get caught in her bike chain and cause a crash.

She speeds up as I approach, and I veer into the left lane to pass her. As I'm going by, I glance at her and startle so badly that I almost lose control of my bike. She's Fake Laurissa.

My bike rattles over the gravel at the edge of the path. I straighten the wheel, fighting for control. I'm down in the grass that borders the bike trail, inches from the trees. I get traction, easing my bike back up onto the trail, moving considerably more slowly than I was.

Fake Laurissa is there, riding alongside me. She's got a wooden nightstick in her left hand. She jabs it at my front wheel. I swerve away and scream, "What the hell?" I'm not fast enough. The baton jams between the front fork and the spokes. Instantly, I fly over the handlebars, my bike cartwheeling behind me. An image of the huge maroon car hood from the accident when I was fourteen flits past my eyes. A shrub vaults toward my head; there's a tremendous crack, and everything gets blurry for a moment.

I lift my head, looking around woozily. I'm on my stomach beside a clump of bushes. My bike is a few steps behind me. The front wheel is mangled, the baton still wedged amid its broken spokes. Fake Laurissa steps up to the bike, plants a sneaker on the front wheel, and pulls her nightstick free.

I push myself up and manage to crawl a few feet before I collapse again. A chunk of plastic from my shattered helmet falls past my face. I've got no balance, no strength. I look back—Fake Laurissa is striding toward me, baton in hand. I heave myself another few feet away. Dead leaves crunch under my knees.

Fake Laurissa kneels on my back. I try to push up, to throw her off, but I can barely even lift my head. "What are you doing? Why?" I moan. No answer comes. She slides the baton under my chin, gripping it at either side of my neck, and pulls upward. My throat is being crushed. I can't breathe. I can't breathe. I. Can't. Breathe!

I buck wildly, but she barely even moves. Why, I want to ask again, but no sound can escape the inexorable pull of the baton. Only the leaves answer, crunching under my flailing arms. I reach behind me and grab fistfuls of Laurissa's clothing. It's smooth, slick and strong. I can't tear it, can't move her by tugging on it.

The edges of my vision fade to black, and the world darkens around me.

26

Jake

The pressure on my throat eases suddenly. I gasp and cough. Loamy air so sweet I can taste it floods into my mouth and nose. My body flares, coming alive like a fire given fresh fuel.

Fake Laurissa beats the nightstick against the ground, so hard that the thunks vibrate the back of my head and bits of shattered leaves float around my face. "I need," she smacks the nightstick down again, "to do," *smack*, "this." *Smack.* "I promised him I would."

"Who?" I gasp. "Why?"

She's gripping the baton as if ready to strike, standing over me. Her face is contorted and red. She looks angry enough to kill me. I don't understand why she didn't. I don't understand why she wanted to in the first place. She kneels, bringing her face close to mine and speaks in a low, menacing voice. "You've got one chance to survive. You've got to die."

"What?" Another fit of coughing overtakes me, and it's all I can do to gasp the one-word question.

She ignores my comment. "You leave here now. You don't go home. You don't ever use your real name again. If I tell him you're dead . . . I get what I want, and you get to live."

"I . . . Mom, Laurissa—"

"They'll be fine if you disappear now."

I know this is not true. They'd be crushed if I disappeared.

"If you don't," Fake Laurissa continues, "well, he doesn't care who gets killed. Just so long as you do."

"Why are you doing this? Who's *he*?" I want to ask more questions, but I can barely squeeze the words out past the burning in my throat. "Who are you?" I ask between gasps.

She gets up and strides over to where her bike is lying at the edge of the path. I climb to my feet and stagger after her.

"What the hell is going on?" I ask.

She mounts the bike and puts her foot to a pedal. She looks back, and I see her eyes are bright, as if she might burst into tears. What does she have to cry about? She turns away, and I grab for her bike, trying to stop her. My need for answers outweighs my fear. I get a grip on the pouch mounted under her bike seat. The old Velcro holding it in place rips free as she pedals away.

Should I call the police? I can't just disappear, whatever Fake Laurissa said. There's no way I could do that to my mother. I'll ignore her on small things, sure, but to disappear would be beyond horrible. And where would I go? What would I do? I have no idea if it's even possible to disappear— how do you get a new name? How do you pay for things?

A coughing fit seizes me, so violent that I double over for a moment. I rub my throat. It hurts to touch, but I don't stop—it seems to help with the coughing. I must have a horrendous bruise.

I take my phone out of my pocket and stare at it a moment, thinking about dialing 911. Then I put it away. I need to get away from this isolated stretch of trail, get somewhere safe. I need to think this through.

I stuff the pouch from Fake Laurissa's bike into my backpack and retrieve my bike. The front wheel is wrecked beyond all hope of repair. The fork looks bent, too, but I can walk along the path by rolling the bike on its back wheel. I head for the pocket park I know is ahead. It's visible from Fall Creek Parkway, and there are usually people around.

How did Fake Laurissa know I'd be here? I hadn't planned to ride this way. I haven't been on this trail for months, at least not that I can remember. It's a long way from my house, and I usually prefer to ride out into the country, not into the city. There's no way she could have known where to find me. But she did. Fear seizes me, so intense that it cramps my gut, and I have to stop, trying to slow my racing heart.

When I can move again, I start jogging. I'm still wobbly, and the dead weight of the bike isn't helping, but I have to run, have to move, have to get away from here. How is she following me? I left the hospital almost naked—if she planted some kind of bug on me, it'd have to be . . . inside me, somehow. I run faster. But even as I break into a sprint, I realize this isn't a problem I'll be able to outrun.

27

Betsy

I bike along the trail to the spot where I'd stashed my back-pack and clothes. I stumble down the river bank into a dense wooded area close to the river to change. My stupid Muslim outfit goes into my backpack.

I pause before stowing the nightstick. How can I make myself carry through with my plans? Why couldn't I kill him? "Betsy, you are such a stupid, weak-kneed, wuss of a . . . ." There's no insult bad enough for what I am. The only thing that comes close is "girl."

I want to beat trees with the nightstick until it cracks. I want to hurl the nightstick into Fall Creek. I want to hurl myself into Fall Creek. But I don't have the energy. Instead, I Velcro the nightstick onto my backpack and shoulder it.

I trudge up the bank to my bike. Now I look like an ordinary girl out for a late-afternoon bike ride, my legs and arms exposed to the breeze. Except for the nightstick. Most girls don't bike around with a nightstick on their back.

I ride to the Goodwill on Keystone Avenue, avoiding the bridge and park at the north end of the trail. I donate my costume: no receipt, no paper trail. That's when I discover that my seat pouch is missing. I'm supposed to donate the bike, too, and buy another one at a bike shop a few blocks from here, but my money was in the pouch. That way, even if I couldn't return to my backpack, I'd have resources.

I race back to the trail, pushing the broken-down Schwinn for all it's worth. A quick hunt through the area turns up no sign of my seat pack. I pull my bike off the path and start searching the brush along its edge. After about five minutes, a guy stops and offers to help. I shrug and tell him no, I'm just looking for a lost contact lens. Over the next couple of hours, it happens three more times. Two of them are alone, but then a guy out biking with his girlfriend or wife stops and offers to help. He's so persistent that I have to grab the nightstick and pretty much order him to leave.

When twilight falls, I'm forced to give up my search. There's nothing in the seat pouch that can lead to me. It's all part of the cover, part of the plan to confuse things and throw suspicion onto the most likely suspect. Most murders are committed by someone the victim knows. A husband or boyfriend is the usual perp, but girlfriends and wives commit murder too. Dad says that if there's anything linking the real Laurissa to the crime, the cops will fixate on that and quit looking for any other explanation.

The lost money is no big deal. But it irks me to change the plan, to keep the bike. I bought it with cash, so it would be almost impossible to trace it to me. But I wonder: What else is going to go wrong?

28

Jake

By the time I reach the park at the north end of the trail, I'm gasping, out of breath. I pull my phone out of my pocket and, without really thinking about it, dial Mom's cell. The call goes straight to voicemail, and I hang up.

I double over. I'm afraid I'm going to hurl. I'm hyperventilating. *Get it together, Jake*, I tell myself. *You can handle this.* I can handle it. I can. But I need help. I dial Laurissa's cell.

She picks up immediately. "Hi," she whispers. "I'm in that seminar at the law school I told you about. With my friend Charlotte. Call you back at lunchtime?"

I'd completely forgotten. I blurt out my whole story in a rush, barely pausing to breathe.

"Hang up. Call the police. Now," Laurissa's voice is loud now, authoritative. "I'll be there in eight minutes. Maybe nine."

I'm still trying to catch my breath.

"Jake. I'm already halfway to my car. Did you get that? Hang up and call the police. Okay?"

"Okay." I disconnect and dial 911.

The police beat Laurissa to the park. An unmarked car with a flasher in the front window pulls up after barely a minute has passed. Captain Beaner gets out. He looks around as he approaches me. The park is busy—there are half a dozen fishermen down by the water and two mothers watching a passel of kids play on the jungle gym. I'm sprawled out on a bench near the bike trail, my wrecked bike lying in the grass in front of me.

When he gets close enough to see the shattered helmet still perched atop my head, he reaches for the radio at his hip. I overhear him telling dispatch to send an ambulance.

"Take it easy," he says. "Help is on the way."

"How . . . why are you—"

"I was the closest unit," he says. "What happened?"

While I'm telling him the whole story about Fake Laurissa trying to kill me again, a patrol car pulls up, lights flashing. A uniformed officer gets out. Beaner tells me to wait and ambles over to the car. After a moment, the uniformed officer gets back into his patrol car and drives away.

An ambulance arrives, sirens wailing. The paramedics rush out, and for a while, I'm occupied by their questions, their tests, and their gentle examination of my skull. My bike helmet has a hole the size and shape of a grapefruit. It appears to have done its job, though. I'm grateful to Laurissa for buying me the best helmet in Bil's shop—she may have saved my life. Again. The paramedics are worried about a possible concussion, but they can't find anything broken.

Laurissa's blue Prius pulls up. The paramedics are checking the scrapes on my hands and knees. Beaner is still asking me questions. I feel dazed, like I'm trying to watch three movies at the same time.

Laurissa charges into the chaos. "Thank God you're here," I say, giving her a one-armed hug. One of the paramedics is holding my other arm captive, picking grit out of my palm.

Beaner turns to her, "Ma'am, would you mind waiting by your car for a few minutes?"

Laurissa doesn't answer, and Beaner chooses not to press the issue. I'm stuck there for another hour while the paramedics try to convince me to go to the hospital—the last place in the world I want to go—and Beaner questions me. Eventually, the paramedics give up, Beaner hands me a small gray slip of paper—another incident report—and I'm free to go home.

We load my wrecked bike onto the rack on Laurissa's Prius, and she drives me home.

I don't remember the pack I took from Fake Laurissa until we're ensconced on the couch in my living room. I'm telling Laurissa the story for the third time when I realize that I left that part out. I unzip my backpack and take out the black canvas bike pouch.

Inside the pouch, there's a small, brightly patterned cloth purse. "I have one exactly like that," Laurissa says. "It's Vera Bradley—a wristlet."

I'm not sure why she named her purse Vera or exactly what

a wristlet is, but it doesn't seem important. I open it—inside, there are a couple of tubes of lipstick, a compact, and a red leather wallet. I pull out the wallet.

"That's just like mine, too. Coach."

I open the wallet. There are ten old, worn twenty-dollar bills inside. I put the money aside and pull the cards out, fanning them on the coffee table.

"Mother of Sauron!" Laurissa curses.

"What? What is it?"

She doesn't answer. Instead, she reaches into her purse—it's a lot larger than the purse Fake Laurissa was carrying—and takes out a wallet that's a dead ringer for the one I'm holding. She pulls out her cards and lays them alongside Fake Laurissa's. They're exactly the same. A black Amex. A driver's license. A UnitedHealthCare card. Even a library card. I pick up both driver's licenses and compare them. They're identical, except for the photo. Same address—Laurissa's real address. Same driver's license number. Same holographic seal the State of Indiana puts on the front to make them difficult to fake. It seems impossible that anyone would have the power to fabricate a cover story this perfect. But someone has. And I have no idea who they are.

29

Betsy

When I finally pedal up to our house, well after dark, Dad isn't home yet. He must have pulled a double shift. He's been doing a lot of those lately.

I'm deeply asleep when a powerful flashlight shining directly into my eyes wakes me. "Why," Dad says in a voice so close to a growl that it's nearly unintelligible, "is Jake Solley still alive?"

"Dad . . . my room?" I'm too sleepy to think straight. He's not supposed to come into my room like this. I'm seventeen, for God's sake.

"Why!" he roars.

"He fought me off. I'll get him next time. Maybe bring a taser or—"

The back of his hand smacks into my cheek, rocking my whole head sideways. I saw him winding up for the blow, but I didn't believe it, didn't make any move to defend myself. My father would never hit me. Even now, with the taste of blood between my teeth, I don't believe he would hit me.

"Your mother would be ashamed of you," he says.

"Maybe—"

"I'm ashamed of you. You're weak. A failure. Disgusting."

"I'm sorry," I say, but I can hardly believe the words coming out of my mouth. I feel like someone else is talking while I watch. Someone else's cheek is on fire. Someone else is curled on my bed, nursing a pain that only begins with her face. It's all I can do not to cry.

My father turns and leaves the room, closing the door with precisely enough force to make it latch. Once he's gone, my façade cracks, and I curl up on my bed and sob. I pull a pillow against my face and muffle the noise so my weakness won't disturb him.

30

Jake

The pair of shiny black Amex cards look totally out of place on our battered wooden coffee table. I pick up both of them—Fake Laurissa's and real Laurissa's. They're heavy—not plastic, but some kind of metal. There's a Roman centurion on the front in an oval, which makes it look like some kind of currency. The account numbers on the front are the same. I flip the cards over—the signatures look identical.

Laurissa has her phone out. She takes her card from me and dials the number on the back. A muffled voice comes on the line, and Laurissa responds, "Hi, Jason, this is Laurissa Davis. I need to know if any additional cards were issued on our account in the last six months or so." There's a brief silence, and then Laurissa reads the card number and gives him a security code. "I see. . . . Could you tell me if *I've* requested any additional cards in the last six months? . . . I realize that, but can you check your records for me? Surely my own requests aren't confidential from me? Okay, thanks." Laurissa hangs up.

"Apparently, I requested a duplicate card almost two months ago, while you were still in the hospital," she says.

"But you didn't."

"No. I wonder what she's been using it for?"

"You don't know?"

Laurissa doesn't answer—she's on the phone again.

"Joe?" she says into the phone. "I need to see all my credit card charges for the last two months. . . . Can you just email me the file? . . . Fine, I'll log into the server." She hangs up.

"Who was that?" I ask.

"Dad's accountant. Won't email them to me—says it's not secure. Should be up on Dad's server in five minutes."

Laurissa waits maybe three minutes before thumbing something long and complex into her phone. She flips through pages of itemized statements. "It's all legit," she says finally. "Why would you go through the trouble of getting a copy of my black card and then not use it? Was she going to try to frame me for your murder?"

"Maybe. Maybe it was a cover? Nothing makes sense."

She calls Amex back and tries to get the phone number used to request the duplicate card—the concierge tells her he can't pull up that information, and when she finally gets through to someone who can, she finds out that the number was blocked. A call to the Indiana Department of Motor Vehicles to ask about the bogus driver's license is completely fruitless. UnitedHealthCare and The Indianapolis Public Library are similarly tightlipped.

Laurissa tosses the cards down in frustration. I pick up the fake driver's license, staring at the photo. The license says Eyes BRO, Hair BLK, which is true for both Laurissas, even though they look nothing alike. "The only thing we know is real is her picture."

"Why did they have a fake ID made with a real picture?" Laurissa asks.

"Maybe in case she gets stopped?" I say. "She can show it to a police officer, and it looks legit?"

"Maybe."

"So anyway, since we know the picture is legit, we should search using that."

"That's brilliant." Laurissa whips her phone out again and takes a picture of the photo on the license from about two inches away.

In minutes, we're plugging the photo into search engines. Google Image returns a bunch of similar photos but none of the same person. Facebook won't let us search by image, and when we try the suggest tags feature, we get nothing. We find a couple of customized photo search sites, but they're no better—we get famous people, similar-looking people, or no results at all.

"This isn't working," I say.

"Thank you, Mr. Obvious."

"Every one of these cards is a dead end. We've checked everything."

Laurissa has picked up Fake Laurissa's wallet, and she's examining it thoughtfully. "We haven't checked everything. This wallet needs repair, don't you think?"

"No," I say. It's pristine.

"So you're a manly man—rip out this seam." Laurissa hands me the wallet, pointing out the seam in question.

"Why?"

Laurissa explains her idea to me—it sounds like it just might work. But hard as I try, I can't damage the wallet. I get a knife from the kitchen. Even with the knife, I have to work at it for fifteen minutes or so to get one of the seams to give way. Someday, I'm going to give my mom one of these—her wallet is continually falling apart.

Just as I'm thinking of her, Mom sweeps in through the door. I grab all the fake cards from the coffee table and jam them back into the bike pouch. I don't want to try to explain the day's craziness to Mom—she's got more than enough on her mind as it is. Attempting to track down Fake Laurissa will have to wait until morning.

31

Jake

Laurissa has promised to eat dinner with her family, so Mom and I eat dinner together. Mom makes meatloaf, which I love. Her secret is that she puts lots of super-finely chopped vegetables in it, which keeps it moist and adds flavor. I spend ten or fifteen minutes working alongside her, mincing carrots, celery, and an onion.

The smell of baking meatloaf reminds me of the only place I've had meatloaf even half as good as Mom's, Shapiro's Deli in downtown Indy. Remembering Shapiro's triggers an even more intense memory. I was riding downtown, despite Mom's rule that I should never go east of Lynhurst Drive or south of 38th Street. It was a good rule—there are some rough neighborhoods in that part of town. But back then I didn't see the point. I figured I could safely bike anywhere. I was a fast, confident rider—who could catch me, let alone stop me?

I learned my lesson the hard way. I was waiting to cross Michigan Road. A guy I hadn't even noticed suddenly straddled the front wheel of my bike. He laid one hand on my handlebars and opened his vivid red and black Chicago Bulls jacket with the other. I saw the handle of a knife, strapped with the sheath hidden under his baggy pants.

"Give me your wallet," he growled, so close to my face that I could smell alcohol on his breath.

I reached toward the pouch mounted behind my seat, where I kept my wallet and keys. There was nothing else I could do. He was blocking me from moving forward, and road bikes don't go in reverse. The cars zipping by on Michigan at fifty miles an hour might as well have been airplanes, for all the good they did me. There was no one else around. My hand shook so badly that I couldn't get a grip on the zipper.

The guy grunted, obviously disgusted with my inability to retrieve my wallet. He stepped around to the side of the bike, grabbed my seat pouch, and ripped it free. The whole bike rocked sideways as the Velcro gave.

"Get off the bike."

No, I thought. I was riding my Dad's bike. Not the best racing bike, but completely irreplaceable. Losing my wallet was no big deal, but losing my bike would be a catastrophe.

He still had a grip on the handlebar, but he was standing beside the bike now. I stomped on the pedal and hurled myself into the traffic on Michigan Avenue.

Brakes squealed and tires burned as drivers desperately tried to avoid the lunatic cyclist in their midst. One car flashed past so close that it clipped my front wheel, and I very nearly wiped out. By the time I was across the street, I was probably doing twenty-five or thirty miles an hour—a flat out sprint. I barely slowed until I reached home.

I told Mom that my seat pouch fell off somewhere, that I lost it. I was afraid she'd ban me from riding completely if she knew I'd violated her "do not ride" zone. I'd lost a few bucks, my house key, my wallet, and my library card. Getting everything replaced ran about thirty bucks. Mom was annoyed, but not nearly as angry as she would have been if I'd told her the truth.

Over dinner, I tell Mom about the memory of the mugging.

"You were riding downtown?" Mom asks. "When you were . . ?"

"Twelve or thirteen," I say.

"I think you would have told me about something like that."

"I was afraid you'd ban me from riding."

"Hallucinations, false memory, paranoia," Mom said. "It fits a lot of the symptoms in that book about brain injury."

"Would a hallucination be that detailed?" I ask.

"I don't know. Maybe not."

I want to argue, but don't. After all, how can I be certain she's not right? Maybe none of my memories are accurate. The thought lodges in my gut and suddenly just the smell of the meatloaf is nauseating. I excuse myself from the table and bolt to my room.

32

Betsy

When Dad—no, Father, I can't think of him as Dad any-more—has worked a night shift, like he did last night, he sleeps all day. I mope around, watching a lot of bad television when I should be doing homework for my summer class. My stomach is killing me. Around noon, I run out of Rolaids and walk to the gas station to buy more. I don't even think about the bruise on my face until I get home. It's hideous, a smashed purple and blue flower blooming across my cheek. I could dab some concealer on it, but what's the point?

I log on to the Stormbreak forums and delete a bunch of posts some libtard troll put up overnight. I get a couple private messages and reply perfunctorily. I don't feel like talking to anyone. Normally, a whole day to spend talking

163

to friends online would be heavenly, but today, I'm just not feeling it.

When dinnertime rolls around, Father's still asleep. It's Friday—I don't have classes tonight, so I decide to make dinner. I get a package of pork chops from the freezer and defrost them in the microwave. We don't have anything fresh, but we do have frozen green beans.

Father appears not long after I start frying the pork chops. I swear, if he were in a coma, the smell of frying pork chops would wake him. My stomach clenches when I see him, but I force a smile onto my face. I leave the stove and open the fridge. "Want a beer?" I ask.

"No. Water," he says.

I pour a glass from the pitcher in the fridge and hand it to him, then go back to tending the chops.

He takes a deep draught from the glass. "Look, Betsy—"

"It's okay," I say, although I feel like I may vomit right into the frying pan.

"It's not okay. I shouldn't have raised my hand to you. It'll never happen again."

"Okay." I flip the chops with a fork. A drop of grease splatters against the back of my hand. I bite my lip against the pain, ignoring it.

We're silent until we're seated at the table. I break the silence and bless the food.

"Amen," Father says, stabbing a pork chop with his fork and levering it onto his plate, "and thank you for making dinner."

"You're welcome." I let some green beans roll off the serving spoon onto my plate. They remind me of logs rolling down a hill, accelerating as they go.

For some reason, my mother comes to mind. The way her sweatshirt felt against my cheek the last time she hugged me, after I'd been suspended from school. How safe I felt. "You really think Mom would be ashamed of me?" I can't believe that question fell from my idiot mouth.

His fork stops on its way to his mouth, a chunk of pork chop skewered on it. He sets the fork down, then picks it up again and eats the bite, chewing slowly. I wait.

"It was nothing," he says finally. "The anger talking."

"I don't remember her being involved with The Sons, is all."

"She never helped with any operations."

"I want to look for her. If you'd help, I know we could—"

"No."

"But I want to—"

"Drop it. If she wants to be found, she'll contact us."

I nod, accepting his answer, at least outwardly. But I'm not sure I believe him.

33
Jake

Laurissa and I are at The Fashion Mall—the fanciest mall in the city—when it opens at ten the next morning. This is not the mall my mom takes me to, although I have been here before. Once. Laurissa's wearing ripped jeans—not the kind I own, with the knees torn and grass-stained from yard work—but ones that look like someone spent a hundred hours with an X-Acto knife, ripping them just so. She's wearing a T-shirt with a stylized YSL on it and black high-heel boots that are almost as shiny as her shades. Dieter follows close behind us, scowling.

I feel completely out of place. Laurissa and I are dressed about the same—I'm wearing jeans, a really soft *Waikiki Beach Bum* T-shirt that I got at Goodwill, and sneakers. But I'm guessing my whole outfit didn't cost as much as her T-shirt. And her diamond teardrop earrings probably cost more than my house. I don't remember seeing her wear jewelry before. Or high-heels or shades, for that matter. I hope we'll go straight to the Coach store and get this over with.

But we don't. "We need to make the right kind of impression," Laurissa says. So we start at Nordstrom. Laurissa shops like a Tasmanian devil—if she were a Tasmanian devil with a black Amex and the desire to load its bodyguard down with Nordstrom bags.

Laurissa flashes her black Amex at a clerk and says, "I need a new wardrobe. And I only have half an hour. Would you be a dear?" They ask to see her ID, which seems kind of insulting to me, but she's already got it out. I guess she's used to being carded. In moments, we have three clerks helping us. One is picking out clothing and taking it to Laurissa in the changing room. Another runs back and forth from the changing room to the sales counter. A third is standing at the cash register, ringing up purchases as quickly as she can scan them.

When we leave, Dieter is lugging five huge Nordstrom bags. I offer to carry a couple of them, but Laurissa says no. "We're going to load you down, next."

We hit the Abercrombie & Fitch and repeat the whole scene. They have almost nothing in Laurissa's size, so I wind up carrying only two bags.

Laurissa is smiling savagely as we leave. "I love shopping there. Fat black girl with an unlimited card is their worst nightmare."

"You're not fat!" I protest.

"I know what I am. I could buy the whole store, literally

everything, but they've got nothing to sell me. You'd think they'd figure out that not everyone is some bony white chick."

"Glad you're having a good time." I love spending time with Laurissa, but I'd prefer it if we were almost anywhere else. "Doesn't it bug you? Buying stuff just to make an impression on the clerk at Coach?"

"No. Why?"

"It just seems . . . profligate is the word, I think."

"You sound like my dad," Laurissa says.

"I didn't mean—"

"It's okay. Look, Jake, money is just a tool. I don't care about it for its own sake, like my dad does. What matters is what I can do with it, how I can use it to help the people I love. Like you. So yeah, this is fun."

"Oh. I hadn't thought about it that way." I resolve to quit raining on her parade and follow as she sashays toward the Coach store. We make quite a procession—Laurissa, unburdened; me, with a bag in each hand; and Dieter behind us, glaring his disapproval and carrying five bags, all of them on his left arm—three hanging from his forearm and two clutched in one ham-sized fist.

The only person in the Coach store is the generically pretty white woman staffing the desk. She looks up and says, "Welcome to Coach. I'm Janet. How may I help?"

Laurissa plops the red leather wallet down on the counter with a dramatic flourish, makes a pouty face, and says, "My bag broke."

The clerk slides over to the computer terminal, puts a plastic smile on her face, and replies, "We'll be happy to replace or repair that for you, Miss . . ."

"Davis. Laurissa Davis."

The clerk types something. I edge around the counter, trying to get to a spot where I can see the screen. The clerk's face brightens considerably, and she says, "I'm so sorry you had trouble with your wallet, Miss Davis. Since you're a preferred customer, I can waive our normal handling fee for a repair. Or perhaps you'd like a full-credit exchange? Maybe an upgrade to a newer style? We just got some fabulous new bags in our—"

"A new style?" Laurissa says. "I only got this one two months ago."

The clerk glances at her screen. "Our records must be in error, then? I show you purchased that item almost two years ago. In September."

"No, no," Laurissa says. "That one was a gift. I bought this one," she gestures at the wallet on the counter, "about two months ago."

The clerk picks up the wallet, opening it and inspecting a leather tag sewn to the inside. I back up a little more and squint to read the screen past her shoulder. She types something into the model number field and pulls up a list of transactions. She tabs backward through the list. "Oh, I see the problem. You paid cash so it didn't get associated with your account. I'll just fix that."

"Thanks," Laurissa says.

I watch as the clerk pulls up a detailed record. The only information in the customer field is a first name: Betsy. Everything else is blank. The clerk enters Davis in the last name field, selects Laurissa from the drop-down list of Davises that appears, and just like that, all the fields are replaced with Laurissa's information. "Can I offer you a free replacement?"

"No . . ." Laurissa is wearing her pouty face again. "I want this one repaired."

"No problem. Shall we send it straight to your home?"

"Yes. What address do you have?"

The clerk says, "111 Willow Spring," which is Laurissa's home address.

"No, no," Laurissa says, "send it to the other address. The one I gave you when I bought it."

"You . . . didn't give us another address. I'll just put it in now."

"Nevermind," Laurissa says. "Just send it to the address you've got."

We leave the store. As we trudge through the mall, Laurissa says, "You see anything on the screen?"

"Yeah. The only field that was filled in was for first name: Betsy."

"Well, that was a waste of time."

"Maybe not."

"She paid cash and didn't bother to give them information for the warranty—there's no way she used her real name."

"I bet it was a reflexive thing—the clerk said 'Hi, I'm Janet,' or something like that and she says 'I'm Betsy' without thinking about it. A tiny mistake in the big scheme of things. If she'd lied, she would have said she was Laurissa."

"It's not much to go on. There's got to be a zillion girls her age named Betsy in Indianapolis."

"It's kind of an old-timey name," I say. "It might not be that bad. And we have her picture."

"It's still not much."

I shrug. I know more than I did an hour ago. Fake Laurissa is a real person probably named Betsy, and she was in this mall and bought a wallet just two months ago. Somehow, I will find out more. Somehow, I will locate Betsy. And learn why she wants to kill me.

34

Jake

On the way home, I start to drift—not quite falling asleep, but close. As we near my house, a plane roars overhead, triggering another memory. I remember my bike ride the day of the accident, the tanker trucks lined up alongside the road. The memory comes with an overwhelming feeling of dread. I want to scream "No!" but I can't say anything, can't stop my remembered self from swerving around the first tanker truck and racing alongside it.

The tanks open, and the memory of the overpowering reek is nearly enough to make me gag, even though the backseat of Laurissa's Mercedes smells like leather polish, not sulfur. The roar of the airplane overhead merges with my memory of another plane. The truck door opens in front of me, too close to avoid, and I slam into it, startling fully awake.

"You okay?" Laurissa asks.

I'm panting like I'd just done a race-finishing sprint on my bike. "Yeah. No." I tell Laurissa about the memory.

"Maybe that's what Captain Beaner was talking about?" Laurissa says in a rush. "The information he wanted about the plane crash on 6/11."

Laurissa and Dieter come home with me. I invite Dieter in, but he wants to guard Laurissa from outside the house.

I dig Captain Beaner's card out of my wallet and dial his number. He picks up on the second ring, which surprises me. I figured a captain in the police force would have a secretary or at least some kind of Byzantine voice mail system guarding his telephone.

"I remembered something that could be related to the plane crash," I say. "There were tanker—"

"Wait one second," Beaner says.

There's a buzz, a click, and a long wait—more like one minute than one second—and then Morris comes on the line instead of Beaner, "You remembered something? Tell me."

I tell him about the tanker trucks.

"We need to discuss this in person. Are you at home?"

"Yeah."

"I'll be there soon. Don't leave." Morris hangs up.

I make turkey and lettuce sandwiches for Laurissa, Dieter, and me. I slather Laurissa's with the spicy mustard she loves, and put a generic version of Miracle Whip on the other two. Laurissa takes a sandwich outside to Dieter—he won't come in, not even for lunch.

Laurissa and I spend the rest of the afternoon on the Internet, searching for girls in Indianapolis named Betsy. Laurissa doesn't say anything about my ancient garage-sale computer or the slower-than-molasses Internet. I know her home setup is roughly a thousand times better, so I appreciate her lack of comment.

We can't figure out any good way to search using just a first name and location so we try popular surnames in white-pages.com. There are eight Betsy Smiths, seven Betsy Johnsons, five Betsy Browns, six Betsy Millers, four Betsy Davises, three Betsy Wilsons, three Betsy Andersons, six Betsy Taylors, and so on, and so on.

Fortunately, the site lists an age range for each Betsy, and most of them are way too old to be Fake Laurissa. But still, after about two hours of searching, we have a list of well over a hundred possibilities. And we're nowhere near finished.

Morris still hasn't shown up by mid-afternoon, which strikes me as odd. His definition of "soon" must be completely different from mine.

Laurissa and I take a break to stretch and then return to searching for Betsy on the Internet. Two more hours produces the same results we got before: nothing.

We're interrupted by a knock on the door. I get up from the computer and roll my arms for a moment before answering it. There's another, harder knock as I start down the hall. Behind me, I hear Laurissa's phone ring. I glance through the window beside our front door. There are two men in conservative gray suits, one tall—6'3" or more—and the other a short, dark-haired man. The tall guy has blond hair that's retreating from his forehead, and he's a few pounds overweight. His eyes show too much white, so he looks a little startled or crazy. He holds up a pocket-sized leather portfolio and lets it flop open so I can see his badge and I.D. I can't read any of the words except his name, Special Agent James Tapper, but the badge is clear enough: It reads F.B.I. Three dark sedans box in Laurissa's Mercedes. Behind them there's an unmarked white panel van. Dieter is standing beside the Mercedes, talking to a woman in a gray pantsuit. Laurissa is talking into her phone behind me, but I can't make out the words.

"Open up. FBI," Agent Tapper yells, loud enough that I can hear him through the door.

I unlock the door and start to open it. He pushes into the foyer before I can step out of the way. "Mr. Solley?" he asks.

"Yes, but most people call me Jake."

"Face the wall. Put your hands behind your back."

"What's going on?"

"Now!" he says in a voice so authoritative that I comply without really thinking about it.

The dark-haired guy steps up behind me. I feel cold metal against my wrists and hear a click.

"What are you doing?" I say. "Why are you handcuffing me?"

"Mirandize him please, Agent Soufan."

"I didn't do anything!" Without intending to, I've started yelling.

"You have the right to remain silent," Agent Soufan says in a monotone.

"I don't understand! What's this about?"

"Anything you say can and will be used against you in a court of law. You have the right to talk to a lawyer and have him present while you are questioned. If you cannot afford to hire a lawyer, one will be appointed to represent you before questioning, if you wish."

"What's going on?" I ask.

"You know exactly what's happening and why, Mr. Solley," Tapper says as he snaps a pair of latex gloves over his hands.

Soufan continues, "Do you understand the rights I have just read to you? With these rights in mind, do you wish to speak to me?"

"Actually, I have no freaking clue what's happening," I say.

Laurissa puts her phone in her pocket and comes to the edge of the living room. "Don't say anything, Jake."

"What? Why? I didn't do anything."

"Say nothing!"

Tapper turns toward her. "Are you related to the suspect?"

"No," she says, "but—"

"You will leave the premises now."

What's he doing ordering my girlfriend around in my own house? It's lucky I'm handcuffed.

"What are you charging him with?" Laurissa asks.

"Agent Soufan brought an extra pair of handcuffs. One more word, and you'll be modeling them," Tapper says.

Laurissa holds his eyes for a moment and then pushes past him. As she steps behind me, she grabs my hand and gives it a brief squeeze. Then she's out the front door. Her phone is out, and she's already dialing. Summoning help, I hope, although I'm not sure what kind of help Laurissa could possibly get for someone who's just been arrested by the FBI.

Tapper starts frisking me with his gloved hands. He reaches into my front pocket, pulls out my cell phone, and drops it into a plastic evidence bag.

"What am I being charged with?" I ask.

"Obstruction of justice," Tapper says.

I take a breath to start protesting but remember Laurissa's parting words. Say nothing.

When Tapper finishes searching me, he turns to Soufan. "The mother?"

"She's been notified," he responds and turns toward me. "We'll make sure your mother knows where you are."

As we leave, four men in white plastic jumpsuits enter the house. Laurissa is standing with Dieter beside the Mercedes, talking into her phone. She catches my eye and puts her fist over her heart, moving it in a circle. I'm not sure exactly what she means, and I'm too dazed to respond.

The agents lower me into the back seat of one of the sedans. Soufan drives, and Tapper rides shotgun. I ask where we're going, but neither of them responds. My stomach is roiling, and I try to breathe deeply, which helps a little. We're headed toward the north side of Indianapolis.

The car pulls up at what looks like an ordinary suburban office building. Soufan and Tapper hustle me to an elevator. In no time at all, I'm sitting at a dented metal table in a room with pale green walls and a linoleum floor. Three sturdy metal chairs surround the table. Otherwise, the room is utterly devoid of decoration—there's nothing but a boxy thermostat placed oddly high on the wall facing me. The only door is on my left.

Tapper and Soufan leave. The click of the lock as the door closes feels dangerously final.

35

Jake

I wait in the tiny interrogation room for what seems like an hour. Several times I stand up and pace. Once I try the door, turning my back so I can reach the knob with my cuffed hands. Locked. I don't call out, don't say anything. I'm sure they want me to talk, maybe to beg to be released—there's got to be a point to leaving me alone for this long.

Eventually, the door opens and Soufan comes in. "Let me get those cuffs off you. They've got to be getting uncomfortable."

I stand and turn, and Soufan removes the cuffs from my hands. "I don't understand why I'm here," I say. Soufan slips the cuffs into his jacket pocket. "Have a seat, Jake."

I sit down behind the table, and Soufan drags a chair to the end of the table and sits so there's nothing between us.

"I know how you're probably feeling, Jake. You're scared and nervous—that's okay, but there's nothing to be scared of here. We'll just have a little discussion, clear a few things up, and get this resolved."

"Do I need a lawyer?"

"I can't advise you on that. You play any sports, Jake?"

"I'm a bike racer."

"Oh really? My son loves to ride. He doesn't race, though. There a lot of races around here?"

"This time of year? There's one in driving distance almost every weekend." Why is Soufan asking me this stuff? I don't get it, but it's a relief to talk about something I understand.

"You ever win anything?"

"Yeah. I almost always win the junior races. In some of the small races I'm allowed to compete with the pros. I get smoked in those."

"So you were riding your bike on 6/11?"

"Yeah. I was training. Riding the cornfield loop. That's what I call it, anyway. Doing a recovery ride."

"Where were you?"

"Before my accident, I used to ride an eight-mile loop west of the airport. I've ridden it hundreds of times. If you have map or something, I could mark it out for you."

Soufan takes a pen and tiny notebook out of his pocket and scrawls something. As he puts them away, he says, "We'll bring you a map. What time did you leave for your ride?"

"I don't remember exactly. Probably around 5:15. I usually set my alarm for five."

"*Ya salaam*, son. That's hardcore. I can't get my kid up before noon on the weekends."

"*Ya . . . ?*"

"Just means I'm impressed."

I shrug. I'd been thinking about moving it back to four. If I ever want to make it to Belgium, I'll need to step it up a notch or two. Although now, with everything that's happened, I wonder if it's still possible.

"When did you notice something unusual?"

"On my first lap, I saw a tanker truck parked by the side of the road."

"Where?"

I give him the nearest intersection. "On the second lap, there were five. On the third lap, there were fifteen or sixteen. I was riding past when they started to open. There was a sulfur smell so intense I nearly gagged." I expect Soufan to take out his notebook again—this is the important stuff, after all. But he doesn't. "A cab door opened, and I hit it full speed. I don't remember anything after that."

"Nothing?"

"No. Nothing until I woke up in the hospital."

There's a knock at the door. I twist in my seat—Agent Tapper has opened the door. He's holding my phone in a plastic evidence bag. They have a short conversation in low whispers, then Soufan turns to me and says, "I'll be back in a few minutes, Jake. You like something? Cup of coffee? A snack?"

"Love some water," I say.

"Smart move. Coffee around here tastes like brown pond scum." He shoots me a wry smile.

I'm tempted to ask him how he knows what brown pond scum tastes like, but I quash that thought—snark isn't going to help me.

I wait for a lot longer than a few minutes. It seems like another hour. I try the door—it's locked. Again. I wasn't particularly thirsty when I asked for water, but now I'm parched.

When Soufan finally does come back, he's carrying a Styrofoam cup of lukewarm water. I thank him and gulp it greedily. Soufan takes the plastic bag that contains my phone out of his jacket pocket and sets it on the table. "Where did this come from?"

"I bought it at Walmart."

"When?"

"About a year ago." I don't get what my phone has to do with anything. And I want to go home. I wish he'd get to the point.

"Where did you get the PlaneSploit program?"

"What are you talking about?"

"You know what I'm talking about, Jake."

"No. I don't."

"You're not being entirely truthful with me, Jake."

"Actually I—"

"Honesty is the best policy, here, Jake. If you were my own son, I'd tell you to be completely up front. Who gave you the PlaneSploit program?"

"What's a PlaneSploit program?"

"How'd you get it? Was it on the SD card in your phone?"

"My phone doesn't have an SD card." I'd thought about buying one; my cheapo phone constantly ran out of memory.

"Look, Jake, we already know all about it. There's no reason to be less than fully candid with me. We know someone gave you the PlaneSploit program on an SD card. We're going to find out who. It'll be best for you if you just tell us."

"What's a PlaneSploit program?"

"The person who gave it to you may have called it SIMON. Who was that?"

"Nobody gave me anything."

I'm getting exasperated, but Soufan is perfectly calm. "I've got all night," he says. "All week. All month, if need be. The Deputy Director has pulled me off my other cases. We can continue this for as long as it takes. So why don't we clear it up now, Jake? Where were you when you got the SD chip with SIMON on it? Did someone give it to you in person? Was it a dead drop?"

"I don't have any program called SIMON or PlaneSploit."

"It's in your phone, Jake. Right here. Denying it isn't helping you." Soufan taps the edge of the evidence bag.

"I don't know how it got there," I say. "What about the tanker trucks? Maybe they had something to do with the plane crash?"

"When I left the room, Agent Tapper checked out your story. That road was closed on 6/11. They were repaving it. You couldn't have ridden down it that day. You need to be truthful with me, Jake."

I lean back in my chair. That's impossible. My brain may have been scrambled, but I'm sure my memories of that day are true. They were so vivid when I was riding in the backseat of Laurissa's Mercedes just this morning. It seems like years ago now. "There wasn't any road closure. Nobody was paving any of the roads on the cornfield loop."

"You aren't helping yourself here, Jake."

I lean forward, "I'm telling the truth!"

"I know how it is, Jake. Maybe you're afraid. Whoever gave you the program threatened you. Threatened your mother. You didn't want to go along with it, but you didn't have a choice.

The FBI has resources that can help you. Protect you and your mother. But you have to start by being fully honest with me."

"I am!"

"I don't believe you're responsible for the plane crash, Jake. You're just seventeen. About the same age as my son. You were tricked. It's not your fault; it's on whoever gave you the program. Why should they get away with it, while you're stuck here with me? You can do the right thing, the moral thing, and help us bring them down."

"I wish I could help you, but I don't know what you're talking about."

"Look, Jake, I know you're scared and worried. We know you aren't the bad guy here. And as soon as you tell us who is, we'll be done, and you can go home and get your life back."

"I can't help you. I would if I could," I say.

Soufan starts the whole line of questioning again. He obviously believes I had something to do with crashing the plane, somehow causing it with nothing more than my cell phone. We go over and over and over the same questions. Soufan is calm, cool, and implacable. His tie is just as firmly knotted after hours in this claustrophobic room as it was when he sat down.

The interminable interview is finally interrupted by a knock at the door. Soufan gets up and opens it. Tapper is standing outside. There's a short, whispered argument— Soufan is annoyed at the interruption—and then Soufan steps out and pulls the door shut behind him, leaving me alone. I stare at the wall—it's an unnatural shade of pale green. I want out of here, want to ride until my legs blow up amid the authentic greens of cornfields and woods. But I can't. I'm locked in this puke-green room for something I didn't do.

36
Jake

After about ten minutes, both Soufan and Tapper come into the room. "Agent Tapper is going to take over for a while," Soufan says. "He's like a human lie detector—you won't be able to get away with anything. You'd better just tell him the whole truth."

"I have been," I say, but Soufan's not listening. He leaves, latching the door behind him. Tapper is carrying a tablet computer. He ignores the chairs, sitting on the edge of the table.

"Jake," Tapper says in the tone of voice you use to scold a disobedient dog, "where did you acquire a copy of the SIMON program?"

"I already told Soufan. I don't have any program. Not SIMON, not PlaneSploit."

He leans forward until his face is inches from mine. "Where. Did you get. The program?"

I try to back away, but my chair only moves an inch or two before hitting the wall behind me. "Why do you think I have it, anyway?"

"We received a tip earlier today. From a very trustworthy source—"

"Who?" I ask.

"That's not relevant. What is relevant is that we've confirmed it. You have a copy of SIMON on your phone. I need to know where it came from."

"I already told Soufan. I have no idea what you're talking about."

Tapper leans closer until his nose is almost touching mine. "You're trying to play a game with me, Jake. I don't like people who play games with me. Do you know what I do to people who play games with me?"

"No . . ."

Tapper screams at me so loudly I flinch. "I make their lives." He slams his palm into the tabletop. "A complete." He slams his palm down again. "Hell!" His last strike leaves a fresh dent in the tabletop.

I try to scoot back again, but there's nowhere to escape to. What does he want from me? "I don't know what you're talking about," I tell him for the third time.

"There's no point in lying to me, Jake. We already know all about you and the program. We know you didn't write it. We know exactly who did—the copy on your phone was written by a white hat hacker, Hugo Teso. Took him more than three years. It's not something some kid could do in his basement. What we don't know is how you got a copy. Or whether there are more copies out in the wild. That program is stored on exactly six computers in the world: at the FBI, FAA, Boeing, Aerobus in France, nSense in Denmark, and the BKA in Germany. We need to know how it got from there to you. Who gave it to you? And who did the modifications to your version of SIMON?"

"This is the first time I've ever heard of it. Can my phone even run this program you're talking about? It's the cheapest phone Walmart sells."

"Obviously it can. Since it did."

I can't think of anything to say but what I've already said *ad nauseam*. "I've got no idea what you're talking about."

"You need to open up, Jake. Start telling the truth."

"I've been telling you the truth! I don't know anything about a program named SIMON, and I don't have a copy of it on my phone." I'm so keyed up that my hands are shaking. I put them under the table, clenched against my thighs.

"See, this is what I'm talking about. We know you're lying. There was a copy of SIMON on your phone. Who gave it to you?"

"I'd never heard of SIMON until you guys told me about it. I don't even buy apps for that phone—I'd rather spend the money on my bike."

"You know Jake, the Deputy Director told me that he's got six votes on the House Oversight Committee to allow the FBI to use extraordinary rendition in terrorism cases, like the CIA used to. You'd be loaded on a plane in the middle of the night, transferred to Romania, Bulgaria, or Egypt. Spend time in a room painted green—floors, walls, and ceiling. They do that so it's easier to spot and clean the bloodstains, you know. They've got dental chairs with restraints on them. Metal hooks that hold your mouth open. That kind of thing."

I don't want to hear any of this garbage. I wish I could unhear it. I clench my fists even more strongly, and when I reply, I'm just about yelling, "I can't tell you what I don't know!"

"This is serious, Jake. If you were a foreign national, we would have turned your case over to the CIA. They wouldn't have sent two friendly FBI agents to pick you up. They would have sent a drone equipped with a very large missile. You're an American citizen, so you get a chance to do the right thing. To help us catch whoever gave you that program."

"I'd help you if I could," I say.

"I want to help you, Jake. I know how it is. The guy who gave you SIMON threatened you, right? Said he'd hurt you if you talked to anyone. You're scared. We can protect you. But you've got to come clean."

"There is no guy."

"Where'd you meet him, Jake?"

"There is no him."

"Maybe he threatened your mom, maybe your girlfriend. Laurissa, right?"

"Give it a rest already! There is no guy! He didn't threaten anyone! My phone is just a phone. I don't have any secret program on it. What's this program got to do with plane crashes, anyway?"

"You already know the answer to that question, don't you Jake?" Tapper leans forward, staring me down.

"What, there's some kind of hack that can bring down a plane with a cell phone? I don't believe it."

"Guy who gave you the program didn't tell you what it did, did he? Maybe you thought you were just sending info to someone on the plane?"

"There is no guy."

"Now you're scared out of your mind. You think the guy who gave you the program, the guy who set you up, is who you've got to worry about, right, Jake?"

How am I supposed to get through to this guy? I don't respond.

"This is personal, Jake. I lost family on 9/11 when the twin towers came down. I will do what it takes to keep that from happening again. No liquid shit of a kid is going to stop me."

I glare at Tapper. "Don't I get a lawyer? Isn't my mother supposed to be here?"

"I can't advise you on that," Tapper says. He stands and shrugs out of his suit jacket. He turns and hangs the jacket over the thermostat on the wall.

Why did he cover the thermostat? It looks exactly like the digital thermostats at my school. But this one is positioned far higher than any thermostat I've ever seen. In fact, it's at exactly the spot where I'd put a camera if I wanted to record everything that happened in this tiny room. "That's not a thermostat, is it?"

Tapper sets his tablet computer down in front of me. A video is playing on the computer. "You recognize her?" Tapper asks.

I do. The video shows a girl from above; all I can see is the top of her head and part of her face. And it's dusk—there's just barely enough light to get a clear picture. Still, I know instantly who it is—Laurissa. She's pacing, her iPhone plastered to her ear. "My girlfriend, Laurissa," I say.

"That's right. Where is she?" Tapper asks.

She's walking back and forth on a slate patio. I catch a glimpse of a flower bed that looks familiar. "Looks like her backyard." Where is this going? How does Laurissa figure into anything?

"Right again. You're looking at satellite imagery, taken about six minutes ago. Let's switch to real time." Tapper swipes his fingers across the tablet, and a new image appears. Laurissa is still pacing in her backyard, but now the picture is from an even higher angle, so all I can see is the top of her head.

Tapper opens some kind of console on the tablet and enters a couple of commands. Then he puts the video back up. Only one thing has changed. Now there's a vivid red dot on the crown of Laurissa's head. It wavers slightly, but never leaves her head, tracking with her even when she turns.

Tapper leans close and whispers in my ear. "You know what that is, right? You've seen a laser sight—you've probably used one in a video game. This isn't a game. There's a Predator drone with a custom sniper package mounted on a gimbal. It's flying circles about two thousand meters above her house. It'll take out a criminal holding a knife to a hostage's throat without mussing the victim's hair. I tap a set of commands into this tablet, and the drone takes the shot. It never misses."

The room wobbles around me. I've forgotten to breathe, and the lack of air is making me dizzy. I can only manage to whisper, "You're bullshitting me. Someone's got to be operating that drone—"

"You're wrong," Tapper continues whispering in my ear. "There's nothing but a computer flying it. And I," he taps his tablet twice, "control the computer. I can injure Laurissa. I can kill her anytime I want to. I've even got a patsy lined up. He'll fire a rifle into the air over near Eighty-Sixth Street—same caliber as our drone uses. He'll say he was celebrating a birthday. Bullets don't just go up—they come down, too, at nearly the same velocity. It'll be a tragic accident. He'll cry while he apologizes to her mother in court. It'll look real. Maybe he'll do a few weeks in jail, some community service. I'll owe him a big favor. Only you and I will know it wasn't some random accident. But Laurissa will still be crippled. Or maybe dead, Jake."

I bend over in my chair trying to think. Is this real, or just some horrific creation of my scrambled brain? It doesn't seem real, but I've got to treat it that way. Otherwise . . .

Would he really do it? Tap those commands into his tablet? Kill Laurissa, who has nothing to do with this? Can I take the chance that he might? "What do you want to know?"

There's a knock at the door. Tapper blanks the screen on his tablet and answers the knock. Soufan pushes into the room and lifts Tapper's jacket off the thermostat. Soufan's face is set in a grim mask. He whispers at Tapper, but he's speaking so forcefully that I can hear him. "We've been over this. You can't keep cowboying your way through everything, James."

"This is personal." Tapper's teeth are bared. If he were a dog, he'd be growling.

"Let's take this outside," Soufan says.

"I lost my father on 9/11," Tapper is practically shouting.

"I know," Soufan replies calmly. "And I'm sorry for your loss. But we all lost something."

"What did you lose?" Tapper scoffs.

"We should take this outside, James." Soufan glares at the door of the tiny interrogation room.

"That's what I thought. Nothing."

"About 60 American Muslims died on 9/11."

"Your family?"

"No. But it touched off a wave of anti-Muslim hysteria. More people started lumping all of us in with the extremists. Started assuming all Muslims are the same. And that's when OPR started making me take polygraphs twice as often as anyone else in the bureau."

"Oh, boo-hoo," Tapper sneers.

"Outside. Now." Soufan says through gritted teeth. He shoves the jacket at Tapper.

They step out of the room, and the door locks behind them. I hear muted shouting.

A while later both Tapper and Soufan return to the room. Once we're all seated, Tapper asks, "Were you aware that you had a copy of the avionics hacking program colloquially known as SIMON on your cell phone?"

"No." Tapper gives me a hard look and nudges his tablet. I hastily change my answer. "Yes," I say.

"Were you aware of the function of the SIMON program?"

"No . . ." I say warily, but Tapper seems to accept that answer.

"What did you think the program did?"

I think furiously, remembering something Tapper said. "It sent messages to passengers? On the plane?"

"Why would anyone want to do that?" Tapper asks. "Almost every plane has Wi-Fi. Wouldn't the passengers just use their cell phones if they need to communicate with someone on the ground?"

"I don't know," I say.

"Who gave you the program?" Tapper asks.

"A guy . . . he didn't give me his name." I watch Tapper carefully—he seems to be buying this shovelful of bullshit. "I met him at school."

"Where exactly? What dates? Times? We'll pull the security camera footage."

"Not at school, exactly. On the other side of the street. Before school."

"How many times?"

"Three or four."

"What dates?"

"I don't remember"

"What did he look like?" Soufan asks. His voice is a relief after Tapper's rapid-fire questions.

I describe the most generic-looking guy I can think of—5'10", brown hair, brown eyes, white, no distinguishing marks. Tapper takes over again, grilling me on my imaginary guy for a while, clearly frustrated.

Tapper leans forward, his face almost against mine. "He gave you the program?"

I force myself not to withdraw, to meet Tapper's intense gaze. "He put it on my phone."

"And taught you how to use it?"

"Yes."

"Why'd you go along with it? Why'd you help him?"

I blurt out the first thing that comes to my mind. "Same reason I'm 'helping' you. He threatened Laurissa. Just like you."

"Who's Laurissa?" he asks.

I do a double-take. Not ten minutes ago, he finished whispering his plan to kill her into my ear. He's smooth. "My girlfriend, Laurissa. You know exactly who she is."

"Yes, now I do."

"You knew when you were threatening her a few minutes ago."

Soufan glares at Tapper, who responds with a slight shake of his head. "You need to answer our questions," Soufan says.

"That's why he covered up the video camera," I say. "So he could—"

"Nobody is threatening anyone here, Jake." Tapper's eyes are hard, and his hand is resting on the blank screen of the tablet.

"Honesty is the best policy here, Jake," Soufan says.

"Yeah, right," I say. But I've gotten the message. They may disagree on methods, but they both want information I don't have.

"So," Tapper says, "the guy who gave you the program told you to use the program on June 11th, west of the airport, or else . . ."

"Or else he'd hurt Laurissa."

"And you did."

I glare at him. "I'd do anything to protect her. Tell any lie I needed to." Soufan stirs uncomfortably in his seat, but Tapper seems unfazed.

Tapper asks about details of the program supposedly loaded on my cell. He wants to know how I accessed the program, what password I used, what it looked like on the screen. This goes on for more than an hour before he changes tack again. He switches back to asking me about the "guy" who "gave" me the program, makes me describe him and our "meetings" again.

Then we go through my day on 6/11 in exacting detail. What time I got up, what I wore, even what I had for breakfast, although I can't remember most of it. I tell the truth as much as I can, right up to the point where I supposedly got out my cell phone and used the SIMON program.

Soufan says little—he sits at one end of the table, taking notes occasionally in his notebook even though the thermostat is no doubt recording everything. It's strange—a few hours ago, Soufan told me the road where I saw the tankers was closed on 6/11. Now, as I'm rehashing the day, neither of them brings that up. I wonder if they lied about the road closure? Yesterday I wouldn't have believed that an FBI agent would lie like that.

Just when I think we're finally finished, Tapper starts over. I'm yawning continually—it's got to be close to dawn. I can't remember what lies I told.

When Tapper reaches the end of his questions, he returns to the beginning for a fourth time. My butt aches, and I desperately need to pee. I stick it out, though. So long as he's listening to me answer his pointless questions, he won't shoot Laurissa.

Finally, Soufan interrupts. "He's wasted. We're getting gobbledy-gook. Let's pick it up later today."

Tapper nods and yawns.

"Can you call my mom? Let me see her, at least? I've done everything you've asked me to—I'm trying to help."

"Some of your answers are total bullshit, Jake."

"I'm doing my best! Let me see Mom and sleep."

Tapper nods again. Soufan pushes his chair back slowly

and stands, stretching his arms over his head. He ambles out of the room and Tapper follows, pulling the door shut. There's a metallic click as the lock engages, like the noise a revolver makes when it's cocked and ready to fire.

37

Jake

I slump in my chair, trembling a little from my rattled nerves. Nothing happens. Finally, I get up and check the door: locked. I return to my seat, lay my head on the table. I can't fall asleep, but I drift and my mind starts feeding me a waking nightmare.

My bike was hurtling toward the open door of the tanker truck, and wham! Everything goes black.

My bike was hurtling toward the open door of the tanker truck, and wham! Everything goes black.

My bike was hurtling toward the open door of the tanker truck...

The nightmare repeats dozens of times before a noise jolts me back to the cell. The door opens—a pair of uniformed sheriff's deputies comes in. I tell them I need to use the bathroom, and they take me to one on the way out of the building. They both go into the bathroom with me, although neither follows me when I choose to use a stall.

When I'm done, the sheriff's deputies cuff me and walk me to the entrance. The sun is already well above the horizon—I was in that puke-green interview room all night and part of the morning. I get about two breaths of outside air. Despite the August humidity, the fresh air feels great. Then they load me into the back of a van that reeks of vomit and bleach. Neither of the sheriff's deputies will tell me what's going on. The van starts and stops repeatedly, then hums along fast for about twenty minutes—we must be on an interstate. When it finally stops, we're in an underground garage. They hustle me up a flight of stairs and into another interview room, even more dingy than the last, but there's no digital thermostat/spycam in this room. Another deputy removes my handcuffs and leaves.

I wait for perhaps another half an hour. Then the same sheriff's deputy opens the door, and my mother walks in. Her hair is limp and dull, her eyes cavernous. I'm out of the chair and hugging her before I even notice the guy following her in.

At first I do a double-take—he looks like one of the kids I've seen wandering the halls of my high school. But then I realize that he's slightly older than he appears. And the kids at my high school generally don't wear wrinkled blue suits. He swipes his blond hair back from his eyes and then rubs the front of his suit jacket as if trying to smooth it out. He's carrying a backpack by one of its shoulder straps. The backpack is so overstuffed with file folders and papers that it won't zip shut.

"Are you okay?" Mom asks. "Have you gotten anything to eat? Any sleep? I've been trying to get them to let me see you for—"

"Yes, I'm okay. No, I haven't had anything to eat." As I say this, I realize I'm ravenous. Then I remember the red dot on Laurissa's head, and my hunger vanishes.

Mom glares and turns to the guy I haven't met. "They're mistreating him."

"Maybe we should all sit down," he says.

"I don't want to sit down." Mom's hands are balled into fists. "I want my son out of here!"

"I know, I know." He holds his hands up, palms out. He's either trying to placate Mom or surrendering to her. "But for now, let's just sit down and talk about this calmly."

Mom and the new guy sit in chairs across from me. Mom doesn't introduce us, but I'm pretty sure the new guy's not connected to Tapper or Soufan. I turn toward him. "Who're you?"

"I'm your P.D., Bailo Brown." He holds out his hand, and we shake.

"Bailo?" I ask.

"Yeah." He spells it out for me. "But you say it like buy-low. My mother was Belgian." He fishes around in his backpack, pulls out a manila file folder, and opens it. There's one piece of paper inside with a few unreadable notes scrawled on it.

"And what's a P.D.?" I ask.

"Public Defender," he says.

"He's going to get you out of here, honey," Mom says.

"I can't guarantee that," he says. "I'm going to make sure you get the defense you're entitled to by the Constitution and Gideon v. Wainright."

I eye him skeptically. "Gideon what?"

"Basically, I'm your lawyer."

I'm doomed. This guy looks about as lawyerly as Bil from the bike shop. No, scratch that. If you could get Bil to put on a suit instead of bike shorts, he'd inspire far more confidence than Brown. Mom is staring at me like she wants to drink me in. She looks tired, but there's a hint of hope behind her eyes. I decide to play along. "So, what now?"

"I need to do an intake interview. I got assigned to your case ten minutes ago, so your arrest records haven't caught up to me yet. Walk me through everything that happened to you. I need the truth. Everything you say now is protected by attorney-client privilege. I'm not going to judge you in any way—I just need to know the facts so I can defend you effectively. Okay?"

"Okay." I tell my story for what seems like the hundredth time. Then I tell him about the FBI interrogation, about Tapper's threats. Mom springs out of her chair and paces while I talk.

"We need to get him out of here. Right away," Mom says to Brown when I finish.

"There's a process we have to—"

"What if we sue the bastards?" Mom asks.

"You'd have to talk to a private attorney about that," Brown says.

"You're just going to let them get away with this?" Mom's voice is about an octave higher than normal.

"The only thing our office handles is defending our clients. Even if everything Jake is telling us is true—"

"You asked for the truth, and now you don't believe it?" I say.

"Jake, calm down," Mom says, although she's the one who's anything but calm. "You've been through a horrible accident. Not everything you've remembered has been true. We should at least consider the possibility that—"

"I'm telling the truth!"

"I know you think you are, honey."

"Okay," Brown says. "First, he's pretty much said he confessed already. Second, we don't know yet whether he'll be charged as an adult or a child. Based on the information I have now, I'm guessing they'll charge him in adult court. So after the initial hearing—"

"What's the initial hearing for?" I ask.

"It's just a presentation of the charges against you. The judge will set your bail at the hearing. It'll probably be on Thursday or Friday."

"Two days!" Mom says.

"Maybe three if they ask for a continuance, but if he's charged as an adult, they'll have to set bail by Thursday whether there's a hearing or not," Brown says. He's talking in a rushed monotone and shoving my file into his backpack. This part is routine to him. "You probably won't have to say much at the initial hearing," Brown says. "Just stand still and keep your arms at your side. Be quiet and respectful at all times. Answer any questions as briefly as you can and tell the truth."

"Okay." I sway in my chair and plant my elbows on the table to prop myself up.

"After that's over, we'll know exactly what the charges are, and I'll meet with the D.A. and try to work out a deal," Brown says.

"What kind of deal?" Mom asks.

"Depends on the charges," Brown says, "but usually I can get them to drop the worst charges in return for a guilty or no contest plea."

"But I haven't done anything," I say.

"That's irrelevant," Brown replies. "The reality is that if you go to trial, the outcome is likely to be worse for you—a lot worse. It's your decision to make, but in most cases, I strongly advise against a trial."

"So even if I'm innocent, it's better to plead guilty?"

"Usually, yes."

"That's unbelievable," I say.

"Welcome to the justice system," Brown replies.

Mom and the lawyer say a few more things I don't really process, and then they get up. I push myself to my feet, shake the public defender's hand, and give Mom a hug.

"It will be okay," she whispers. "And I will get you out of here, somehow."

I hug Mom back as strongly as I can. I know she thinks that she can get me out of this place. But I don't believe it. Either she doesn't trust everything I'm telling her, or she's vastly underestimated Tapper.

Then she's gone. I catch a glimpse of a guard closing the door behind her and hear it click. I collapse back into my chair, my head against the cold metal table. I catch a whiff of Mom's rose-scented shampoo and fight back the urge to cry.

38
Jake

I doze in the interview room for what must be hours, my head on the table. I'm awakened when two guards come into the room. They're in uniforms that look similar to the sheriff's deputies', but they don't have badges. They walk me down a long corridor. The doors we pass are all labeled: INTERVIEW ROOM #3, DEBRIEFING ROOM, INFIRMARY, and so on. We go through a security door—one of the officers waves at the security camera above our heads. There's a short pause, followed by an obnoxious buzzing sound and a loud click as the door opens.

They take me to a room where I'm forced to strip to my underwear and put on an orange jumpsuit and slippers. My clothes disappear into a box that one of the guards hands off to an attendant.

We pass through another security door, turn a corner, and enter a hall that's lined with cages about six feet wide and ten feet deep. Metal bars form the front wall and door of each cell; the side and back walls are cinder block. There's a bunk bed, a couple of chairs, a small table, and a combination sink and metal toilet in each cell. Inmates glance at us as we pass. A few of them get up and come to the front of their cells, gripping the bars and following my steps with hungry eyes.

Near the end of the hall there are several vacant cells, but the very last one is occupied. There's a guy lying on the lower bunk. He looks so much like me, it's startling. Same sandy-blond hair. Same blue eyes. Same powerfully built legs. Similar face. His chest and arms are bigger than mine, and he looks a little older. He's wearing an orange jumpsuit and slippers that are identical to mine. He could easily pass as my older brother.

One of my guards waves at another security camera. There's a short pause, and then the cell door buzzes open.

"In you go," the other guard says. He pushes on my back firmly enough that I have to step forward to avoid falling. The door clangs behind me. The guards' boots clomp against the concrete floor, fading quickly from earshot.

From up close, the cell looks dingier than it did from the hall. The metal sink and table are dented, and the toilet bowl is stained. It reeks of urine and bleach.

"Um, hi," I say to my older clone. He's watching me but hasn't moved. His hands are tucked behind his head, elbows splayed.

"Guess I get the top bunk," I say.

"Yep," he says. "Fresh meat gets the leftovers." He isn't scowling or anything. His face is relaxed, placid even.

"Seems fair." I wander over to the sink. It strikes me that I'm turning my back on my cellmate and glance over my shoulder. He hasn't moved.

I turn the tap on and cold water trickles out. There's no hot. A short, ratty toothbrush teeters on the edge of the shelf above the sink. I decide I don't need to brush my teeth, and I cup my hands under the faucet and rinse my mouth. The water is flat and tasteless. I splash my face and run my wet hands through my hair.

I can sort of see myself in the scratched and foggy metal mirror screwed into the wall. My eyes are black pits in the landscape of my face. My hair is wild—I'm pretty sure that if I jammed my finger into an electric socket, it would get neater. At least it's long enough to cover the scars on my skull.

I need to use the bathroom again, but no way am I going to do it in front of this guy or the open cell wall.

I climb up the ladder and settle into the top bunk. The pillow is about as thick as five sheets of construction paper. I bunch it up under my head and pull the sheet over myself. I don't undress, don't even take off the slippers. I start drifting asleep almost immediately.

I hear a voice from below, "So what are you in for?"

I'm half asleep, and I answer without thinking, "They think I crashed a plane."

"Really? Wicked. How many people died?"

"I don't know. I had nothing to do with it."

"They just made it up?"

"Yeah."

"Ain't that a bitch."

I roll over, hoping he'll shut up.

But he keeps talking. "I got sent up for something I didn't do, too. Assholes say I downloaded some illegal shit onto my computer. I've never seen that crap in my life. I was just helping a buddy out, keeping some of his shit on my computer while his was in the shop. Don't see why helping a buddy means I've gotta do time, do you?"

I wonder what kind of computer file would land a guy in this place. If illegal music or movie downloads would do it, half the computer users in America would be in jail. Then it hits me: child porn. They've bunked me with a pedophile. So much for getting any sleep.

"If I tell them where I got the files, maybe they'll let me out. Said they would. Think I'll tell them tomorrow. I mean, I'm not a snitch, but sometimes you just gotta do what you gotta do, right?"

"I guess," I mumble.

"Maybe that'd work for you. Tell them what they want to know."

"I don't know anything."

"Hey, that's cool, if you want to play it that way. But you don't have to. I'm no snitch, and nobody's listening to us in here."

I'm not sure how he'd know whether we're being listened to or not. I mean, if they can hide a recorder in a thermostat, it'd be easy to hide one in here. Behind the mirror, maybe. That reminds me of another question. "You know why we're in here together? And why this end of the hall is empty? The other cells I saw were crowded."

"We're in the Federal wing. Separate from the regular riffraff. Special, huh?"

"But why put us in together if this wing is empty, anyway?"

"Hell, I don't know. Why do the Feebs do anything they do?"

It hits me like the pavement during a bike crash: He's a plant. What will he do, in this isolated cell, if I don't answer his questions? If Tapper's willing to threaten Laurissa, why not have this guy beat on me for a while? I roll over again, putting my back into the corner between the bed and wall.

He breaks the short silence, "So tell me straight up, what did you do, anyway?"

"Okay, okay," I say. "I'll tell you the real story."

I feed him the same line of bullshit I fed Tapper. At least, I think it's the same—it's hard to remember exactly what lies I told, but maybe he'll believe me and nothing worse will happen in this tiny cell. We talk all afternoon and half the night, when I just want to drift off to sleep and leave this insanity behind. Finally, after hours of ridiculous chatter—him trying unsuccessfully to maintain the fiction that he's just an inmate, me trying to keep my lies straight—he relents and pretends to go to sleep.

I breathe a sigh of relief and try to sleep. Instead, I lie there rehashing the disaster of my life. Tapper wants whoever is responsible for the crash. Because of whatever he found on my phone, he thinks he can get at them through me. Captain Beaner seems to have a different agenda from Tapper—they're both obsessed with the plane crash, but Beaner doesn't seem to think I caused it. Detective Morris seemed more interested in the fake firefighters and the murder of the cop outside my hospital room. I'm still no closer to discovering who Fake Laurissa was, or why she wanted to kill me. It all adds up to one thing: I can't trust any of them.

39

Betsy

A couple of days after the debacle on the Fall Creek Trail, Father comes home from work early. He's got something of a grin on his face. Just the corners of his mouth are turned up, but for him that's Cheshire Cat territory. It's not the fact that I've got his favorite breakfast, a ham-and-cheddar omelet, keeping warm in the oven. He hasn't seen that yet. Maybe he smelled it?

"What's got you so happy?" I ask.

He gives me a sharp look, but the grin comes back almost immediately. "That problem we had? It's pretty much fixed."

I follow him into the kitchen, racking my brain for a way to get more details out of him without breaking his OPSEC rules. The rules are necessary, I guess, but right now they're a real pain in my ass. "So the problem has, um, expired?"

"No, but it's as good as solved."

"What happened?"

"Best if you don't know."

Best for whom, I wonder, as I slide the warm omelet across the table toward him.

Later, when he's asleep, I call around to some of the other brothers, trying to get info. Nobody will tell me anything. Joshua might talk to me—he's been hitting on me pretty much since the day I turned sixteen. Eww. But even if he would talk, he's in the backwoods of North Carolina.

I call Joshua's cousin, Tobin, who's also a member of The Sons of Paine, to ask if there's any way to get in touch with Josh. It turns out there is. They have a burner cell in the cabin and normally get a bar of service from a tower in a town about a day's hike away. It's not supposed to be used except in emergencies, and I have to hint to Tobin that I'm rethinking my stance on Joshua to get him to give up the number. If that conversation gets back to Joshua, it'll raise his hopes, and I feel bad about that because there's no way I'm ever going to agree to so much as a date with him.

I try three times throughout the next day before I reach Joshua. "How's your arm?" I ask when I finally get through.

"S'okay," he says. "Bullet just grazed me. Going to be a heckuva scar there, but I don't mind. Girls like scars, don't they?"

"I don't know. Maybe you ought to ask a *girl*." I load the words with all the sarcasm I can muster.

"Aww, honey. I meant you. Do you like scars?"

"I don't have an opinion one way or the other." This isn't the best way to start a conversation in which I'm asking for information, I realize. "It's nice to hear your voice," I say. "And I'm glad you're okay."

"That's sweet of you to say, Betsy."

"You know anything about what's been going down in Indy the last day or so?"

"They don't tell me nothing. And I'm stuck out here in the back of beyond."

"Figures. Father won't tell me anything, either. And I'm in the middle of it."

"He's got your best interests at heart."

"I know. I start to say goodbye, but another question occurs to me. "I want to know more about my mother."

"Oh?" A moment ago we were two friends chatting. Now there's a long, awkward silence.

"I want to find her."

"Wouldn't she have reached out to you by now if she wanted to be found?"

"Maybe. I don't know. Did she have any friends in The Sons? Has anyone heard from her?"

There's silence on the line for a moment, then a beep. The connection goes dead. I assume the call dropped and try to call back. No one picks up. Two more attempts go unanswered. Maybe the call didn't drop. Maybe Joshua hung up on me.

40

Jake

The click of the cell door awakens me. I glance around—there's no sign of my cellmate. The bottom bunk has been made with military precision. Tapper is standing in the open doorway. I desperately need to use the bathroom—my whole groin is on fire.

"Hop down and stand in the corner of the cell," he orders, pointing at the space between the toilet and the wall.

"Why?" I ask.

"Just do it. I could drag you, but I don't feel like working that hard."

I back into the corner of the cell, watching Tapper the whole way. I notice the black globe of a security camera in the hall outside. Tapper approaches, stepping closer and closer until he looms in front of me, trapping me in the corner and blocking the security camera from my view.

He pulls a phone from a jacket pocket and shows me a still photo on its screen. It shows Laurissa with the red dot from a laser sight on her forehead. "You told me you didn't have your contact's real name. So I'm giving you two days to get it for me, Jake," he says quietly. "If I don't have your contact by midnight on Tuesday, I'll pull the trigger."

"No." My voice is shaky, and I take a deep breath before continuing. "You wouldn't. Murder her in cold blood? Just for some name I can't get you?"

"I will," he says flatly.

"Why?" I whisper.

"Someone has to be willing to do the hard thing, Jake. Our freedom and security are paid for with the blood of patriots. Your girlfriend's going to be one of those patriots if you don't give up the name I need."

"This has nothing to do with freedom or security."

"More people will die if we don't take down whoever gave you that program. You're lucky to get two days out of me." He pockets the phone and moves away from me. I sag against the corner of the cell, feeling the rough concrete wall against my palms.

Tapper gestures impatiently. "You want to get out of here or not? Time's wasting." He taps the outside of his pocket, where his phone makes a rectangular bulge.

I follow him down the cell-lined corridor, and he waves at the camera at the end. The first of the double doors opens with a heavy metallic *ker-chunk*. A guard hands Tapper a shallow cardboard box. He looks over the contents and then hands it to me. "Get changed," he says, waving me into the same room where I put on the jailhouse jumpsuit.

All my stuff is in the box, even my phone, which stuns me. Why would they give me my phone back? It's clearly the same one, with the same spider-web crack. I give up trying to figure it out and change quickly.

Tapper leads me past the interrogation rooms and infirmary and through another set of metal security doors. We emerge into some kind of visiting area with booths and heavy plate-glass windows equipped with microphones. But we don't stop. Tapper leads me through yet another pair of security doors, and we emerge on the public side of the visiting area. Mom, Laurissa, and a black man I've never met are standing in a tight knot, waiting for me. I'm relieved to see Laurissa— to know there's not a drone targeting her at this instant.

Mom crosses the room in seconds, wrapping me in a hug so strong it threatens to empty my near-bursting bladder. Mom's talking, but she's crying, too, so I can't make out what she's trying to say.

When Mom finally lets me go, Laurissa and I hug. I look over her shoulder at the guy I don't recognize. He's small, slender, and immaculately dressed, wearing black wingtips, a dark gray suit, and a pink tie. A perfectly matched, pink handkerchief peeks from his pocket. He's carrying a brown leather briefcase that gleams like antique furniture.

"Who's that?" I mutter as Laurissa breaks our hug.

"Your new lawyer," she says.

"Mom already found a lawyer."

"He's better."

"I'm not your lawyer yet, Mr. Solley," the man says. He

produces two documents and a sleek plastic clipboard from his briefcase. "You need to sign this document, firing your current counsel, and this document, retaining the firm of Chesterfield, Cooper, Evans, and Yanklovich."

I look at Mom, and she nods. I take the papers, clipboard, and his proffered pen, signing in the spaces at the bottom of each document. I notice that Mom has already signed them all. "Which one are you?" I ask.

"LaMont Cooper, Esquire at your service," he says, holding out his hand.

We shake. I look around—Tapper has disappeared. "Am I free to go?" I ask.

"Let me check with the desk sergeant," Cooper says. I wait while he talks to a uniformed sheriff's deputy behind a counter at the back of the room.

"I talked to my brother," Laurissa says.

"Brand?" I say.

"Yes. He's majoring in computer science, remember? He's working on a program for us to scrape Whitepages.com."

"Scrape?"

"It'll get us a list of every Betsy in the right age range within a hundred miles of Indianapolis."

I start to thank her, but Cooper strides across the room to rejoin us and interrupts. "I got your bail waived."

"Just like that?" Laurissa is obviously skeptical.

"Well, the prosecution waived it," Cooper says. "I'm not entirely sure why. It's a bit unusual."

"So I can go home?" I ask.

"Yes. There will be a preliminary hearing in a few days. You'll need to attend that. We'll start preparations immediately."

Cooper leads the way out of the jail, followed by Mom, Laurissa, and me. As we emerge from the building into the bright sunshine, I notice movement in Laurissa's hair. I look closer. The bright red dot of a laser sight flickers through her jet-black curls. It wavers a little, tracking her movements as she steps down the stone stairs toward the street. Fear turns my knees to Jell-O. I collapse onto the staircase, and the urine I've been holding since last night releases in a flood.

41

Jake

Laurissa pretends that watching her boyfriend piss himself on the courthouse steps doesn't bother her, but she doesn't fool me. "It's a perfectly normal response to the stress of the situation," Cooper says. He holds out a hand to help me up, but I stand on my own and reach for Laurissa. I need to get her under some kind of cover. Fast.

Urine runs down the insides of my legs. My shoes squelch—my socks are soggy. "We need to get to the car," I tell Laurissa.

Mom replies, "Our car is in the garage right around the corner." I notice Dieter—or Hans, maybe—standing by the black Mercedes. There's another large black sedan parked behind it with a uniformed driver standing alongside—

Cooper's car, I assume. Both cars are parked in a tow-away zone just a few feet from the courthouse steps.

"Laurissa," I say. "Get in the Mercedes. Quick." I don't know if the roof will stop a bullet, but it's better than standing around outside. Sure, Tapper said he'd give me two days, but what if his finger slips on his tablet? What if something goes wrong?

"I figured I'd ride with you." Laurissa says. "I don't care about . . . you know."

"It's not about that—you're in danger. Look!" I point at the crown of her head, and notice that the red laser sight has winked out. Mom gives me a puzzled look. Dieter is holding the passenger door of the Mercedes open, his eyes scanning the street constantly.

"It's okay, Jake," Laurissa says.

"Please? I'll see you at the house."

Laurissa leans over as if she's trying to kiss me. Her face is tight, wearing an expression that I can't quite interpret. I must be completely disgusting. I shuffle back two or three steps. She flashes me a tight smile and then turns and slides into the backseat of the Mercedes. I sag with relief.

I shoot Mom a pleading look. I desperately want to get home. She moves toward me, and I rush off in what I hope is the direction of the garage. Mom follows.

By the time Mom and I get home, both black sedans are parked on the street, drivers outside and waiting. Mom pulls up in the driveway, and we hurry inside. Laurissa and the lawyer, Cooper, follow us in. Mom gets them settled in the living room while I rush to my bedroom.

I take a quick shower and change clothes before rejoining

the group. Mom and Laurissa start speaking at once, each asking some variation of, "Are you okay?"

"I'm fine," I say. "It's just that I didn't have the chance to
go to the bathroom all night, and—"

"Perfectly understandable," Cooper says. "We should get
right to preparing your defense."

"How did I get a new lawyer, anyway?"

"Laurissa hired him," Mom says.

"Actually, Mr. Davis retained me on your behalf," Cooper
says. His dapper pinstripe suit makes him look completely out
of place on our ratty old couch, like a Pinarello in a bike rack
full of Huffys.

"What's that costing?" I ask.

"It doesn't matter," Laurissa says.

"It does to me," I say.

"The retainer was $100,000," Cooper says. "We have
authorization for an additional $200,000 if needed."

I feel like I might fall over. I lean back against a wall for
support. "Fork me with a serving spoon. That is a metric shit-
ton of money."

"Jake!" Mom is giving me her deadliest evil eye, the one
she reserves for truly heinous infractions, like drinking straight
from the milk jug.

"Money is just a tool," Laurissa says calmly.

"It might not be sufficient. Miss Davis," Cooper nods at
Laurissa, "tells me that it's possible you may be charged with
terrorism, in which case the USA PATRIOT Act might apply,
and your case would be moved to federal court. If that happens, a properly aggressive defense could easily require two
million or more."

Two million? What planet is this guy from? He could probably buy my whole neighborhood for less than two million. I realize my mouth is hanging open and snap it shut.

It's insane. Too much. I know money doesn't mean the same thing to Laurissa as it does to me, that she's always had plenty of it and has never overheard her mother pleading with a bill collector on the phone for "just one more week." But this is way, way over the top. I'm grateful, but I also feel a little disgusted—not with Laurissa exactly, but with myself for some reason.

Cooper has continued talking—I have no idea what he's been saying. I put my head between my knees, hoping my lightheadedness and nausea will pass. Now Cooper stops abruptly and asks, "Are you ill, Mr. Solley?"

I lift my head slowly. He's staring at me, a look of solicitous concern on his face. "No... Yes, maybe I am sick. Sick of this whole situation. Sick of—"

"Your circumstances are extremely stress—"

"Enough!" I interrupt Cooper. "I just need—leave me alone for a minute, would you?"

"Jake!" Mom says. "You're being rude."

"We're just trying to help," Laurissa says in a soothing voice.

"It is essential that we begin to prepare your defense immediately," Cooper says. "Any delay will compromise our efforts." Mom, Laurissa, and Cooper are leaning toward me. They remind me of a trio of vultures I saw plucking at a roadkill raccoon once, long necks stretched forward, expectantly. I love my mother and Laurissa, and know they mean well, but I feel thoroughly picked over; there's no meat left on this raccoon's bones.

"No, just forget it!" I stand abruptly, and they startle away. I turn from Cooper to Laurissa to Mom as I shout, "I don't need a lawyer, I don't need your money, and I don't need your scolding."

They all start to reply at once. My mother is on her feet, almost in my face.

"I'm out of here," I say. Then I turn to Laurissa, "Stay indoors."

"What does that have to do with anything?" Mom yells. I push past her and rush to the door that connects the kitchen and garage. It slams behind me with a satisfying crash.

I slap the button to open the garage door. I glance at my ruined bike with the bent front wheel and decide to take my old Huffy. It's way too small, but I'm too angry to care. Mom yells something behind me as I peel out, but I keep going.

I push myself mercilessly on the bike. Almost an hour into my pell-mell ride, a shooting pain in my left calf stops me. My leg locks up completely, and I barely manage to bring the bike to a halt without crashing. I collapse into the weedy shoulder moaning and rubbing my calf. I'm so hungry that my stomach feels like a small animal trying to eat its way out of my body.

When the pain subsides to something manageable, I look around. I've been riding on autopilot. I don't recognize the street I'm on, but there's a major road about a block away. I pick up the Huffy and limp toward it.

I must have been riding in circles—I'm on Kentucky Avenue only a few miles from my house. I could walk home, but the way I'm limping, it might take a couple of hours. There's food at home, but I'm not ready to face my mother. Instead, I cross the street to the Decatur Branch Library.

It's early afternoon—I've lost too much time already. I've got to find something to offer Tapper before he carries through on his threat to shoot Laurissa.

I realize that I've got one lead: Betsy. Maybe Laurissa's brother will come through with his computerized White Pages search. But even if he doesn't, maybe there's another way to find Betsy. Sic Tapper on her and get him off my case. I park my Huffy at the rack and drag my sweaty body and gimp leg into the library.

Passing through the sliding doors is like stepping into another world. I leave the world of lawyers, plane crashes, and death threats and step into a large room so colorful that it feels fictional. But I ignore the enormous stuffed animals and bright chairs in the children's section, ignore the tall display of young adult titles, and turn toward the row of computers.

I claim one of the two open stations—the one at the end of the row, where my stench will disturb only one person, not two.

I don't search for Betsy directly—Laurissa and I tried that already. Remembering that day makes the space behind my eyes hurt. I want to call Laurissa and apologize for running out on her and her lawyer. I need to talk to her, tell her about Tapper's threats.

Instead, I log onto Hushmail and create a throwaway account. Then I open Word and work on composing a message. After about six tries, I wind up with this:

MISSING BETSY
When you visited me in the hospital, just your presence took my breath away, and I forgot to ask for your phone number. Then you

*crashed your bike into mine on the Fall Creek Trail. Now I can't
get you out of my head.*

*I'd suffer through anything—a plane crash, a fire, or jail
time—just to speak with you again. I want to shout my obsession
with you to the world, but I'd settle for your email or phone number.
I feel as though I may die if I don't hear from you. Whether you plan
to crush me or make my wildest dreams come true doesn't matter—
just email me at Jake543@Hushmail.com.*

I post it everywhere I can think of—the Missed Connection
section on Craigslist, Backpage, and the online personals of
our free local weekly, Nuvo. I know that won't be enough.
Surely she won't be reading random classifieds. I'll need to do
something more dramatic to get her attention.

By the time I finish, the cramp in my leg has faded to a
mere annoyance. I trudge out of the library, mount the Huffy,
and begin a slow, cautious ride home.

It's dusk, and the dark gray pavement blends with a
lighter gray sky. Even the cars rushing past me seem bleached
of color. If a few personal ads are the only thing I can come
up with, my girlfriend is going to die. I have to do something
more, something so over the top that everyone will notice.
Even if Betsy doesn't, someone will point it out to her. She
will have to contact me, if for no other reason than to finish
the job she has already botched twice: trying to kill me. If I
survive that, I can offer Betsy up to Tapper in exchange for
Laurissa's life.

What makes a post on the Internet go viral? It probably
needs to be a video, not a classified ad. And it should have cats,
preferably kittens. The Internet loves kittens. Maybe I could

borrow a kitten from someone. Or adopt one? Did they allow
teenagers to adopt cats at the Humane Society? Probably not.

Lots of viral videos feature someone getting kicked in the
nuts. Or falling off a skateboard onto his nuts. There is one
advantage of balls over kittens: I already have a perfectly good
pair. Whether they'd survive my attempts to attract Betsy's
attention on the Internet remained to be seen. Kittens and
balls? The Internet is a strange place.

When I get home, Mom is alone in the living room, pacing back and forth as if she were trying to wear a hole through
the floor and drop into the basement.

"Where's Laurissa?" I ask.

"Where have you been? You can't just walk out on your
lawyer. He's—"

"He's not my lawyer, he's Laurissa's."

"And you owe that girl a huge apology. She's trying to help
you. She's been a rock. There's no excuse for treating her
like—"

"I know, I know. You're right." I don't feel like discussing
Laurissa with my mother. "Where is she?"

"She went home. But we need to focus on you. On keeping
you out of jail. I've been so worried." Mom stops her pacing
long enough to crush me in a suffocating hug. "We have an
appointment with Mr. Cooper tomorrow at 8:00 a.m. sharp."

"I can't—"

"You're going. And you'll be on your best behavior. No
running out. That's final." Mom releases me from the hug and
puts the back of her hand against my forehead, checking me
for fever.

"I don't have time."

"What could possibly be more important than meeting with your lawyer?"

"Laurissa. Her life is in danger."

"Jake. You keep saying that, but how could she possibly be in danger? This has nothing to do with her." Mom seems satisfied with my temperature, and starts picking through my hair, inspecting my scars.

"It has everything to do with her!"

"No, this is about you. And getting these ridiculous charges against you dropped. You need a lawyer for that, a good lawyer."

"Tapper's going to kill Laurissa if I don't tell him who's behind the plane crash. Despite the fact that I don't know a damn thing about the plane crash."

"That's crazy, Jake. The FBI protects people—they don't threaten them."

"It's nothing but the truth. When have I ever lied to you?"

"Every time I ask you why your showers take so long."

"Mom! That's not even funny. And this is serious."

"I know. And I know that you believe that Laurissa is in danger—"

"She is!"

"Let me finish! I know you *believe* that Laurissa is in danger. But Dr. Malhotra says that victims of traumatic brain injury can become paranoid, even have hallucinations. Doesn't it seem more likely that you're having some kind of after effect of your injury? At least more likely than an FBI agent trying to hurt Laurissa?"

"But it's true!"

"You 'remembered' getting mugged. That wasn't true. Paranoia can make things seem true that aren't."

How could I argue with that? No matter what I said, Mom would blame my head injury. If I couldn't convince even *her* that the danger to Laurissa was real, how would I convince anyone else?

42

Jake

I finally escape to my room. The moment I'm alone, I text Laurissa, "Stay inside!"

She texts back. "Why?"

"Where are you?"

"My bedroom. Why do you want me to stay inside?"

I start to type out a text about Tapper's threats, realize that it's going to take forever, and call her instead. There's a long silence after I finish explaining everything to her.

"You there?" I ask.

"Yes."

"So you'll stay indoors? At least until I figure out how to find Betsy? And get Tapper off our asses?"

"I'll ask Brand how the program he's writing is coming."

"Yeah. But stay indoors. Okay?"

"Jake . . . your mom said you were experiencing some paranoia."

Not this again. "It's not—"

"I know it seems real, but think about it. What seems more likely, that your brain is malfunctioning or that the FBI is out to get you?"

"It's not the FBI. It's just Tapper. I've got to run. Talk to you later?"

"Wait, no, we haven't—"

"I've got to go. Stay inside! I love you."

"Be careful, Jake. I love you too."

A Google search turns up dozens of free classified ad sites. I post my "Crashing Into Betsy" ad on all of them. I make a video using the webcam built into my laptop and post that on YouTube. I check my new email account at least a dozen times throughout the evening. It gets more than a dozen spam messages, but only one legitimate response: "Aw, that's a cute story. Send me a pic. Maybe I'll crash my bicycle into you." I stab the delete key with my finger.

I also text Laurissa compulsively. The first time I ask if she's inside, and she replies right away, "Yes, don't worry."

The second time, she replies, "Yes." She replies that way to the next three or four texts, and then responds to the next text I send her with, "Chill, Jake. I'm not going anywhere tonight. It's sweet that you're worried, but you don't need to check on me every ten minutes."

I hold off nearly an hour before texting her again. I just . . . I need to know she's okay. "Are you okay? Are you inside?" I text. I pace back and forth beside my bed while I wait for her reply.

"I'm going to bed now," she replies. "And turning my phone off. I'm fine. Quit obsessing."

I slump back onto the bed, sinking into the rumpled mess of sheets and pillows. The crack in the ceiling above my bed seems wider and longer than I remember. Would my life ever get back to something resembling normal? Would I still have any of the people I love at that point? My mother thinks I'm crazy, and I'm driving Laurissa nuts.

I lever myself upright, stumble across the room to my computer, and resume my efforts to find Betsy. I leave my phone on the corner of my bed, silent and alone.

43

Betsy

While Father's sleeping off yet another double shift at work, I bike to church—our old church, Two Swords Baptist. I'm not supposed to leave in the middle of the day like this without telling Father, but I'm feeling less and less inclined to care about what he wants. And I'm seventeen, for God's sake, not some little girl. Besides, I plan to be back long before he wakes up.

Pastor Hobbes knew my mother. He probably baptized me. I'm relieved to learn from the sign outside the church that he's still preaching at Two Swords.

The church secretary sends me back to Pastor Hobbes's office without even calling him. His door is open, and I peek through, finding him at his desk with a dozen or more open books spread in layers around him. I knock on the jamb to get his attention.

"What is—" Pastor Hobbes glances up, sees me. "Wait, don't tell me . . . Betsy, right? You've really sprouted up."

"Wow." How did he recognize me? I don't look anything like I did when I was ten.

"Come in, come in," he says. "This is a pleasant surprise."

"Am I interrupting? I can come back later," I say.

"No, I'm trying to prepare for the Sunday service. I probably need an interruption. Come on in. Sit down."

I sit in one of the two plush armchairs across from Pastor Hobbes's desk. He steps around the desk and takes the other one. Then he grabs the bowl of hard candy from his desk and holds it out toward me.

"I'm not really into hard candy anymore," I say. "I'm more of a chocolate fiend, now."

Hobbes sets the bowl aside. "It's so good to see you. How have you been?"

"Okay. I finished my junior year at North Central. And I'm taking accounting classes at Ivy Tech."

"That's excellent. And church?"

"We're going to Dry Run Creek."

"Ah." Hobbes leans back in his chair. "Pastor Lee is a good man, but he just doesn't have the fire in his belly."

"I know what you mean."

"You'd be welcome back here," Hobbes says.

"I think Father wants to keep going to Dry Run."

"I meant you, Betsy."

I'm not sure what to say to that. I'm afraid I'm blushing, which is ridiculous. "Oh. Um, thanks."

"Anyway," Pastor Hobbes says, "I'm sure that's not what brought you here."

"No," I say. I'm not sure how to bring up this topic. Just ask if he knows why my mother left me? Why she's been out of contact all these years? How pathetic is that? "I, um, you knew my mom, right?"

"Yes. Very well." Pastor Hobbes laces his fingers together in his lap, a gesture that seems relaxing, somehow.

"I . . . just . . . what I really want to know is why she left. Why she's never contacted me. Why I can't find her. Hasn't she ever tried to find me? Doesn't she care?" The words rush from me, and by the end, I'm biting my lip to suppress a sob.

Pastor Hobbes takes a moment to reply, speaking in the gentlest voice I've ever heard, "I don't have the answers to your questions, Betsy."

"I know they were arguing a lot. They tried to keep it hidden, fought behind the closed bedroom door, but I overheard. But lots of parents argue, right? That's not enough to make most moms bug out."

Pastor Hobbes leans closer to me. "There's something on your cheek."

I brush at my cheeks, but don't feel anything.

He touches my chin with two gentle fingers, turning my head so the light catches my right cheek. "You're bruised."

He's seeing the mark my father left when he hit me. I'd meant to cover it up with concealer before I came here, but somehow I'd forgotten. "I fell."

Pastor Hobbes nods. "Your mother fell a lot, too, those last two or three years. She'd wear lots of makeup, sometimes even sunglasses indoors."

Father hit my mom? It seems incredible, but I believe it. I remember noises at night, noises I had tried to forget. Noises I didn't want to hear. I wrap my arms around myself and close my eyes. A teardrop hits my wrist.

Pastor Hobbes reaches out to me, holds his hand between us, palm open. I unwrap my arms and take his hand. "I tried to convince your mother to get help, to take you and leave. There are places, safe places, right here in Indianapolis. Places you could go. Now."

"I fell," I say almost reflexively. "And anyway, it won't happen again. He promised."

"It will happen again. Until you leave, and he gets serious treatment. It will get worse. You need to get away. Right now."

"I . . . I can't."

"You can. I'll move heaven and earth to help you, Betsy. I owe it to your mother. I owe it to God. I owe it to myself."

"You tried to help my mother, didn't you?"

"Yes."

"And she left us."

"She didn't go to any of the shelters I recommended. If she had, she would have taken you."

"Why didn't she?" I'm clutching his hand so hard that my own hand hurts. I can't imagine how he's bearing it.

"These things follow a pattern. The abuse starts. It gets steadily worse. And sometimes, either on purpose or accidently, the abuser kills his victim. I don't believe your mother left you, Betsy. I believe she's dead."

44

Jake

Monday morning, Mom drags me to Cooper's office down-town. We sit at one end of a long conference table while Cooper and two other lawyers quiz me. Aside from the three lawyers, there's also a paralegal, who Cooper introduces, but I promptly forget her name because she never says another word. All of them take notes, despite the sleek triangular recorder in the middle of the table.

Laurissa isn't there. I worry about whether she's safe and send her a text, but she doesn't respond, which only makes me worry more.

The conference room has a commanding view of down-town Indianapolis. When we start the meeting, it's clear and sunny outside. By lunchtime dark clouds have moved in,

obscuring the window. Cooper tells the paralegal to order sandwiches from the deli downstairs so we can work through lunch.

I text Laurissa again and sigh with relief when she texts
me back, "I'm fine. Quit obsessing."

I tell the lawyers everything—exactly what I remember.
Cooper promises to investigate Tapper, but I can tell that he's
trying to placate me. He doesn't really believe that part of my
story. At one point, he jots a note on a post-it and hands it to
the paralegal. She leaves the room briefly, and when she
returns, she hands a thick pamphlet to Cooper, who passes it
to my mother. Mom tries to hide it, but we're sitting right next
to each other. The pamphlet is titled "Mental Health
Professionals of the Greater Indianapolis Area."

By the time we finish, it's late afternoon. Rain lashes the
side of the building, racing in streaks down the panes. Mom and
I get soaked running for the parking garage. I welcome the
rain—it means there's no way Laurissa will spend time outside.
Can a drone operate in weather this bad? I don't know.

Laurissa texts to tell me that she can't come over today—
her dad is insisting on having a family dinner. She says she'll
see me tomorrow. I worry that I'm pushing her away with my
nagging texts about her location. But I can't help myself. I can
barely think about anything else.

When we get home, I try calling Agent Soufan at the
Indianapolis FBI office, but I have to leave a message. Then
I park myself at my computer and resume the tedious work
of trying to attract Betsy's attention. I post in chat rooms,
discussion boards, in the comments on blog posts, on every
social media feed I can get access to. I create accounts for
dozens of sites. I spam the Internet far more thoroughly

than that Nigerian prince who wants to help empty out your bank account.

Mom interrupts me, trying to get me to come to the kitchen for dinner. I flatly refuse. About an hour later, she tiptoes back into my room and sets a plate of food beside my computer. I eat mechanically while continuing to work—after I finish, I'm not even certain what I just ate.

I must have fallen asleep at some point. I wake with the side of my face pressed against the keyboard. Morning light is streaming through the window. The computer makes a soft clicking sound, typing a line of gobbledygook over and over again in the chat room window on my screen. The keyboard noise hasn't woken me, though—the theme from *Mission Impossible* has. It's playing from somewhere behind me.

I lift my head groggily—where could the music be coming from? I don't own an alarm clock or radio. I swivel in my chair, looking for the source of the noise. My phone is lit up and playing the *Mission Impossible* theme. That's not my ringtone. I've never even downloaded that music.

I stumble over to the bed and pick up my phone. Weirder still, the caller ID shows a picture of Tom Cruise. And the caller's name *is* Tom Cruise? I must be dreaming. Phones don't download new ringtones on their own. And as far as I know, Tom Cruise doesn't have my number. I pinch my own thigh, hard, but don't wake up.

The call, if it's real, should have gone to voicemail by now, but it hasn't. I slide my thumb across the screen and slowly lift the phone to my ear.

"Tom Cruise, running in movies since 1981," the voice says. It's not Cruise; it's Tapper.

"Very funny," I say.

"But you're not laughing."

"No."

"Good, because neither am I."

Everything is too weird—overwhelmingly weird. I start pacing diagonally across my room. "I don't have the *Mission Impossible* theme on my phone."

"I know. I fixed that for you. But that's the last nice thing I'm doing for your sorry ass. It's time."

Laurissa. He's talking about Laurissa. "It's not time. I've got the rest of the day." I want to text her, see if she's okay. But that would mean taking the phone away from my ear.

"You're wasting all your time on personal ads, anyway. Who is Betsy?"

How does he know about my ads? Maybe my Internet campaign is starting to work? I start to explain how Laurissa and I found the name Betsy, but Tapper interrupts me.

"Never mind about Betsy. I need your contact. Now."

I'm thinking furiously, and something suddenly clicks into place. I'm so frazzled that I tell Tapper exactly what I'm think-ing: "It's Beaner. It's got to be him. He's the only one who had access to my phone. He planted the program."

"You told me your girlfriend had access to it, too."

"Yeah, and my mom. What, you think everyone is a terrorist?"

"I don't think any of them gave you the program. I think you're covering for someone, Jake. For the guy you met near your school."

"I'm not. That was bullshit. There was no guy. I was scared."

"Let's see. Is it more likely that an ordinary police officer somehow acquired a program that's top-secret, sensitive and compartmented information, and planted it on your phone for no reason whatsoever? Or that you're lying to me about who really gave you the program?"

"I'm not lying!"

"I think you're more scared of the guy who gave you the program than you are of me, Jake. This 'Betsy' is a red herring. I think your head is screwed on exactly backward. You've got to quit staring at your own butthole and give me what I need."

"I'm telling you the truth!"

"I can see that I'm going to have to prove to you that I'm more worthy of your fear than your contact."

"Don't hurt Laurissa. Please don't hurt her." I'm nearly sobbing into the phone. What kind of heartless monster is Tapper?

"Nobody ever said anything about hurting anyone," Tapper says. He's lying. Trying to cover himself? "But I can bring the full weight of the law down on you, Jake. I can make your life miserable in ways you can't even imagine."

Suddenly it hits me: If Tapper can turn my phone on remotely, presumably listen in to my calls, others could, too. Maybe there are more ears at the other end of the line than just his. "You did threaten Laurissa. You took me aside in the back corner of the cell and—"

"Paranoid fantasies. And an unproductive line of thought, Jake. You should be focused on getting me your contact."

"You said you'd shoot her with a—"

"Think about what you're doing, Jake. My patience is exhausted. You need to come clean."

"I'm writing it all down. If anything happens to Laurissa, I'll tell the world. I'll leave copies of my story on the web and have friends ready to publish it if anything happens to me."

"Call me when you get your head on frontward. My number is in your contacts."

The connection goes dead.

I thumb over to contacts and look up Tapper. I know I didn't add him, but if he could turn my phone on remotely, adding a contact must not have been difficult. But there is no listing for him. Then I look up Cruise, and there it is, Tom Cruise, with a number and area code I don't recognize.

I text Laurissa. "Don't come over this afternoon. Just stay put. Stay indoors."

"I'm coming," she texts back. "You need me. And I need to help."

"Please. Just stay home. Inside."

"I'll see you around two."

I check the time—I've got a few hours. I open a new file on my computer and start writing.

I type furiously, feverishly recording everything I know about Tapper. Every conversation I've had with him, every threat he's made as verbatim as I can remember it. I'm in a writing zone, a trance state. Everything fades but the keyboard. I hammer my fingers against the keys, and they click softly in response. My fingers ache after only five or six pages of typing, but I push on, trying to get it all down.

Finally, my retelling catches up to the present. I write every detail I can remember of the phone conversation with Tapper, aka Tom Cruise. When I finish, I add my name and date.

I save the file and send it to my mother; my lawyer, Cooper; to my own email address; to Laurissa; and to Tapper. I want him to know that there's an accurate record of his threats out there. I don't expect anyone will believe me—my mother thinks I'm suffering paranoia induced by traumatic brain injury, and if your own mother doesn't believe you, who will? But maybe it will give Tapper pause. If I die, or—God forbid—Laurissa is killed—my description of Tapper's threats might suddenly carry a lot more weight.

By the time I finish, I'm utterly exhausted. But I can't afford to sleep. I unplug my computer, disconnect the keyboard and monitor, and clear the whole thing off my desk. Then I rearrange my room, so that my desk and computer are over by the window, where I can watch the street in front of my house. I hook everything up again and resume my online quest to attract Betsy's attention, but I get hardly anything done because I'm glancing out the window about every five seconds. Despite my work, I'm left with a terrible certainty lodged deep in my gut—it won't be enough to protect Laurissa. I've only put myself in a position to watch her get shot.

By two o'clock I'm in a daze. I keep drifting off, my head lurching down to the keyboard. I get up and pace, try doing jumping jacks, but nothing seems to help. My head is dipping toward the desk yet again when I catch movement out of the corner of my eye. I snap awake, leaning toward the window. Laurissa's black Mercedes is pulling up in front of the house.

I vault to my feet, sprinting for the front door. Mom is in the living room. She says something as I race past, but I'm too focused to listen. I throw our door open just as Laurissa emerges from the passenger seat of the Mercedes. A tiny spot of color dances in her hair—the red dot of a laser sight.

45

Jake

The dot bobbles as Laurissa steps toward me. I'm sprinting across the porch, building up speed. My eyes are fixed on the point of red light. My vision seems to narrow until there's nothing left but Laurissa's head, the light, and the edge of the porch. The dot steadies as Laurissa moves toward me and the house.

She's most of the way across our yard, maybe ten or twelve feet from the porch. I launch myself off the porch, arms outstretched, like a maniac football player going for an illegal head tackle. I crash into Laurissa. She screams, and we fall to the sidewalk together in a spectacular wipe-out.

Something punches the left side of my butt, and then I hear a distant pop, like one of those little firecrackers sold in bricks. It doesn't sound like a gun, at least not like the resonant retort of a gun on TV.

I don't feel any pain, don't feel anything at all. Even though my head is right next to Laurissa's mouth, her screams don't hurt my ears—she sounds distant and hollow.

I push myself up on my hands and knees, keeping my body between her and the sky. There's no way Tapper will shoot me—he wants information he thinks I have. I glance down, checking to see if Laurissa's okay. She's not. There's a pool of blood forming under her legs, slowly seeping out into the sidewalk, and forming a deeper rivulet along a crack.

"What the hell, Jake?" she says.

"Where are you hit?" I ask. I see one of the Brothers Grimm—Hans, I think—running toward us.

"You tackled me."

"Where are you bleeding?"

"My arm's all skinned up." Laurissa is trying to sit up, trying to push me off her, but I won't budge. There's no way a skinned knee would bleed this much—she's been hit somewhere. I try to check without giving up my position shielding her from the sky. Before I can figure it out, Hans reaches us. He tosses me aside as if I were a football rather than a full-sized person. I land in the grass beside the walk.

"Oh my God, what happened?" Mom yells from the porch, rushing down to us.

Laurissa shouts, "Let me go!" Hans has her wrapped up in a bear hug. He runs toward the Mercedes, carrying her.

"Laurissa's bleeding," I tell Mom.

Mom runs down the stairs to where I'm splayed in the grass. She stops and stares toward my legs. "It's not Laurissa. It's you."

Hans throws Laurissa into the back seat of the Mercedes and slams the door. Almost immediately, it starts to open again. Hans rams his leg against the door, closing it and holding it shut. He fishes a key fob out of his pocket and pushes a button, locking Laurissa in.

I twist my torso until I can see the backs of my own legs. There's a huge tear in my jeans starting below the waistline and ending in the middle of my left butt cheek. Blood is pouring steadily from a groove in my flesh that matches the tear. As soon as I see it, it starts to hurt.

Hans has reached the driver's seat of the Mercedes. It peels out, wheels spitting grit. A cloud of black smoke envelops me, and I choke on the stench of burning rubber.

Mom rips her T-shirt off and wads it up against the wound in my butt, pressing hard. "Laurissa. Is she okay?" I ask.

"Her bodyguard will take care of her," Mom says. "Let's get you inside."

I notice a gray blob on the sidewalk—a lead bullet that has suicided against the sidewalk—and I pick it up. It's hot and heavier than I expect.

I hope to God there's no one with a cell phone nearby. This would make the weirdest picture ever taken—my mother, in a beige old-lady bra, holding her shirt against her son's butt. Then I realize that I'm saying exactly the wrong thing to God, that I don't care if a thousand photos of this bizarro situation are taken and posted in every dank corner of the Internet. I silently ask to replace my no-cell-phones prayer with a simple thank you that Laurissa and I are alive.

Mom tucks my arm over her shoulders and half drags me back up the porch steps, through the entryway, and into the kitchen. Mom's hand is clenching my butt so hard that I wonder if she'll squeeze off my left cheek, leaving me to sit lopsided for the rest of my life. Despite her grip, I'm trailing blood on the carpet.

Mom levers me down to the floor on my stomach. She reaches around to unbutton my jeans. I resist for a minute, but it's futile. In seconds she has both my pants and underwear around my knees.

Mom's got one hand on her T-shirt, and she's kneeling on the floor straight-armed, bearing down on my wound. She reaches for her pocket with her other hand and retrieves her cell phone. Her hand is shaking so badly that the phone slips, dropping against the linoleum next to me with a thud. She reaches for her phone, snags it, and then drops it again while she's trying to lift it to her ear.

"Let me do it," I say. I reach for the phone. Mom puts both hands on my butt, bearing down even harder.

I punch Laurissa's number into Mom's phone. "Call 911," Mom orders, but I ignore her. Laurissa doesn't answer, and I leave a frantic message. "Are you okay? Call me!" Then I hang up and call 911.

I tell them I've been shot. They ask for my address and say they're sending both an ambulance and a police officer. Then they tell me to do pretty much exactly what Mom's already doing—apply pressure to the wound with a clean cloth. I'm not sure Mom's T-shirt qualifies.

I return Mom's phone to her and reach down to my ankles to retrieve my phone from my pants. Maybe Laurissa didn't answer because she didn't recognize Mom's number. But there's no answer when I call on my phone, either.

It seems like almost no time at all passes before I hear sirens; they're the soundtrack to my life, lately. The ambulance arrives first. The paramedics burst in carrying a stretcher. I don't recognize either of them.

Nor do I recognize the cop who arrives almost on their heels. His nameplate reads R KENT. When I try to tell him about the drone, he gives me a dry look and sidelong stare. A Buddhist monk might begin to doubt his own sanity under the pressure of that withering gaze.

The paramedics put clean gauze over my wound and wrap it tightly, stretching the bandage around my hips. I tell them I can walk, but they insist on loading me onto the stretcher, facedown.

The cop's radio squawks and he rushes off—something about a 10-32 nearby. I have no idea what a 10-32 is, but I'd bet my bike that someone just sent in an anonymous tip about a firearm being shot into the air somewhere nearby. Tapper's single-minded commitment to his plan is terrifying.

Mom follows me into the ambulance. I'm still clutching my phone in my hand. I dial Laurissa, but the call goes to voicemail again.

I notice that there's a Snapchat notification and thumb the icon. I have one message; it's from Tom Cruise, complete with a picture of him in a black getup from one of the *Mission Impossible* movies. I open the message and immediately kick myself mentally. I need to save this! I know there's a way to do it—some of the Cro-Magnons at school pass around nude selfies of their girlfriends screen-captured from Snapchat—but I've never learned how. I clench the phone in frustration as the photograph fades from the screen: my mother, with a red targeting sight on her forehead and the words, "TWO DAYS."

46

Jake

I endure the bumpy ambulance ride with gritted teeth—it only improves when the paramedics bundle me into the emergency room. I'm at the same hospital—Methodist—where my brain surgery was done. Where the two firefighters tried to shoot me. Everything moves at the pace of a grandma on a one-speed Schwinn. Once they realize that I'm not going to bleed to death, they park me in a tiny exam room, still face down on the gurney.

I call Laurissa again. She doesn't answer. I'm frantic. I try to get off the gurney, but Mom holds me down. We argue. She says she'll call an orderly and have me strapped down if she has to. I relent and settle for checking my phone every five seconds.

Mom stands beside the stretcher, holding my hand. I wish she'd go out to the bustling ER and demand some service. I'm on borrowed time—or she is.

I try calling Laurissa's home number. That goes to voicemail, too. I leave another message.

Mom's phone rings. Her end of the conversation is a string of yeses and thank yous—I have no idea who she's talking to.

As soon as she disconnects, I ask, "Who was on the phone?"

"Officer Kent. They've already caught the guy who shot you. He was over on Rockville Road firing some kind of military-style rifle into the air."

"He didn't fire the bullet that hit me. And it wasn't aimed at me, either." I glance at my phone. There's still no word from Laurissa.

"There are two witnesses," Mom says. "And of course it wasn't aimed at you—Officer Kent said the guy was testing out a new gun. And anyway, what kind of jackhole is too stupid to realize that bullets fired up have to come back down?"

"The bullet that hit me came from a drone. Tapper—"

"I didn't see a drone," Mom says.

"Tapper said—"

"Dr. Malhotra recommended a psychiatrist. We'll see if we can get your appointment bumped forward a couple of days," Mom says.

"I emailed you a description of exactly what Tapper said, of the way he threatened Laurissa. I predicted this attack in advance, Mom!"

"I saw your email, honey. That's part of the reason we need to see the psychiatrist. It was gobbledygook. I'm sure you'll be able to write coherently soon, but your brain may need a little more time to heal."

Could she be right? I was rushing and stressed out, but I'm sure I was making sense. A man in navy blue scrubs enters the room and introduces himself as a physician's assistant. He wheels me to a larger room with a wide array of equipment, where they're finally going to stitch me up.

The physician's assistant asks me about a hundred questions, tapping the answers into a tablet computer. People bustle in and out—a nurse who says nothing to me and a man who introduces himself as Dr. Doll.

I'm still lying face down, my butt in the air, mooning them all, but I'm past caring. I answer the PA's questions as tersely as I can.

The most painful part of the whole procedure is, ironically, the painkiller. I wonder if they've loaded up the syringe with pure habanero pepper extract as a twisted emergency room joke. But the intense pain fades, and in moments, my backside, hip, and most of one leg are completely numb. I barely notice as Dr. Doll cleans the gash. The stitches don't hurt either—there's just a strange tugging sensation as the thread forces the furrow in my flesh closed. I wind up with a whole railroad track across my ass—twenty-seven stitches.

We leave the hospital with a sheaf of papers on wound care. I have strict instructions not to sit down or lie on my back for a week. I ignore it all, trying to hurry Mom out of the ER. There are only two things that matter to me: Is Laurissa okay? And will my mom be? I have forty-two hours left.

47
Betsy

Could Father have killed my mother? It seems unbelievable, impossible. I decide that I don't believe it. Pastor Hobbes must have the messed-up families in the Old Testament on his brain: Cain and Abel, Lot and his daughters, Abraham and Isaac.

Still, he was right about the fights, I suppose. I do remember a lot of arguments. I don't remember Mom having bruises or black eyes.

We must have some old photographs. Maybe I'll see bruises. Or maybe I'll only see my mother wearing sunglasses and too much makeup. Father removed all the pictures from the walls not long after Mom disappeared, but I assume they're in boxes in the attic.

While Father's at work, I pull down the overhead stairs to the attic. A tuft of loose insulation floats down, spinning idly in the breeze.

The attic is scorching. I'm sweating from the moment I reach the top of the stairs. There are only five boxes up here, all marked Christmas.

I go through them anyway. There's nothing weird in the boxes: a plastic tree, coils of lights, a nativity set, and dozens of ornaments. I find one—a plasticine baby Jesus—that's inscribed, "Betsy's First Christmas." There's a whole series of these, ending with my tenth Christmas.

We used to have more personalized ornaments. I remember one I particularly loved that had two big snowmen hugging a little snowman and all our first names on it. I finish searching the boxes, but I don't find the snowman ornament. I realize with a shock, everything that had my mother's name on it is gone. It's as if she never existed.

I stumble down the attic stairs, my stomach cramping. I get a couple of Rolaids from the bottle in the bathroom medicine cabinet and chomp them down. I get why Father might not want reminders of his wife around, but throwing out Christmas ornaments with her name on them seems extreme.

When the Rolaids have calmed the bees in my gut, I decide to continue searching for signs of my mother. I tiptoe toward the lion's den—my father's bedroom. I don't know why I'm making an effort to be quiet; nobody's in the house but me. I twist the knob and step inside.

I haven't been in this room in years. There's a dresser, a desk with a computer, a queen bed, and a bedside table. Nothing else. No pictures on the walls. No television. The walls are beige, the carpet is beige, and the bedspread is a generic shade of green. Anyone could live here, or no one.

I open the drawer in the bedside table. Father's Remington 1911 pistol is in there, along with a few dog-eared gun magazines. I pick up the pistol and check it—the safety is on and there's a round in the chamber. I put the gun back, close the drawer, and search the rest of the room.

There's nothing interesting in the dresser or closet. I was hoping for a box of mementos of Mom. Surely something would be shoved away somewhere?

I go through the drawers of the desk. I find Father's tax returns. This year is in the front, and they continue back exactly seven years. Nothing older than that is in this drawer. Nothing with my mother's name on it. Every trace of her has been expunged from Father's life and files. I try to boot up his computer, but the login is password protected, and I'm not a hacker.

I put everything back as I found it and leave Father's bedroom. I'm not going to learn anything from snooping around the house. If I want to know what happened to Mom, I'm going to have to confront my father directly.

48
Jake

Mom insists on stopping at the drugstore on the way home from the hospital to fill the prescription for the pain meds, which means waiting around for twenty minutes while they count my pills. I call Laurissa's cell phone again, and my call goes to voicemail—again. I try her house, and her dad picks up.

His voice rumbles like far-off thunder, "Davis Residence."

"Is Laurissa there?" I ask.

"This is Jake?"

"Yes."

"Don't call here again."

"Wait! What?" Mr. Davis always seemed like he liked me. Or at least tolerated me. Laurissa's mother was the one who clearly wished I'd disappear from her life.

"Look, Jake, I like you."

"But then why—"

"Let me finish, please."

"Can I please ask just one question?" I say.

"What?" Mr. Davis's voice has dropped about an octave, into a flat-out growl.

"Is Laurissa okay?"

"Yes," he says in a considerably gentler tone. "She is. She just skinned her arm on the sidewalk. Now listen."

"Yes, sir." I can barely breathe out the words. He's going to ban me from even talking to Laurissa?

"I admire your grit. Your determination. You're poor as dirt, but somehow you've made yourself into a hell of a bike racer."

What does this have to do with anything? I want to talk to Laurissa. "Can I—"

"You remind me of myself when I was your age. You're driven. I like that."

"Thank you. But can I—"

"So when Laurissa asked to use part of her trust on your legal issues, I agreed. It's almost impossible to say no to her, anyway. She's going to make a hellacious lawyer someday."

"Yes, she is."

"But here's what I cannot and will not tolerate. You cannot put my baby girl in danger. That's not negotiable. Not by you, not by her, not by God on high."

"I don't want her in danger either, sir," I say.

"My daughter came home covered in blood. Anyone involved in that sort of thing is not someone I want her associating with."

"Most of that blood was mine."

"We'll continue to fund your legal defense, but in return, you're not to have any further contact with my daughter. Is that understood?"

"Yes." I breathe the word like it's my last.

"Are you okay, son?"

"No."

"I'm sorry to bring you bad news after you've been hurt. But it is what it is."

"I'm okay physically." And that's true, for what it's worth. It could have been so much worse. "Twenty-seven stitches. But I'm fine."

"I'll tell her. But from here forward, you're not to speak with my daughter."

"But can . . . can I at least say goodbye?"

"I'm sorry, Jake." Mr. Davis hangs up.

I sag into the seat of one of the pharmacy chairs. Mom rubs my back. "It'll be okay, Jake," she says. I don't respond.

On the way home, I try Laurissa's cell phone. My call goes to voicemail. I need to speak to her like a drowning man needs a life ring. But that's not my only problem. I've got to find Betsy. Got to do something about Tapper. I call the Indianapolis FBI office and work my way through their voicemail system until I'm connected with Soufan's line, but he doesn't pick up. I've had it. I leave two sentences on his voicemail: "I thought you wanted information about Flight 117? Call me!"

"Cooper said communication with the FBI should go through him," Mom says.

"Yeah. You're right. I'll call him when we get home." But I won't. Cooper doesn't believe that Tapper is out to get me.

He thinks I'm crazy, just like Mom. Calling him would be nothing but a waste of time.

I sag against the car door, thinking about my Internet campaign to contact Betsy. It isn't working. Either she is choosing to ignore me, or she hasn't seen any of my posts. The latter seems more likely—why would she be looking at Craigslist or any of the even more obscure sites where I've posted my ads? What I need is to attract more attention, to make my plea so popular that Betsy, or Fake Laurissa, or whoever she is, can't ignore it. She needs to remain anonymous. I need so many people to see my ad that she'll be forced to contact me, if only to ask me to take it down. Maybe she'll try to kill me again. Even that would be preferable to waiting for my mother to get shot. I need to make a viral video.

I'm entirely the wrong person to create a viral video; I don't even like the Internet very much. I have classmates who spend every waking hour connected to Tumblr or Snapchat. After an hour online, I get twitchy. I need the wind in my hair, the pressure of the pedals under my feet, the time with nothing but my thoughts and the passing scenery for company.

When we get home, Mom tells me to go to bed. I grunt my agreement, go into my room, shut the door, and boot up my computer. Sitting pulls at my stitches a little, but it's not painful—I still can't feel much at all in my hip or leg.

I pull up a list of the top YouTube videos of all time. I'd thought that cats and porn ruled the Internet, but these videos are all pop stars and drugged toddlers—not helpful. I don't see a single cat video on the list, although some of the music videos are almost pornographic. Obviously, I need to revise my notion of what's popular on YouTube.

I click through to the videos and start watching them, just a few seconds of each. I'm too tense to watch more. Every second I'm wasting on YouTube annoys me. My meds have kicked in—my head is floating upward while my body stays anchored to the chair and my neck is stretching, but I don't care. My fingers twitch across the mouse, switching videos so fast that the videos don't have time to load. I see only a flickering black screen adorned with YouTube's loading icon.

I lift my head from the keyboard. I must have passed out briefly; maybe I forgot to breathe. I close my eyes and slowly suck down lungfuls of air, swelling my stomach outward with each breath, like I do when I'm riding, to deliver maximum oxygen to my legs. After a few moments, I feel calmer. My head is still floating, riding the smooth, narcotic wave of the pain meds, but when I open my eyes, some of the twitchiness is gone.

There's a video of a guy getting kicked in the nuts on my computer screen. The video cuts, and now there's a guy falling off his skateboard onto a handrail, split-legged. Then a kid doing a backflip on a balance beam—only he lands on his balls—and no, I don't mean the balls of his feet.

My mind wanders to a memory: Eustace Belcher talking to me in the school cafeteria. We weren't friends, not exactly. Eustace just kind of glommed onto anyone who wouldn't walk away from him and regaled them with the plots of the movies he'd watched the night before. He was easily the best person in school to ask for a movie recommendation—he'd seen everything—but he had no spoiler alert filters whatsoever. He got the movies off a Swedish pirate feed, and given the quantity of movies he'd seen, I'm not sure if he ever slept. Except in class, where he was a certified ninja at desk-sleeping.

Anyway, during one of Eustace's movie blathers, he told me about some comedian who'd nailed his balls to a wood plank. I remember nothing of that conversation with Eustace except for that singular fact: Some guy nailed his balls to a chunk of wood.

There's no way I'm going to put my hairy balls on YouTube, but the idea has wormed its way into my head like a maggot. I leave my room, stumbling slightly on the way out. The painkiller is making me loopy.

In the basement I find a hammer and a box of large nails. There's a thick layer of dust on the box—my dad must have bought the nails, which means they've been sitting on the shelf for more than eleven years. Would he approve of what I plan to do with them? Despite my hazy memories of him, I'm sure he wouldn't. But unlike him, I can't load us all on a plane and fly us somewhere far away. I have to protect my family with the considerably less lavish resources at my command. Like this box of nails he left behind.

Back in my room, I lock my door and start my webcam. The ready light is Mr. Yuck green. Its glare holds more than a hint of reproach. I steel myself, addressing the light with the same unblinking determination it shows.

"You told me your name was Laurissa, but I know your real name is Betsy. I know more about you, but I won't say anything more if you'll only speak with me again. Five minutes of your time is all I ask. All I can hope for. I'm desperate. I've only got two days left. I'll do anything to reach you, Betsy, anything. Let me prove it to you."

I take a deep breath. I'm not really ready for this part of my plan. How could I be? How could anyone be ready for this? I

lay my left arm flat atop the smooth, wooden surface of my
desk, palm down. My desktop is cool and tickles the hairs on
my arm. The computer is picking everything up perfectly—my
face is set in a grimace on the screen.

I take one of the nails from the box. It's three inches long,
with a sturdy round head and a point that was made by shear-
ing off the tip on four sides, sort of like the tip of the
Washington Monument. The label on the box says it's a fram-
ing nail.

I push it against the flesh of my forearm and try to grab the
hammer. The nail falls off my arm. I can see why the insane
comedian nailed his ballsack—he needed two hands free, one to
hold the nail and one to swing the hammer. I push the nail into
my flesh hard enough to draw blood, but it still won't stand
upright long enough for me to whack it with the hammer.

A bead of blood wells from the hole in my arm and rolls
down the side, plopping against the desk. The wound barely
hurts at all—much less than the anesthetic for the stitches in
my butt did. I'm sitting kind of lopsided, trying to keep weight
off the stitches on my left side. I'm not even supposed to be
sitting down, but I'm probably not supposed to be trying to
drive a nail into my arm either, so whatever.

I pick the nail back up, but this time I put the tip against
the web of flesh between my pointer and middle fingers. By
closing my fingers, I can hold the nail upright. I lift the hammer, aim carefully, and smack it down against the nailhead.

This time the pain is indescribable. Instinctively I try to
draw my hand back toward my body, but I can't; I've nailed
myself to the surface of the desk. Pulling on the wound sends
fire pulsing up my arm. Tears leak from my eyes, mingling

with the sweat dripping from my forehead. My image on the computer screen leers back at me, my face twisted to the point that I can barely recognize myself.

I open my fingers. Blood wells around the shaft of the nail, running onto my desktop. The unblinking green eye of my webcam sees it all. I grit my teeth and grab another nail from the box, placing it against the skin between my middle and ring fingers.

"You need to contact me, Betsy. I will do anything, absolutely anything, to speak with you again."

I smack the hammer down on the new nail. This time I can't hold it in; I scream as the nail bites my flesh.

I'm still trying to talk into the webcam, to speak to Betsy, but I'm gritting my teeth against the pain, and I'm not sure any intelligible words are making it out of my mouth.

I place another nail between my ring and pinkie fingers. Smack! Three nails hold my hand to the desk now.

Mom is banging on my door. "Jake, if you don't open the door right this minute, I'm going to break it down."

"Can't!" I yell. I try to tell her I'm nailed down, but I can't get the words out around the prison of my gritted teeth.

I place another nail, the fourth, between my thumb and pointer finger. The hammer glances off the side of the nail and it skitters away, leaving my hand scratched but not punctured.

Mom's hitting the door with something heavy now, trying to break it down. It won't take her long—the door to my room is cheap and hollow. It makes a booming sound with each blow she lands.

I take a fresh nail from the box and drive it through the web of flesh between my thumb and finger, screaming as it rips my flesh.

The door splinters as the butt end of a fire extinguisher abruptly appears alongside the knob.

I shut off the recording and type a title for my video one-handed. "Guy Crazy for Betsy Nails Hand to Desk." While I'm doing that, Mom pulls the fire extinguisher out of the door, reaches through the hole, unlocks the knob, and charges into my room.

"What the hell is going—" Mom falls suddenly silent as she takes in my desk: My hand firmly attached to it. The blood spreading around my fingers, coating the blond maple top with a red stain. She turns her head away, swallowing hard.

I put my Hushmail address in the video description and hit enter, watching as the blue bar labeled "Uploading" slowly grows on my screen.

Mom gathers herself and charges forward to stand beside my desk chair. "Baby, why? What on earth were you thinking?"

I try to respond, but can't form anything more coherent than a moan. The nails are driven through my hands and about an inch into the wood. I hold my hand as still as possible—any movement sends excruciating spikes of pain racing up my arm.

Mom seizes one of the nails in her fingers. Her face screws up and turns cherry-bomb red. Her whole hand is white with the strain. The nail surrenders with a screech, ripping free of the table and my hand. I scream, and the blood wells anew from my wound. The hammer is lying in easy reach, its nail-pulling claw shining red with light reflected from the puddle of blood on my desk. Mom ignores the hammer, grabs the next nail, and rips it free. I scream again from the pain, but inwardly I'm in awe. A gorilla couldn't have ripped those nails free, but evidently enraged mom beats gorilla the same way rock beats scissors.

Mom pulls the last two nails. I sag against my chair in relief. All four holes are bleeding, but they don't hurt as much now. And I don't have to keep still.

Mom disappears behind me for a couple of seconds, then returns with a T-shirt, wrapping it tightly around my hand. "You stupid, stupid boy," she mutters.

Maybe she's right, but I know the pain I'm feeling is temporary. If this works, if it draws Betsy's attention, I won't care about the damage I've done to my hand. The computer dings—my video has finished uploading.

"We're going to the hospital. Again." Mom hauls me to my feet and rushes me out the door. She keeps up a running stream of questions as we move through the house at a near jog, "Why? What were you thinking? How could you do this to yourself? How could you do this to me?"

By the time I can get a word in edgewise, we're in the car backing down the driveway. "I don't need to go to the hospital," I say. "It's just four little puncture wounds. We can wrap them in gauze or something."

Mom has backed the car out into the street. She slams the gearshift into drive, and the tires squeal as we drag race down our residential street. "Jake, you need help."

"Mom, I can explain. The guy who shot at Laurissa with the drone—"

"There was no drone."

"We didn't see it, sure, but that's because it was in the clouds or maybe behind a tree or something."

"No. Officer Kent called me. They caught the guy who did

it. He confessed. There was no drone, Jake."

"That was part of Tapper's plan. To frame—"

"Maybe it was the injury, maybe something else. But we've got to face the fact that there's something going wrong in your head, Jake. I'm going to get you the help you need."

"I need to go back to my computer and—"

"No. There's an excellent inpatient psychiatric department at Community Hospital. Cathy Nikose's son went there after he took those pills."

The car windows shift suddenly—they're sealing me in rather than sealing the world out. "I can't go there. I've got to—"

"All you have to do is rest and get better. That's what I want you to focus on." Mom wrenches the car through a right turn so violent that I feel sure we're taking it on two wheels.

Mom gets stuck in a line of cars at a red light. She's twitchy, bouncing in her seat. I feel the same way for totally different reasons. I can't be trapped in some psychiatric ward. Whether Mom believes me or not, her life is in danger. I have no idea whether my video worked, whether my crazy schemes for finding Betsy and placating Tapper will work, but there's no way I can afford to be locked in an inpatient ward. Mom must be crazy with worry, and I know I'm only going to make it worse, but I can't—won't—get trapped now.

I wrap the T-shirt tighter around my hand. Blood is caked between my fingers, sticking them together. I tuck the loose end of the T-shirt under the wrapped fabric. I can't knot the bandage one-handed, but I manage to get it fairly secure.

Traffic is brutal. We get stopped again at a light by an apartment complex. Mom has quit telling me about the care at Community. Instead, she's cursing under her breath. I unbuckle my seatbelt. And as Mom yells a protest, I open the passenger door and run for it.

49

Jake

The car bangs up onto the sidewalk behind me. Mom's trying to follow, yelling something out the still-open passenger door. I dart across the grass, cutting between two apartment buildings spaced too close for our car to fit.

I run across a quiet cul-de-sac and pass between two more apartment buildings. At the far side, there's a grassy hill that leads down to a lake. I jog to the edge of the water and slow to a walk. Down here, at the bottom of the hill, I can't be seen from any road. I pick my way around the lake, following the shoreline. By the time I reach the far side, night has begun to fall.

I climb the bank. There are more apartment buildings on this side so I cut between them. When I emerge onto the road beyond, I recognize where I am—not far from the Wayne Branch Library.

I need to see if my video uploaded. Is anyone watching it? Has Betsy responded? I reach for my phone, but realize that I left it on my desk. I curse myself and decide to head for the library.

I cross the road and cut over a block, trudging down an obscure residential street. The streetlights pop on one by one, casting a dull yellow light that makes my skin look sallow and sickly.

The painkillers start to wear off, and my hand throbs in time with the beating of my heart. The stitches on my butt pull with every step I take, but the physical pain seems unimportant. I desperately want to call Laurissa. To hear her voice, her calm tones like a streetlight on a foggy road before the break of dawn. If I had my phone, I'd try. But I'm guessing her dad took her phone. Otherwise, she would have answered my earlier calls.

I'm moving slowly now. The trek to the library seems to take forever, slogging through a night that only gets darker with every step I take.

The library parking lot is empty—all the lights are off except a solitary streetlamp. I drag myself across the pavement, my feet weightier with every scraping step. The lobby beyond the glass doors is dark. I tug on the cold steel handle anyway; the doors are locked.

Maybe someone is there who will take pity on me and let me use a computer after hours for a few minutes. But my frantic knocking doesn't bring anyone to the door.

I stumble around to the side of the library. There are no cars parked there, and the door marked "Staff Entrance Only" is sealed tight. What do I do now? My mother wants to lock me up in a mental ward, my girlfriend can't talk to me, Agent Soufan isn't returning my calls, and Agent Tapper is going to kill one of the two people I love most unless I give him information that I don't have. There's a fenced enclosure for AC units near the door. I step into the corner between the back wall and the chain-link fence. My legs buckle, and my back slides down the rough brick wall until I'm crumpled on the concrete, sitting against the library. Curled into the corner, I give in to my despair and cry softly until I fall into an uneasy sleep.

50

Betsy

The first words my father says to me when he gets home from work are, "Goddamnit, Betsy!"

Does he know I've been snooping through his stuff? How could he? Or maybe he heard about my visit to Pastor Hobbes? Heard that I've been asking about my mother?

"Have you seen this shit?" Father's holding out his phone. There's a YouTube video queued.

"Nooo," I say. I feel like a mouse tiptoeing among dancing elephant feet.

"Watch it."

I do. It shows Jake nailing his own hand, trying to get attention. My attention. It's stupid and also a bit terrifying. How did he get my real first name? My cover was perfect. It

275

should have been impossible for a nobody like Jake to penetrate. "Everyone will think he's nuts," I tell Father after the video finishes. "Who's going to believe anything he says now?"

"He knows your face. He knows your name. You know almost all the brothers. It's too dangerous. I'll deal with him myself." Father takes his phone back and starts punching buttons furiously.

"What do you want me to do?" I ask.

"Just a minute."

I step beside him so I can see his phone. He's pulled up a weather site, and he's looking at sunset times.

Father puts his phone away. "Go to the library. Contact him with a throwaway account. Tell him to get all that shit off the Internet. Set up a meeting, in the park, by Fall Creek near the bike trail bridge. Tell him to come alone. Make the meeting at exactly 6:40 p.m., two hours before sunset."

"Okay," I say, "but do you suppose you could . . ."

Father isn't listening. He has turned his back and is already halfway across the house. He's headed toward the garage, toward the safe where he keeps his long guns. Including his sniper rifle.

51

Jake

The sound of a shoe scuffing against concrete wakes me. I yawn, slowly turning my head toward the noise.

There's a young, blond woman fumbling with a key card, trying to unlock the back door. She's wearing a sleeveless dress, and her arms are muscled. She looks like she'd be more comfortable clinging to a sun-drenched cliff than staffing a desk at a library. She wears oversized glasses with red frames.

"Excuse me," I say, struggling to my feet despite my stiff legs.

She lets out a yelp, drops her key card, and jumps backward. Her hands fly up to either side of her head, and her feet shift back into a fighting stance. Maybe she's not a rock climber. A boxer? Her feet are positioned like a boxer's, but

I've never seen any boxer hold his hands as high as hers; she's leaving her stomach wide open.

"Sorry," I say. I hold my hands up, palms outward. "I didn't mean to startle you. I'm just here to use a computer."

Her fists drop about an inch. "What happened to your hand?"

I turn my left hand over, inspecting it. The T-shirt/bandage is filthy. A crusty streak of dried blood adorns my forearm. "Umm, it's kind of complicated."

She drops her arms some more. At least now she no longer looks like she's about to pummel me. "You want me to call someone? Your mother?"

"No!" I realize I'm shouting and try again with a more normal tone. "No, I just need to use a computer. But thank you."

"Your mother did that to you?"

"What? No!"

"Mm-hmm." Now her arms are crossed.

"It's complicated," I say again.

"Were you out here all night?" she asks.

"Yeah. Sorry. I fell asleep." I'm not sure why I'm apologizing. And saying that I fell asleep is about the worst explanation ever for hanging out all night at the back door of the library.

The librarian is looking more skeptical by the minute. "You have anyone you can call? Someone who can help?"

"Um . . . I really just need to use a computer. If you don't mind?"

"We don't open for another half hour."

"Can I just . . . wait back here?"

She stares at me for a few moments, arms still crossed. "Never mind. Come on in."

The librarian retrieves her key card from the ground. I notice that she doesn't bend over to grab it. Instead, she squats, and her eyes never leave my face. She unlocks the back door, holding it open for me. I step through into a dim hall, lit only by the rectangle of light streaming in the door behind me.

"You have a library card?" She touches the wall behind me, and fluorescent lights pop on, slowly brightening as their tubes warm up.

"Yeah. But I don't have it with me."

"Take a right at the end of the hall." I walk down the hall, and she follows me a couple of paces behind. "Do you have any kind of ID?"

"Not on me. I left my wallet at, well, behind." I turn the corner and see a large, open area packed with carts of library books. I stop at the edge of the light leaking from the hall—I don't want to stumble around blindly. Behind me, the librarian hits a switch, and more fluorescents pop on.

Two walls of the room are open—I can see the shelves of the library proper beyond. In here there are a half-dozen desks stacked with books, papers, and a truly baffling assortment of paraphernalia.

At the center of one desk, there's a large stuffed animal that's some kind of cross between an elephant and an octopus. Another desk is half covered with at least a hundred Lego figurines standing in ranks. A miniature Foucault pendulum swings silently nearby. And in one corner, there's a life-sized cardboard cutout of Benedict Cumberbatch.

The librarian picks up a small brass nameplate that reads Lena Heck. She has to reach awkwardly through the neck hole of her dress to fasten the old-style pin on it, and I catch a flash of bra—white and plain, boring. I always assumed librarians wore sexy lingerie under their frumpy clothes; Lena is the opposite—she has frumpy underwear under an interesting dress. She goes to a different desk and rummages around in one of the bottom drawers for a moment, coming up with a plastic box marked with a red cross and the words FIRST AID.

"Follow me," Lena says.

"I just need to use a computer. Please?"

"I can't have you bleeding all over the keyboard. Let me look at your hand, and then I'll set you up. Okay?"

I nod and follow her to a cramped staff bathroom. She turns the water on warm and opens the first aid kit, perching it precariously on the edge of the sink.

Lena extracts a pair of disposable latex gloves from the kit. As she snaps them on, I notice that her nails are cut short like a nurse's—or a boxer's, I suppose. "Let me see that hand," she says.

I offer her my hand, and she slowly unwraps the T-shirt. The shirt is so crusted with blood that it crackles, and flakes fall off like miniature leaves to wash down the drain. It's stuck tightly to my hand, and as she pulls it free, I wince and suck in my breath sharply as some of my scabs are yanked off. Fresh blood wells from two of the wounds, drops spattering against the porcelain.

"Crack my spine," Lena mutters under her breath. Then she asks, "Who did this to you?"

I can't tell her the truth—she might march me to the same psychiatric ward Mom was aiming for. "It's . . . complicated."

"You said that already. At least twice." She wets down a square of gauze and begins washing the dried blood off my arm and hand, slowly approaching my actual wounds. "What's your name?"

"Jake. Look, I appreciate the help and all, but I just need—"

"To use a computer. Yes, I know." She keeps washing my hand, a painful process once she gets around to the actual nail holes. She dries my hand with a couple of paper towels, which are rough and come back bloodstained. The antibiotic ointment is a relief, cool and lubricious against my skin. She cuts small rectangles of gauze, draping them over the webs of my fingers. Then she takes a roll of gauze and wraps it between and around my fingers and hand until my whole left hand is pretty much mummified. My fingertips are free, though. I wiggle them experimentally—I can type, although it won't be comfortable.

"Thanks," I say.

"Hmm. You're welcome. The public computers boot up automatically when the library opens in about twenty minutes. I'll set you up on mine instead."

Three desks are occupied when we return to the office. I get strange looks from the other librarians, and one of them approaches Lena; evidently, patrons aren't supposed to be in this area. Lena brushes her off, saying she'll explain later.

She boots up her computer for me, typing in a password so fast that I can't catch it. She opens a web browser and offers me her chair. "Will you be okay for a minute? I need to make a call."

"Sure, thanks." I hope the call she's planning to make isn't related to me, although I have a sinking suspicion that it might be.

She strides to the far side of the room, picks up a handset from an unoccupied desk, and starts paging through a laminated flip chart, looking for a number.

I pull up my YouTube account and sign in. Did it work? Did anyone see my video? More importantly, did Betsy?

My most recent upload is nothing but a black box. I click on it and get the message, "This video has been removed for violating YouTube's terms of service. For more information, click here."

It was all for nothing. I curl up and hit my head against the keyboard, where it types unprintable words I don't have the energy to say out loud.

52

Jake

I lift my head from the keyboard and look around. Lena is muttering softly into a phone at the back of the room, staring right at me. She flashes a weak grin when she sees me looking her way. I turn back to the screen—I don't like the maternal glint in her eye.

I log on to my throwaway Hushmail account—I've got forty-six messages. Which is bizarre since I opened the account less than two days ago.

I start working through the emails. The first seven are spam, but the next is someone urging me to get treatment and providing a link to a help line for cutters. After that there's someone who wants to know how I did the trick with the nails because it looked so real. Then one from someone who wants me to have the number for the National Suicide Prevention Lifeline. Another fan wants to know why I was too big a wimp to drive the nails through my bones, like a "REAL badass." Another person sends me the link to a counseling center in Indianapolis that takes clients on a sliding scale—if you're poor enough, they'll see you for free.

Evidently, my video didn't get taken down instantly. At least a few people saw it. I rush through all the messages. Near the end of the queue, there's one from WodjanShahrakhhani@ hushmail.com that reads, "I got your video taken down. Meet me at the park near where I crashed your bike today at 6:40 p.m. Delete everything else you posted about me, and come alone, or I won't be there. —Laurissa."

The next message is even stranger. It's from Betsy7654@ hushmail.com and reads, "Do you have a death wish? Run!"

I want to charge out of there, get to the park right away. It's halfway across town. If I have to walk, it might take most of the day. But for some reason, I think about my mother. She's probably still looking for me. I've never disappeared overnight before.

I glance behind me—Lena is hanging up the phone. She can't have been talking to Mom; she doesn't know my last name. I dash off a quick email to Mom, telling her I'm okay and will be home soon. Almost as an afterthought, I add, "I love you" and have to choke back sudden tears.

Lena lays a hand on my shoulder, and I quickly close my email. "You okay?" she asks.

"Yeah. Fine."

"I have to run out to the circulation desk. I'll be right back."

She leaves, and I start deleting the ads I placed on Craigslist, Backpage, *Nuvo*, and dozens of other sites. I'm fairly sure I get them all, but it's not like I kept a list when I was placing them. When I finish, Lena's still at the circulation desk. She's standing—I can see most of her back through one of the openings connecting this room with the rest of the library. She seems to be looking toward the front door of the library.

I get up and walk casually to the phone Lena used earlier. I pick up the receiver and dial *69. A mechanical voice comes on the line. "You've reached Marion County Child Protective Services. If you know the extension you—" I hang up and glance toward the circulation desk just in time to see Lena rush out and greet two people coming through the main library doors: a young black woman in a suit and a white police officer.

53

Jake

I want to run, but nothing would draw more attention than an all-out sprint. My heart is hammering, but I manage to turn and saunter into the hall at the back of the library.

The hall is empty, so I dash to the staff entrance at the other end. I heave a huge sigh of relief when I see the crash bar on the door—I'm not locked in. I let myself out into a dazzlingly bright morning. An alarm wails behind me, and I run for it.

I cross the side yard of the library and plunge into a scrubby wood. I glance backward—Lena, the police officer, and the young woman in the suit are just emerging from the back door of the library.

"Jake, wait!" Lena yells. "They just want to help!"

I force my way through the tangled underbrush at the edge of the woods. I've taken fewer than ten steps when I reach a railroad embankment. I scramble up it, slipping on the gravel, and jump down the far side in about three loping steps. There's another strip of brush to crash through, and then I'm at the back of a row of houses. Most of the yards are fenced. I spot one with a four-foot, chain-link fence, but no sign of a dog. I jump over it despite the shooting pain in my butt and hand.

I vault several more fences, running through backyards, staying off roads as much as I can, and changing direction several times. When I finally slow down, I see no sign of pursuit.

I come to a corner and check the street signs—I'm not terribly far from my house, on a road I've biked on. I walk home, sticking to side streets.

Mom's car isn't in the driveway. I find the key in its usual hiding place and let myself in.

The door to my room is ruined, huge splinters of wood hanging from the jagged, roughly round hole Mom made in it. My desk is even worse; it's coated in crusty, dried blood. I retrieve my wallet, keys, phone, and phone charger. I glance at the phone—I have a text from Zach about a bike race this weekend, which I delete. There's also a voicemail, but I don't recognize the number. In the kitchen, I check the cabinet where Mom hides her emergency cash. There's twenty-six dollars. I take it all, despite feeling guilty about wiping her out. I've known she keeps cash here for years, but I've never taken anything from her before. I wish I didn't have to now. I grab some peanut butter crackers from a cabinet and a bottle of water from the refrigerator and jog to the garage to get my Huffy.

♦ ♦ ♦

I get to the park almost three hours early. It occurs to me that I've met Betsy/Fake Laurissa twice, and she's tried to kill me twice. This meeting might be different, though—she could have killed me the last time we were here, but she didn't. For all that she tried to suffocate me and crashed my bike, she's just not a killer.

But if I'm wrong—if she is planning to take another shot at me—then there's no reason to make it easy on her. I study the area. It's a grassy slope dotted with concrete benches and ancient trees. The strip of cleared land is fairly narrow, bordered on one side by Fall Creek Parkway and on the other side by Fall Creek itself. On the far side of the road, there's a modern, three-story apartment complex. Along the river bank, there's a boat launch and a concrete fishing pier. Past the pier, a thick stretch of trees hugs the river.

I push my way into the woods until my Huffy and I are both well hidden. Then I wait with my back against a tree, peering out through gaps in the leaves to watch the park.

I'm dead tired—I have to fight to stay awake despite my apprehension about meeting Betsy again. I set an alarm on my phone for 6:10, just in case I do fall asleep.

I still haven't checked the message on my phone. I press the play button and just about scream for joy when I hear Laurissa's voice. "Where are you, Jake? I talked to your mother, and she said you didn't come home last night. Are you okay? I'm worried. My dad's being a total orc. Add this number to your contacts, but don't call it. Nobody knows I have this phone. I'll call you as soon as I can. I love you. Be careful."

It's all I can do not to call her. My need to hear her voice is almost exactly as strong as my need to breathe was when Betsy was strangling me. If I call her, and her father finds her secret phone, we'll be completely out of touch. I listen to her message again and save it.

I call the FBI office and leave a message for Soufan. "Why aren't you returning my calls? I've got info about Flight 117. Call me."

There aren't any messages from Mom. She thinks my phone is still on my desk. She's probably out looking for me right now. I'm still angry at Mom for trying to have me locked up, but there's a little niggling voice in my head that says she doesn't deserve the worry she's suffering. I send her a text, "I'm okay. I'm sorry," and pocket my phone.

Around four o'clock the park fills up with kids—mothers with their young children, high school kids on their own. Most of them are just passing through, using the bike trail that winds along the river.

My phone vibrates in my pocket. I don't recognize the number, but I answer anyway. I recognize Agent Soufan's voice, "You have information about 117?"

"Tapper is threatening my mother. He shot at my girl-friend. With a drone."

"A drone?"

"Yes."

There's a heavy sigh. "Tapper's a twenty-year veteran. He's earned the Medal of Valor. And you expect me to believe—"

"It's true."

"What you need to do is give up your contact, Jake. Come

over to the right side of the street. I'd be a lot more inclined to listen if you were cooperating."

"He hung the jacket over the recorder in the interview room so he could threaten me."

"I'm not having this discussion with you. Tapper's one of the finest agents in the Bureau. Throwing ridiculous sci-fi accusations around isn't helping you."

"He's got a program to control it on his tablet. Can't you check that?"

"Get me your contact and I'll try."

"There is no contact! That was all bullshit I made up to placate Tapper. If you'd—"

"You can report it to IAD if you want. But they aren't going to believe you, either."

"What's IAD?"

"Call me back when you've got something real." Soufan hangs up.

I sag against the tree trunk and jam my phone back into my pocket. I pluck a leaf off a nearby bush and slowly shred it into about a zillion pieces.

Two old guys show up with fishing poles, coolers, and lawn chairs. They sit on the concrete pier and cast their lines into Fall Creek. By five thirty, all the kids have cleared out, replaced by joggers and cyclists, moving fast along the trail. The fishermen are starting on their second six-pack. Nobody has noticed me, or if they have, they haven't reacted.

Six forty comes and goes. I'm kneeling now instead of sitting, ready to spring up and run if I need to. There's no sign of Betsy. I scan the park anxiously. The sun is low in the sky now, almost touching the top of the apartments across the way.

People are out on their balconies grilling dinner, but the glare of the sun makes them look like black ants against the bright yellow and blue walls of the complex.

I see something moving out of the corner of my eye and glance toward the bike path bridge over Fall Creek. Betsy is cresting the arch of the bridge, pedaling the same bike she was on when she crashed into me, a red Schwinn. Her head swivels, scanning the park, taking in the two fishermen and moving on. She doesn't have the nightstick this time, or any obvious weapon. There's no pack hanging under the seat of her bike. She's wearing another headscarf and a flowing, long-sleeved, pantsuit-type getup. This one is sapphire blue. The cuffs of her pants are restrained with rubber bands, keeping the fabric out of her bike's chain.

She's pedaling slowly, looking around. About halfway up the slope toward the road, she stops and dismounts her bike. I'm fairly certain she doesn't see me. I wait another minute or so, trying to see if she's alone. The only people in the park now are the two fishermen on the pier, and they aren't paying attention to anything but the bottoms of their beer cans.

I leave my Huffy where it is and cautiously work my way out of the overgrown woods. Betsy turns, her clothing swirling around her. I take a couple more steps toward her.

Betsy remounts her bike, muttering something. The only word I hear clearly is "dumbass."

"Betsy, wait!" I call.

She puts one foot on the pedal and pushes off. "I told you to disappear." She's above me on the hill, and the sun has dropped far enough that it's just barely above the roof of the apartment building beyond her. I have to squint to look at her.

"Wait!" I start to run after her, but the sunlight flares bright red, nearly blinding me. I throw up my right hand to shield my eyes, and then I see it: a spot of light so intense that I can see it through the flesh of my hand. I instantly know exactly what it is since I've seen them repeatedly this week—a red laser sight.

54

Jake

The laser sight flicks back onto my face, and I dive sideways behind one of the concrete benches. I hear a rifle shot coming from the direction of the apartment complex, and I peek over the top of the bench and look that way, directly into the sun.

Betsy is on her bike, pedaling away down Fall Creek Parkway. There's a figure silhouetted at the top of the nearest apartment building, aiming a rifle toward me. I throw myself flat again. The top of the concrete bench explodes as a bullet whangs off it, showering me with dust and chips.

A raw fury swells in my gut. I feel coiled, tense and powerful, like I could pick up the bench I'm sheltering behind and throw it at the asshole on top of the apartment building, even though there must be at least two hundred yards between us. I am sick and tired of people trying to kill me and the people I love. I'm going to get some answers about why, even if I die trying.

The fishermen are running across the bridge. Another shot spalls off the concrete sheltering me. I lunge to my feet like a linebacker rushing the quarterback and charge toward a huge, old sycamore about twenty feet closer to the sniper. I'm running pell-mell toward the guy shooting at me. It's not smart, but rage has devoured all the higher functions of my brain.

I hear another shot just as I reach the tree. Police sirens warble in the distance; someone has called 911.

I squat so my head will be lower than the sniper expects and peer around the trunk. I'm just in time to see his silhouette turn and run toward the back of the roof.

I bolt from cover, sprinting up the hill and across the fortunately vacant street. I run between two of the apartment buildings and pull up, breathing hard, peering around the corner and trying to figure out where the sniper went. There's no sign of him at the roofline, but he had plenty of time to move while I covered the two-hundred-plus yards between us.

Movement in the parking lot draws my eye. There's a guy stowing a bag of golf clubs in the trunk of a white sedan, but there's only one club, topped with one of those fuzzy covers golfers use. As he lifts the bag into the trunk, I catch a glimpse of gunmetal gray between the lip of the bag and the club protector.

Now what? Who is this guy?

There's only one entrance to the complex—a two-lane road with a median planted in purple flowers. I run back the way I came and hide in a bush near the entrance.

Only a few seconds pass before the white sedan rolls by. I
have a clear view through the front windshield. The driver is
Detective Morris.

55

Jake

He's alone in the car, wearing civilian clothing. It's a Crown Victoria, I see as it passes, probably an old police cruiser. The license plate has an American flag on it and says "In God We Trust." I memorize the number as the car sweeps out of sight down Fall Creek Parkway.

Betsy is long gone. I notice that the car went in the same direction she had gone. What's the connection between Betsy and Morris? There must be one—Betsy brought me here so Morris could kill me. Why does he want me dead? Could he be connected with Tapper in some way? I'd begun to suspect something was weird with Beaner—he seemed obsessed with the 6/11 crash, but Morris? They can't all be dirty, can they?

I retrieve my bike and head for the closest library, the College Avenue Branch. At the library, I discover exactly how difficult it is to track down information about a police officer. Morris has a Facebook account, but every privacy setting is on high. I can't see who his friends are—even his profile picture is a cartoon rendering of a police officer, not his real face.

Google dredges up several articles about Morris, but they're all tiny listings in the *Indianapolis Star* about minor crimes—he was the arresting officer who caught a burglar in Broad Ripple two years ago. Another article mentions that he attended a "Thank the Police" picnic sponsored by The Old Northside Neighborhood Association last year.

I find him listed in several online directories, but none of them has an address. The White Pages lists a phone number, but when I call it, I get the recording, "You have reached IMPD North Division. If this is an emergency, please hang up and dial 911. If you know your party's extension, please dial it now. For—"

I hang up. I'm stuck. I can't figure out how to find Morris or Betsy. Almost worse, I'm not sure where I'm going to sleep tonight. I plod out of the library and pace back and forth along the sidewalk.

I need resources, someone with connections or money, someone who can help me find out what's going on and who I can report it to. Someone like Laurissa. But if I call her and her dad discovers the phone, we'll be cut off completely. I decide it's important enough to risk texting her. I send a short message, "Need to talk," even though a long one would be no less risky; a notification ding is the same no matter how long the text is.

Then I resume pacing, trying to think of what else I could do. I call Agent Soufan, intending to report Morris, but he doesn't pick up. I pace faster. I've got less than nineteen hours before Tapper starts shooting at my mother.

I pace for a few more minutes before my phone rings.

"I said I'd call you," Laurissa says before I can even say hello.

"It's Detective Morris. He just tried to shoot me at that little park by Fall Creek."

"What?! Wait, are you okay?"

"Yeah. Other than the fact that a police officer wants me dead, and I have no idea why."

"Wait, Morris?"

"Yeah."

"Hold on a sec."

I hear papers rustling in the background, and then Laurissa whispers to herself, "Morgath's balls."

"What?" I say.

"Brand finished the program to scrape Whitepages.com. I've got a printout listing every under-thirty Betsy in Central Indiana. I've been calling them whenever I can get enough privacy."

"You've been—"

"That's not the point. There's a Betsy Morris on the list. But her address and phone number are unlisted."

"Maybe she's his wife or daughter?"

"Maybe." There's a long silence, and then Laurissa asks, "Are you sure you're okay?"

"Yes. Not really. Mom's trying to get me committed to a mental ward, I got shot by a drone, I injured my hand. . ."

"Where are you?"

"At the library on College."

"I wish I could come and get you."

I stop pacing. "You can't?"

"No, I traded my car for this phone."

"You what? How?"

"Well, sort of. I convinced my friend Charlotte to wreck her car, and—"

"Really? How'd you manage that?"

"Dad didn't take my computer away. I IM'ed her and talked her into wrecking her car. She just ran it into a telephone pole. No big deal. It's not like her mother can't afford it; she probably makes more than that car cost every day. So anyway, she suggested to her parents that she could borrow my Prius, since I'm not allowed to use it anyway. And my dad let her come get it, despite the fact that I'm under house arrest, and that's how she smuggled me a phone."

"Whoa." I'm not sure what to say. Laurissa's amazing. I'm pretty sure she could have talked Sauron into destroying the One Ring himself, saving Frodo a ton of hassle and a finger. "You talked her into wrecking her driving record just to bring you a phone?"

"They won't report the accident or claim insurance. They can afford it, and it'll keep her driving record clean."

"That's crazy."

"So, I don't have a car. Not that Dad would let me out of the house, anyway."

"It doesn't matter," I say. "Can you get me anything on Morris? I've got less than nineteen hours left."

"Until what?"

"Until . . ." I see a white Crown Victoria turn the corner off College Avenue, heading toward the library. I squint, trying to see who's driving. Morris. Of course. How the hell does he know where I am? I mutter "sorry" into my phone and run.

56

Jake

I race around the corner of the library, my brain working almost as furiously as my legs. It's got to be my cell phone. Somehow, Morris is using it to track me.

I run through the small employee lot at the side of the library. I need to ditch my phone. Laurissa's voice is coming from it, tinny and unintelligible. I look at the screen, trying to memorize her new number. My foot catches on a curb, and I go flying to the asphalt. I scoop up the phone from where it fell, push to my feet, and keep running.

One of the parked cars has two windows cracked. I slide my cell phone through the window—it bounces on the seat, falling to the floorboards. Some poor librarian is going to get a very unpleasant visit from Detective Morris, but I don't have time to feel guilty. I glance backward—Morris is turning into the patron lot behind me. I dash across College Avenue pell-mell, running into an alley alongside the fire station. Half a block down the alley, I change direction, vaulting over a black chain-link fence, wincing as my weight hits my nail holes.

I zig and zag through the residential neighborhood, sticking to alleys and backyards until I'm sure Morris can't have followed me.

I feel a little naked without my phone, like a telephone pole without wires, disconnected from everything. Laurissa didn't say if she could get Morris's address for me, and now I don't have any way to contact her.

I plod north through residential neighborhoods and apartment complexes, bitterly regretting the fact that I had to abandon my Huffy at the library. Eventually, I reach the back of the Walmart on Keystone Avenue. I must look a mess—sweaty and disheveled, limping along with a dirty bandage on my hand and a lump in my jeans where my butt is bandaged.

I buy the cheapest cell phone they have and a thirty-day, two-hundred-minute prepaid card, which wipes out almost all of my cash. I was planning on buying more food with that money—my stomach has shrunk to a hard knot of nothing in my gut.

As I leave the Walmart, I text Laurissa to tell her I've got a new phone and number. Not thirty seconds later, my phone rings. "Where are you?" Laurissa says. "Are you okay? Why'd you hang up on me?"

"Did you get anything on Morris?" I ask.

"Not yet. I've been lying my head off. My dad's going to be furious when he finds out."

"Lying? About what?"

"I told LaMont Cooper that I was working on a 'Sunday's Supports Our Peace Officers' campaign, and that Detective Morris had won a community vote for Officer of the Year. We're supposedly going to surprise him at home with a new car, big red ribbon and all."

"That worked?"

"Not sure yet. Cooper's law firm has great connections. I guess he knows someone in the mayor's office. It might work. But when Dad finds out that I called his lawyer without his permission and lied to him, I'm going to be grounded until I'm thirty. And he will find out."

I'm not sure what to say. Would this mess wreck Laurissa's relationship with her father as thoroughly as it had wrecked my relationship with Mom? A mere "thank you" seems completely lame.

Abruptly, Laurissa whispers that she hears someone and hangs up. I hope her secret phone hasn't been discovered, but I've got to stay focused.

I head north from the Walmart. I wonder if Morris is connected to the plane crash. He must be—otherwise, why would he be trying to kill me?

I catch a whiff of rotten eggs from a nearby sewer grate. It reminds me of the smell on 6/11 right before I slammed into the truck. I need to figure out what it was, which means another trip to the library. The Wayne Branch is out; Lena Heck would have Child Protective Services there in minutes. Morris could still be at the College Avenue Branch, so that's out, too. I start toward the Nora Branch.

The walk takes nearly an hour. When I reach the library, they're already closed. I find a spot at the edge of the library's lot where I can curl up behind a tree, mostly hidden from the parking lot and road. For the second night in a row, I sleep at a library. As I drift off, I think about my mother—less than fifteen hours left.

57

Betsy

Father is in a rage when he gets home. The first thing he says to me isn't, "Glad you got home safely," or "Sorry I put you downrange of a target I was shooting at." It's, "You tipped him off." His blue-eyed glare should freeze me solid.

"What? Huh?"

"We've failed four times. The common thread is you."

"I swear. I've told Jake nothing."

"How did he know your name? How did he know to dodge behind that bench? Don't lie to me, Betsy." Father is steadily moving closer to me, getting in my face. I want to run, want to curl in a ball and hide. He looms above me like an implacable mountain, even though he's only two inches taller than I am.

"I don't know how he found out my name."

"You told him."

"I didn't!" Still, I suppose my extra email to him on my own account was a terrible idea. If Father finds it, he'll be even more furious. If that's possible, I don't want to be around to see it. My life would be worth less than a handful of spent brass.

"And today." Father's face looks like the bars on a jail cell. "You said something to him. Right before he jumped behind that bench."

"I didn't." Something flips inside me, like there's a point at which I'm so scared it automatically converts to anger. The anger feels righteous and correct, like I just stepped off a rickety porch onto solid ground. "And where do you get off accusing me? You should have had a spotter. I should have been on the roof with you. It was your stupid plan to be up there alone."

Father's right fist rears back and crashes into my jaw, rocking my head back.

I'm almost beyond caring, beyond feeling the pain. "And whose idea was it to use that dumbass laser sight? Maybe that tipped Jake off. You think of that?"

My father throws a left hook, and my head snaps sideways.

I make no effort to defend myself or fight back. "No real sniper would use a laser sight. Totally defeats the whole point."

Another right hook slams into my face.

"And why is it that I had to wear stupid Muslim clothes every single time I did an op, but you went up on that roof in civvies? Defeats the plan of blaming Muslims for everything we do, doesn't it?"

My head is rocked back to the left. I barely feel the blow. Either he's getting tired, or my face is getting numb.

I wipe a hand across my cheek. It comes back coated in blood and spit. I'm not crying. I won't cry. I'm beyond tears. "And whose idea was it to use the two dumbest brothers in the history of The Sons of Paine for that abortion of an assassination attempt. You plan to blame me for that, too?"

He punches me in the gut so violently that I fall backward, curled in on myself. He stands over me, panting, watching me, daring me to say anything else.

I do dare. When I catch my breath I add, "Is this how it happened with Mom? Did you tell her you'd never hit her again? Except that you did. And one day, you hit her a little too hard? Or she fell wrong and left you with a corpse instead of a wife?"

Morris—I can't think of him as my father—rears back and kicks me, like an NFL placekicker launching a ball seventy yards. I feel and hear my body breaking, ribs cracking. "Don't talk about your mother. You aren't fit to say her name. You're just some gaint little girl. Your mother was an angel. You're nothing. Worse than nothing. A failure."

His words reach my ears but don't penetrate. I don't care about him or his words anymore. I glare at his back as he walks away. I no longer want his approval. I want revenge.

58

Jake

I wake long before the library opens, so I'm first in line to get in and claim a computer. I google "sulfur smell and tanker truck," but that just brings up a whole bunch of posts about how to get the gas tanks on semi-tractors to quit smelling bad. "Sulfur smell and gas" brings up an enormous list of pages about farts. There's a CNN article titled "Why the Earth Is Farting," which is interesting—it's about methane releases in the Siberian tundra due to global climate change—but it doesn't seem relevant. I hunt for a while but find only one potentially useful fact: utility companies add a chemical, mercaptan, to natural gas to give it an odor like rotten eggs. Could it have been natural gas in those trucks? How would that have caused a plane crash, though? It seems about as likely as my cell phone causing a plane crash.

Maybe the trucks were there for some innocent purpose. I try googling "sixteen tanker trucks" and "why would you need sixteen tanker trucks on a wooded road," but that brings up news reports about accidents and, of all things, a page about Thomas the Tank Engine.

This doesn't seem to be the kind of question Google can answer. I need an expert. I google "Chemical Expert" and come up with The Wesson Group, which bills itself as a science and engineering consulting company. There's a toll-free number right in the banner at the top of the website, so I pull out my brand-new phone and dial it.

A cheerful sounding woman answers, "It's a great day at The Wesson Group, how may I direct your call?"

"I was hoping to talk to someone who knows something about, um, airplanes and chemistry?" I say.

"And you're calling for?"

"Um, information?"

"We consult for companies, government entities, and law firms. If you need information for a school paper, let me suggest the library."

I almost groan out loud, given that I'm sitting in a library. "Well, thanks anyway."

"Have a nice day," the operator says and hangs up.

Obviously I'm not going to get any help from chemical engineering consultants, at least not unless I can come up with a better cover story.

There's a librarian approaching fast from the direction of the reference desk. I get ready to run, afraid that somehow, against all odds, Lena Heck has tracked me down and has told the librarian here to do a Child Protective Services referral, but it turns out that all this librarian wants is to remind me archly about the rules on cell phone use at the computers.

I look up university chemical engineering departments. They're easy to find—most of them are advertising for students. I grab one of the stubby, eraserless pencils that exist only in libraries and putt-putt courses and jot down telephone numbers for six of them. Then I surrender my computer and go outside.

I sit on the library's lawn with my back against a scraggly-barked tree and start dialing. I get a secretary at Purdue University's Department of Chemical Engineering. When she asks why I want to speak with a professor, I just tell her I'm a senior in high school. Which is true enough—I will be a senior if I survive until the start of the school year.

I endure the university's faux-classical hold music for a few minutes before a man's voice comes on the line and says, "Dr. Nichols speaking." His voice is deep and rich—he ought to be a radio announcer instead of a chemical engineering prof.

"Yes, I was wondering if you could tell me what kind of chemical might be used to cause an airplane to crash—from the ground." I realize as I'm speaking that I should have thought this through better. There's a long silence.

"Who am I speaking with?" Nichols asks finally.

"Jake."

"Jake who?"

"Um, Jake Pinarello," I say.

"And where are you calling from, Mr. Pinarello?" he asks.

I hang up.

I stand up slowly, trying to think of a better reason for asking random professors about plane crashes. My phone rings, but I see that the area code is 765, same as Purdue, and I don't answer. Whoever was calling doesn't leave a message, although I'm not sure they can, since I haven't set up voicemail. Finally it hits me—the perfect excuse for asking about nearly anything. I sit back down and start dialing the other universities.

Nobody—not even a machine—answers at the next number on my list. The third number is answered by a very nice graduate student who tells me none of the professors are in. Finally, at the fourth university, I get another professor on the line.

"Dr. Matthews speaking."

"Hi, Dr. Matthews," I say. "My name is Jake Pinarello. I'm a research assistant for James Patterson—maybe you've heard of him?"

"Of course. He writes those books . . . *Alex Cross*, right?"

"Yes, that's right."

"How can I help?"

"Well, Jim is outlining a new thriller, and he seems to think he's heard of a possible technique for crashing an airplane from the ground, using a number of tanker trucks. But he can't recall where he read about it or what was involved. 'Figure it out, Jake,' he tells me, but I'll be darned if I've been able to track anything down." I wonder for a moment if I'm laying it on too thick, but Matthews answers almost immediately.

"I bet I know exactly what he read—it had to be one of those articles about the Bermuda Triangle."

"The . . . huh?"

"Sure, the Bermuda Triangle," Matthews says. "Let me explain. There really have been a statistically improbable number of disappearances of both ships and planes in the Bermuda Triangle."

"What does the Bermuda Triangle have to do with it?" I ask.

"Everything. People have offered all kinds of hypotheses to explain the Triangle—occult forces, aliens, pirates—you name it. But they never offered any evidence. We've known since the early seventies that there are huge deposits of methane in the sediment at the bottom of the ocean in the Bermuda Triangle and elsewhere. The methane is kept in solid form, a hydrate, by the cold temperature and tremendous pressure of thousands of feet of water. So what happens if something disturbs that methane, say an earthquake or a warming trend?"

After a moment, I realize that he's waiting for an answer, and I'm briefly seized by the same sort of panic I get when I'm called on in class for the answer to a question I haven't studied. "Um, it gets released?" I guess.

"Right! So a huge bubble of methane gas is released. It has just enough surface tension to stick together as it rises from the deep ocean. Any ship caught in the bubble loses all its buoyancy. It sinks almost instantly. There's probably not even time to make a distress call. Australian researchers built small-scale models in 2003 and proved that methane bubbles can cause ships to sink."

"And planes?"

"Same thing. They lose all lift in a bubble of methane. Suddenly, a machine designed to cruise comfortably at thirty thousand feet behaves exactly like a hunk of aluminum. It falls straight down."

"So that's something Patterson's fictional terrorists could do? Engineer a huge release of methane to cause a plane crash?"

"I don't know," Matthews says. "Perhaps not. I'd have to do some calculations. My offhand guess is that it would be nearly impossible to release enough methane fast enough to form the kind of bubble that would cause a plane at thirty thousand feet to lose lift. It'd probably take several cubic kilometers of gas."

"How much is that?"

"Thousands of tanker trucks worth. And there's the problem of how you'd release it all at once. To get it to release fast enough, you'd have to have some kind of nearly explosive mechanism. But it can't be explosive, or the methane would just burn up."

"And the burning methane wouldn't be enough to crash the plane?"

"No. Methane mostly forms carbon dioxide when it burns, which is present in large quantities in our atmosphere anyway and doesn't pose the same problem for aircraft as methane."

"What if you released the methane close to an airport, where the planes are only a few hundred or maybe a thousand feet up?" I ask.

"You'd need a lot less methane, but still a huge amount. Maybe a few dozen tanker trucks worth. I couldn't tell you for sure without spending some time modeling it on a computer."

Maybe just sixteen tanker trucks worth, I think. "Thanks Professor. You've been a huge help."

"No problem. You think Patterson will put me in his book? In the acknowledgements section or something?"

"I'll make sure of it," I say. A twinge of pain flashes through my hand like a physical manifestation of my guilty conscience. I've read a couple of Patterson's books, and I can't even remember if they had an acknowledgements section.

"Call anytime if you have more questions," Matthews says.

I thank him again and hang up. My phone is showing three missed calls—all from Laurissa.

"Good news?" I ask when she answers my return call.

"No. Cooper called my dad. Remember when I told you I'd be grounded until I was thirty if I were caught lying to our lawyer? I was wrong. I'm grounded for the rest of my life."

59

Jake

I'd been thrilled to learn about the connection between methane and plane crashes—it seemed like I was getting somewhere, finally decoding some of the insanity in my life. That sense of elation dissolves instantly as I talk to Laurissa, and I feel at least twice as tired as before. Morris is connected with this whole thing, but how will I prove it if I can't even find him? For that matter, how will I prove it if I *do* find him?

"Well, that's just superb," I say. "How the hell am I going to track down Morris, now?"

"The other problem is that I'm afraid Dad will figure out that I have a cell phone."

"How does he think you called Cooper?"

"I told him that I lifted Mom's phone from her purse. If he checks with Cooper, he'll find out that the call didn't come from Mom's number."

"But he bought it?"

"For now. But he's not happy that I borrowed my mother's phone. He was angrier than I've ever seen him. I thought he might stroke out."

"Are you okay?"

"Not really." Laurissa exhales a breath that's almost a sob.

"I'm sorry," I say, but it doesn't seem like enough. Doesn't even begin to make up for the mess I've created for her.

Laurissa breaks the long silence. "There is some good news. I got Morris's address."

"I thought Cooper called your dad?"

"He did. But I sort of . . . borrowed the notepad Dad keeps on his desk. He must have written down the address while he was talking to Cooper. He'd torn off the top page, but his pen left an impression on the page under it."

"And you lifted the address from that?"

"Yeah, a little shading from a pencil did the trick."

"You're a genius. What is it?"

"972 Maplebrook Court."

"Indianapolis?" I ask.

"Yeah. The zip is 46220."

"Thank you."

"Please be careful."

"I will. I love you."

"I love you, too." Laurissa hangs up.

There's no data connection on my new cell phone, so I go back into the library, wait for an available computer, pull up

Google Maps, and print an actual physical map. The library charges fifty cents for the privilege of using their printer. I have to tell them I don't have fifty cents, so the librarian puts it on my library card like an overdue fine and hands over the map.

Maplebrook Court isn't far—it's in an old neighborhood of small homes on the north side of Indianapolis. I've biked through the area a couple of times. It'll take an hour or so to reach on foot. But what will I do when I arrive? Knock on the door? There's a well-armed police officer living there who wants me dead. I've got to figure something out fast. Tapper is still waiting, and my mother has less than two hours left.

60

Betsy

The noise of the garage door wakes me. I'm curled up on the floor beside my bedroom door. I wrapped my comforter around my body and slept here with my back to the door so it couldn't be opened. I push myself upright and stumble to the window just in time to see Father's police cruiser pull out of the garage. He must be working a day shift, which means I'll have the house to myself for at least eight hours.

My face feels like it's been run over by sixteen tanker trucks. There's a bottle of Advil in the drawer of my desk, but I don't get it. I want to feel this pain. My Rolaids are in my purse beside the bed. I don't get those either. I don't need them.

I let the comforter fall to the floor and stumble across the hall to the bathroom. My face is a horror show. I've got small cuts along my cheekbones on both sides of my face. Blue and purple bruises bloom across my cheeks topped with streaks of dried blood, tears, and snot. My face is swollen unevenly, so I look like a lumpy-headed zombie.

I turn on the shower and set it on pure hot, strip off my clothes, and step in. The water is nearly scalding, but I welcome the heat.

It's not enough to distract me from my situation, though. What are you going to do, Betsy? If I call the police, it'll get back to my father in seconds. If he doesn't kill me, I'll spend the rest of my life in prison for my role in the plane crash. Maybe that would be fair, but it's not an appealing option.

Could I take the advice I gave Jake and just disappear? I'm not sure how. Pastor Hobbes said he'd help me, and I believe him. But I have no doubt my father will be able to find me. No shelter Hobbes could recommend will be able to protect me. I give in to hopelessness, the water pouring around me, hiding the tears leaking from my eyes.

By the time the hot water runs out, I'm done crying. I dry myself off and dress quickly. My father lied to me when he said he'd never strike me again. He lied when he said my mother left us. I've helped to kill people based on his lies. Hundreds of people on that airplane. I've tried to kill Jake Solley, just because he was in a bad place at a worse time.

I want to crumple into a ball and sob, but I know that won't help anyone. I promised myself I'd get revenge, and I'm going to keep that promise, even though my dad will probably kill me. Maybe I can do some good, too, and stop The Sons of Paine from killing anyone else. If I'm dead either way, well, I may as well die on my own terms.

What would hurt my father the worst? I can't fight him physically, and my attempts to assassinate Jake proved that I'm just not a killer. I need to use my strengths. What am I good at? Numbers. Accounting. Not much of a superpower, but it'll have to do.

I head straight for Father's computer. He normally doesn't come by the house while he's working, but he could. I turn his computer on and then off again. It has the type of off switch that you have to hold down for five seconds. If he comes home, by the time I turn off his computer, he'll be in the living room and in plain view of the hallway. If he sees me coming out of his bedroom, I'm dead. Probably literally.

I spend half an hour filling a backpack with the essentials: all the money I have, two changes of clothes, an overnight kit, and bottles of Rolaids and Advil. When I return to Father's bedroom, I wrench his window open as wide as it will go, relishing the hot, outside air. It smells like the pine tree in our backyard. Like freedom. If Father comes home, I'll grab my backpack, dive out the window, and run.

The password screen on the computer taunts me. I type Father's badge number, 8952, and hit enter. Nothing. I try our house number. Nothing. His birthday. Nothing. After six or seven attempts, the computer locks up and I have to power it down and restart. I try his social security number. Mine. His phone number. Mine. After every six tries, I have to restart his system. I spend about ten minutes pecking keys before I figure out that I'm repeating previous guesses. I go to my room, get a notebook and pen, and settle in for a more systematic effort.

I start combining numbers with names, numbers with addresses, changing a's to @'s and 1's to !'s. Hours go by. My notebook slowly fills with failed attempts.

I'm so startled when I suddenly get past the login screen that I nearly fall out of the chair. His password is H@ m89520melet. It seems like a good password to me. I'm probably the only person alive who knows what his favorite breakfast is. Anyone except me would have taken days, not hours, to figure it out.

I open his Internet browser. There's a bank's site in the bookmark bar. I get a login screen when I click on it. The browser has automatically filled in the login name: TheSonsOfPaine. I click on the password field and discover that his Internet browser has saved the password. Just that easily, I'm in.

The Sons of Paine have just over $121,000 in their checking account and $50 in savings. I start paging through the transaction history. Back in March, there's a huge series of deposits for $9,999, just under the $10,000 threshold at which the bank has to report the transactions to the IRS. I count the transactions—there are 270 of them. So, The Sons of Paine received just under $2.7 million, and they've been burning through the money ever since. I click on one of the deposits and pull up a record. Dead end. It was a wire transfer from a numbered account.

I have complete control over the account. I could take the $121,000 and transfer it into my own account. Or better yet, open a new account at a new bank. Maybe a numbered Swiss account, although I'm not sure how to do that. It's not something they've covered in my accounting classes at Ivy Tech. If I run, I'll need that money. It could keep me alive for a few years while I get back on my feet.

I can't do it, even though I know I should. If I have to run, I'm going to need that money. But it's dirty money—horrible things have been done with it. Maybe I should try to do some good with what's left. When I tried to kill Jake, I discovered that I'm just not an assassin. Now I'm discovering that I'm not a thief, either.

I can't take the money, but maybe The Sons of Paine could give it away? What donations would make Father the maddest? I start googling charities.

I transfer $10,000 to The Brady Campaign to Prevent Gun Violence. Then I send $50,000 to the Council on American-Islamic Relations. Father's always complaining about CAIR. That one will drive him mental. I make the donations in his name. When Swan and the other brothers find out that Father spent their money this way, he's going to have a tough time explaining himself.

I give another $50,000 to Islamic Relief USA and then $10,000 to the Violence Policy Center, which Father says is full of anti-gun lunatics. The last $1,000 goes to the Indianapolis Police Foundation. Maybe that will make it all look more legit. I doubt it.

By the time I finish, it's well past noon, and I'm famished. I shut down the computer and carefully arrange the mouse and keyboard the way they were before I came in here. Then I close his window and heft my backpack. How long will it take for Father to find out what I've done? Not long, I'm guessing, but there will be no way to tie it to me. It'll look like he logged in and did the transfers himself.

If he does find out, I need to be able to bug out, fast. I carry my backpack of supplies to the kitchen, keeping it close.

If I hear the garage door, I'll shoulder my backpack and run. Then I fix myself a huge meal. I haven't eaten anything for more than a day, but now, with a short-term plan in place and my revenge accomplished, I find I'm hungry again.

61
Jake

I walk past the house on Maplebrook once, scanning all the windows in the neighborhood, trying to see if anyone is watching the street. It's midmorning, and no one seems to be around. Morris lives in a brick, ranch-style house. There's a two-car, attached garage and a short, concrete driveway. All the windows are covered in tight-fitting blinds; I can't even tell if anyone is home.

I walk about a block farther, thinking about what to do. I'm not going to try peeking into his windows—I figure that'd be a great way to get shot. I need to observe the house without arousing the neighbors' suspicion. If I had a car, I could just park it a few houses down. As I return to Morris's house, I notice the perfect place to hide—there's a huge pine tree with low branches across the street and one door down. I glance around; everything is quiet, no one visible in any windows. I approach the tree casually, like I belong on some stranger's yard. When I reach the trunk, I look around again. Then I reach up and grab a branch, wincing as the bark presses against my bandaged hand. My stitches pull but I climb quickly, ignoring the pain, until I'm hidden more than twenty feet up in the tree's sheltering boughs.

It's a perfect stakeout; nobody ever looks up. I can watch half the neighborhood. Morris's next-door neighbor leaves in a blue Honda, returning a while later with a bag of groceries in each hand. Other neighbors come and go, but Morris's house remains quiet.

I realize it's almost noon—less than half an hour until the deadline Tapper gave me. I pull out my cell phone and dial information to get the number of the Indianapolis FBI office. Then I work my way through the voicemail system to Tapper's extension. He picks up almost immediately.

"It's Jake—"

"I'll call you back," Tapper says.

"It's a new number."

"I know, I've got it." Tapper hangs up.

My phone vibrates about two minutes later. I recognize Tapper's Tom Cruise number and save it in my new phone. "I've got something for you," I whisper. "It's Morris."

"Who's Morris?"

"The other cop who interviewed me after I left the hospital. Along with Beaner."

"You told me Beaner had access to your phone, not Morris."

"Yeah, I don't know how Morris got access to my phone. Maybe Beaner's working with him."

"Beaner was clean. You're just trying to send me on another wild goose chase."

"Morris shot at me yesterday," I whisper urgently. "Why would he be trying to kill me if he's not involved?"

"I want the contact, the person you met with outside your school."

I rack my brains—I need a lie that's just truthful enough to put Tapper on Morris's trail. "I told you, I don't know the contact's name. He's probably someone Morris hired to keep his hands clean—so I couldn't identify him later."

"Hmm." Tapper is silent for a moment. "Could be. I'll check him out. But if you're—"

"I know, I know," I say—and I do. I know exactly what Tapper is about to say, and it's enough to make my hand clench on the cell phone and my whole body red hot with rage. "Anything happens to my mother, I'll never speak to you again, Tapper. You'll never get what you want from me."

"Kid, I care less about your mother than I care about the grease stain my lunch left on my tie. Get me your contact. Tonight. I'm tired of waiting."

What does tonight mean? Midnight? Nine p.m.? I start to ask, but the connection is already dead.

62
Jake

I clutch the tree branch and try to calm down. My breathing is so loud that I'm sure that the people in the nearest house can hear me. Luckily no one is walking around. The rough pine bark digs into the fingers of my left hand. I squeeze harder; the pressure makes the wounds in my hand hurt, but I welcome the pain. I breathe deeply, inhaling the sharp smell of pine sap, calming myself enough to put my cell phone away and resume my stakeout of Morris's house.

By three in the afternoon, I'm both desperate to pee and dying of thirst. If school were in session, there'd probably be busses everywhere about now, but other than a rare jogger or dog walker, the street is deserted. I lower myself out of the tree and hike toward a gas station on the main road.

The station's restroom is filthy—some kind of gray sludge clings to the porcelain sink. I try to wash my hands, but the soap dispenser is out, and the pine resin coating my hands won't scrub off with water alone. The bandage on my left hand gets wet, which only makes the whole process even more disgusting. I give up washing, cup my right hand, and drink. The water tastes vaguely of pine sap.

When I get back to Morris's street, I have to wait at the corner about ten minutes for a young woman pushing a stroller to reach the far end of the street. Then I walk to my tree and scamper back up to my hiding place.

Shortly after four, a gray police cruiser pulls into the driveway. The garage door grinds slowly open. The cruiser pulls into the empty spot next to Morris's battered old white car, and the garage door starts to close. I catch a flash of a blue police uniform before my view is cut off.

Less than ten minutes later, the garage door opens again. There's a flash of movement at one of the windows, but it's obscured by a bush. I can't see inside the garage either; the angle is bad. I quickly drop down a couple levels in the tree. By the time I've repositioned myself, the Crown Vic is already pulling out of the garage. It backs all the way down the driveway into the street and then stops, like the driver has forgotten something. I'm finally in a position to see inside—Morris is driving. He's alone, wearing street clothes—a T-shirt and beige jacket. He fumbles around with the overhead visor, pulls a garage door opener off it, and holds it toward the garage. The door slowly rumbles closed. The Crown Vic pulls away. I glance at the garage and notice one more thing before the door closes completely: a bike visible at the back of the space the

Crown Vic just vacated. I'd recognize that bike anywhere—
Betsy's red Schwinn.

63

Betsy

After my huge meal, I return to my room, lugging my backpack. The meal sits in my stomach like a lead weight. Getting some revenge on Father was delicious, but I know it was incredibly dangerous. I need a better escape plan. Something longer-term than just grabbing my backpack and running. I look up the number for Two Swords Baptist on my phone.

A receptionist answers, and I ask for Pastor Hobbes, telling her Betsy Morris is calling. He answers almost immediately.

"Betsy," he says. "I'm so glad to hear from you. I've been thinking of calling."

I hadn't really planned what to say. I blurt out, "He beat the crap out of me yesterday."

"I'm so sorry," he says gently.

"I need to get out of here. Get someplace safe."

"Yes," Pastor Hobbes says. "I have to report this to Child Protective—"

"No! What do you think is going to happen if Father finds out that CPS is on him? He will find out—fast."

"It's a state law, Betsy. I should have reported your dad after our last meeting."

"Did you?"

"No. I got the sense you weren't ready to deal with it. Let's get you someplace safe, and then I'll report it."

"Like where?"

"There's the Julian Center, the Ruth Lilly home, Queen of Peace—"

"You know Father can find me at any of those places. They're not going to be able to stop a cop from getting in."

"Maybe not. But we have to get you out of there."

"What about an out-of-town shelter? Maybe one in Lafayette or Bloomington? Or better yet, out of state?"

"It might be possible to arrange that," Hobbes says. "Are you safe now, Betsy?"

"Father's gone. I don't think he'll be back for a while. Yes, I think so."

"Let me call around and try to arrange something." Pastor Hobbes gives me his cell phone number, and I write it on my hand. "Call me anytime, day or night." I thank him and hang up.

I trust Pastor Hobbes and believe he'll come through, but I should prepare myself in case he doesn't. I start researching shelters online. Then I wonder if I could get a new identity somehow? I spend hours on the web reading everything I can find on the subject.

I notice the Stormbreak icon in the bookmarks at the top of my web browser. I wonder how Kekkek is doing, but I'm not tempted to log on and check. I haven't been on Stormbreak in a couple of days, now. Will I lose my role as moderator? Probably, but I'm guessing they'll wait a couple of weeks to promote a replacement. I think about that briefly and decide that I don't care.

My ruminations are interrupted when I hear the garage door opening. Father is home. My bedroom door is closed and locked. I throw my shades and window wide open. I slip my backpack on, moving slowly and as silently as I can.

I listen carefully, dreading the moment when I will hear his footsteps in the hallway. I watch the doorknob to my room like a mouse staring at a cat's teeth. If it turns, I need to run instantly. Out the window and down the street. It will only take my father a few seconds to break down the door.

But after just ten or fifteen minutes, I hear the overhead door in the garage grind open again. I glance out my window in time to see Father backing out of the garage in his personal vehicle. I let out a huge sigh, sagging in relief. But then I wonder: Where's he going at four o'clock in the afternoon?

Wherever he's going, I'm safe for now. Now I have a plan, a potential escape route. Grab my backpack, dive out my window, and run. Call Pastor Hobbes. Maybe he'll find a place for me to escape to. But if he doesn't, I need to be ready. I return to my computer and resume my own search for shelters outside Indianapolis. I'm going to survive this mess, whatever it takes.

64

Jake

I stare as the garage door kisses the pavement. Morris and Betsy/Fake Laurissa. What's their relationship? I can't follow Morris's car. But since Betsy's bike is in the house, maybe she is, too? I decide to keep watching the house.

The neighborhood is positively hopping for the next couple of hours, with people returning to their homes, out walking their dogs, or playing with their kids. But Morris's house is dark and silent. Is Betsy even in there? Maybe after failing to kill me, Morris is on the run. He could be on the way to Florida or Mexico for all I know. If he is, I'll never find him. Betsy is my only lead. I keep waiting.

A few minutes before six, there's finally movement at Morris's house. The garage door slowly motors open, and

Betsy emerges on her Schwinn. Her face is battered, big purple bruises covering her cheeks and jawline. I wonder what happened to her. She's wearing jean shorts and a yellow blouse. I've never seen her wear so little—every time we've met, she's been in long, flowing robes that completely cover her arms and legs and scarves that hide her hair. Her legs are spectacular—powerfully muscled, long, and tanned to a deep bronze. I remember them clamped around me on the hospital bed, my panic, and the short, desperate struggle to win one more lungful of air.

A flash of anger propels me down the tree, dropping from branch to branch in a rush. Betsy is turned away from me, pointing a garage door opener toward the house, and the garage rumbles closed. She tucks the remote into a backpack that's imprinted with the American flag, shoulders it, and pedals down the street.

I burst from under the tree, following her at a flat-out sprint.

She turns onto Sixty-Fifth Street, still oblivious to my presence behind her. I'm falling farther and farther back. I'm never going to be able to keep up with her on foot.

I glance around frantically at the houses I'm running past. I see what I'm looking for about five houses up—a bicycle abandoned in a side yard. It's a child's bike with training wheels, bright purple with glittery streamers attached to the handlebar grips. They say beggars can't be choosers, but I'm not even a beggar—I'm a thief, from a kid, at that. But I don't have time to feel bad about the new low my life has hit.

There's a chain-link fence around the yard, but it's short, four feet or so. I vault it, wincing at the lance of pain through my butt and leg, throw the bike over the fence, and leap back to the other side. By the time I've mounted the bike, Betsy is almost out of sight.

I stand on the bike, pedaling for all I'm worth. I probably couldn't sit down even if I wanted to; the bike is smaller than my old Huffy. My knees would hit the handlebars, and I'm afraid I might pull my stitches. The streamers on the hand grips whip and snap in the breeze as I get the bike up to its top speed. The training wheels actually make it harder to ride, since I can't lean into my turns properly. I seem to be earning the name Training Wheels Solley yet again.

Still, I gain steadily on Betsy and have to slow my frenetic pace slightly. I need to keep a few blocks between us because a teenage boy riding a purple-glitter bike kind of stands out.

We ride through neighborhood streets for about twenty minutes. I hang back on the straight parts of her route, letting her get three or four blocks ahead. Then, whenever she turns, I race ahead, trying to get close enough to see her before she takes another turn and loses me completely. She's riding purposefully, focused on the road, not looking around.

Her ride ends at a low, modern office building with a large green and white sign—Ivy Tech, a community college. I pull off the road and stop behind a bush on the other side of the street. She locks her bike to a rack. When she turns to enter the building, I race to follow, leaving my stolen bike lying behind the bush.

As I enter the building, Betsy is turning into a classroom at the end of the hall. I jog down the hall and peer through the window into the room. There are something like forty students inside and a guy lecturing up front. Evidently Betsy was late; all the students have oversized textbooks open on their desks and are taking notes—on laptops, tablets, or old-fashioned spiral notebooks.

I open the door and slip quietly inside. Betsy sees me immediately—her eyes flare in surprise. As I walk toward her, she clenches her fist, and the surprised expression on her face transforms into an angry glare.

I take a seat beside Betsy. The professor interrupts his lecture—something to do with alternate methods of accounting for inventory—and stares at me, saying, "I don't believe you're on my class roster, Mister . . . ?"

I blurt out the first thing that comes to mind. "Pinarello. Jake Pinarello. I'm a transfer student."

The prof eyes me skeptically. "See me after class with your paperwork. Now, as I was saying, the FIFO accounting . . ."

I lean toward Betsy and whisper, "So you're what, Morris's wife?"

"Ew, no," she whispers back.

"What, then?"

"You got a death wish?"

"You didn't answer my question." Someone kicks the leg of my chair. I ignore him. I've got more important things to worry about than whether the guy behind me passes his accounting class.

"I told you to disappear."

"You still didn't answer my question."

"He's my father." Her whole face is tense, like she's screwing it up to spit the words at me.

"Oh." I lean back in my chair, thinking. That puts all her actions in a different light. I thought perhaps she didn't want to kill me or maybe just couldn't. Now I understand why she didn't go to the police, come clean. First, her father is a policeman. Second, could I turn my own mother in? No matter what she did? I don't think so.

I lower my voice still further. "The FBI thinks I was involved in the plane crash. They're threatening my mother."

"Not my problem," she says, much too loudly. "If you'd just done what I told you, everything would have worked out fine!" The student to her right gets up and moves to the front of the room.

"Even if I had disappeared, I would still be wanted, my mother would have lost a son, and those people on Delta 117 would still be dead," I say quietly.

The professor has interrupted his lecture again, and the whole room is silent for a moment. Betsy looks like she might throw up.

"Is this young man causing you a problem, Miss Morris?" the prof asks.

Betsy is trembling now. She keeps her lips tightly sealed, shaking her head no.

"Is he the reason your face is bruised?"

She shakes her head again. Then she jams her textbook and notepad into her overstuffed backpack, stands up shakily, and flees the room. As she passes the prof, she mutters, "Sorry." I get up and follow her.

The prof catches my arm as I reach the door. "What's going on? Do I need to call security?"

"No," I say. "Everything is fine." I twist my arm free and follow Betsy.

She runs down the hall, and I try to catch up. Just as I'm

about even with her, she ducks into the women's restroom. I
hesitate a moment, then push the door open and follow her.

She's standing at the sink with the water running, her
dripping-wet hands pressed to her face.

"This has to end," I say.

She pulls her hands from her face and spins toward me so
fast that I get sprayed with water droplets. "You have no idea
what you're blabbing about," she says.

"I know that Morris—your dad—was somehow involved
in crashing Flight 117," I say. "I know how it was done, too,
with a massive release of methane. The airplane lost lift and
went down instantly. Methane is a common gas, part of the
atmosphere, so by the time emergency crews got to the plane,
all evidence of what had happened was gone."

Betsy dries her face with a paper towel, still staring at me.

"He asked you to kill me because I'd seen it. I had the
dumb bad luck to be riding along the backwoods road where
the trucks were staged. I saw how it was done."

"But you wouldn't die."

"I'm not a big fan of being dead."

"You know, if I killed you now, I'd be a hero to my father
and to his buddies, despite everything I've done. Instead, I
have this." She waves her hand at her battered face.

I'm wobbly with exhaustion and hunger. She probably
could kill me easily. "But you won't. You'd have done it already
if you could."

Her hands and face both clench—red with rage, or maybe
embarrassment. She trembles slightly, staring at me. Then
suddenly she collapses, turning back to the sink, falling over it
so her head nearly hits the spigot, sobbing.

The door opens behind me, and I glance over my shoulder. A young woman takes a step inside and then halts in shock.

"This restroom is busy," I bark. "Use the men's."

She backs slowly out, and the door bangs shut behind her. I wait a moment, until Betsy's sobbing has slowed a little. "There's an FBI agent, Tapper. Is he working with your father?"

"What do you care?" she gasps between sobs.

"He's threatening my mother. Says he'll kill her, just a few hours from now. If I don't get him information on the plane crash."

"That's got nothing to do with me." Betsy has stopped crying. She takes a paper towel from the dispenser and rubs it over her face.

"Your dad planted the program SIMON on my phone, didn't he? Made me a target of the FBI investigation."

"I don't know anything about that part of it. I'm sorry I tried to kill you, but I can't help you." She tries to step around me, but I grab her arm.

"One hundred and fifty-seven people died on that plane, Betsy."

"I can't help them, either."

She wrenches her arm free and steps toward the door.

"Why, Betsy? Why's your father doing this?"

"Look up The Sons of Paine. As in Thomas Paine. They're on the web."

"Will you at least think about helping me? Take my phone number in case you change your mind?"

"You can't go against him. I can't go up against him. We'll wind up as dead as those people on the plane."

"He's already tried to kill me. Four times. I'm not dead."

"You should run. That's what I'm going to do."

Panic seizes me, and I'm silent for a moment. If Betsy runs, where does that leave me? But why would she help me? What can I offer her? "I bet the FBI would protect you. They've got programs for witnesses, right? They can keep a secret even from the police. Who else can do that?"

Betsy stares at me. "Maybe. I'll think about it. Write your number here." She hands me her notebook and a pen, and I scrawl my new cell number on the cover. I don't hand it back to her right away though.

"The people who died on that plane were real people, Betsy. With families they loved, who loved them. My mother is a real person. Maybe you couldn't do anything to stop the deaths of all those people on Flight 117, but you can save my mother. Tell the FBI everything you know."

Betsy rips the notebook out of my hands, whirls, and leaves the bathroom without another word.

65
Jake

As I leave the campus, I pass two security guards headed in the direction of Betsy's accounting class. They don't pay any attention to me, though. I retrieve my stolen bike and return to the Nora Branch Library. I google The Sons of Paine, finding their site in seconds.

The elderly woman at the computer next to me gets up and moves to another open computer a few rows down. I catch a whiff of myself and figure out why. I've only been on the street two nights and most of three days. How do homeless people manage? Do they wash in the White River? Or maybe at the YMCA?

I return to my reading. The Sons of Paine seems pretty innocuous. They've got an "About Us" page that advocates a "return to the values of our founding fathers," whatever that means. They want to close the borders and quit accepting refugees from the Middle East. They want to make America "pure" again, but they never explain exactly what they mean by "pure" or how they plan to accomplish whatever it is they're proposing.

There's a calendar of events, but it hasn't been updated in two years. It lists a Fourth of July ice cream social, a group camping trip in August, and a weekend in the woods on the first day of hunting season in November.

The forums are another matter. They have thousands of posts, some of them made only a few minutes ago. The most common topic is the idea that the U.S. is being undermined by Muslims. They're moving here and outbreeding us. They're imposing Sharia law in the U.S. They've taken control of the Democratic Party and parts of the Republican Party. They're a "stain" on the "purity" of the United States. The Sons of Paine don't just hate Muslims, either. Some of them hate Jews, black people, and Mexicans. But the one thing they all agree on is Muslims.

After a few minutes of reading, I have to look away from the screen for a minute. The level of hatred I'm reading literally makes my stomach turn. It doesn't make any sense—I doubt if any of them have ever even met a Muslim person. They're not exactly common in Indianapolis, although there are a few that go to my high school. And every time I read something hateful about black people, I think of Laurissa, and it's all I can do not to smash the library's computer.

All the posts are under obvious pseudonyms: ThePatriot47, AllAmerican1, 4EverFree, and the like. At least half the forums are blocked—I can't access them. I create an account and password, giving myself the name "LiveFree76." I still can't get into any of the private forums, so I send an access request to the board administrator.

This still doesn't make sense. The guys in the tanker trucks were dressed in Muslim-looking headdresses. The first couple of times I saw her, Betsy wore clothing that would have worked as well in Saudi Arabia as in the United States. I don't see how any of that could be related to this group, which obviously has a huge stick up its butt about Muslims. I wish I'd asked Betsy about it, although it's not like she would have answered my questions.

I keep reading the forums. A lot of posts are mundane. Some guy has a log splitter he wants to sell. There's a huge discussion about what kind of recycled bottles are best for storing drinking water to use in an emergency. Milk jugs start leaking after about six months, but plastic two-liter soda bottles last forever, according to the posts.

My head sags toward the keyboard. I repeatedly face-type strings of nonsense. I give up on reading inane posts and scoot the mouse pad aside. I lay my head beside the keyboard, thinking I'll just nap for a moment.

I wake to a librarian shaking my shoulder.

"Sir? Sir?" she says. "The library is closing in a few minutes."

I lift my head and try to rub the bleariness from my eyes.

"I ignored your sleeping as long as I could," the librarian says. "You looked like you needed it. But you need to head home now."

Home? I wish I could. How long have I been asleep? I drag my thumb across my phone to wake it. The time displays in huge, accusatory numbers across the lock screen: 8:55 pm. What did Tapper mean by "tonight?" I spring out of my seat, running for the door and clutching my phone. Have I missed Tapper's arbitrary deadline? Has he already shot my mother?

66
Jake

I call "Tom Cruise's" number and hold the phone to my ear while I straight-arm my way out of the Nora Branch's front doors.

"You're late," Tapper says. "I should push the button, teach you a little respect."

A burst of sudden fury blooms coldly through me. My mind is as clear as pure ice. "Bullshit," I say. "You were never going to push that button. You can't push that button, not unless you're willing to flush your career and freedom along with my mother's life."

"I don't bluff. I did push the button. Every time you sit down, you know I will push that button."

"Yeah, and that's why you can't do it again. Sure, you can convince some pet judge that the first shot came from a dumbass on Rockville Road celebrating with his new rifle. How likely is that to happen twice? To the same family? The dumbest prosecutor in America is going to investigate that shit. The dumbest judge in America is going to let that go to trial. Even if you get off, will your career survive? I don't think so. So screw you, and screw your threats, and screw your phony-ass patriotism, Tapper."

"You're not going to give up your contact, are you?"

"That was all bullshit I made up because it was what you wanted to hear. You put enough pressure on anyone, and they'll tell you everything you want to hear. I'm no different. That program was planted on my phone by Detective Morris or maybe Captain Beaner. It's a total red herring. Flight 117 was brought down by a massive methane release engineered by Morris or someone connected with him. The same way planes crash in the Bermuda Triangle. There's a Wikipedia article on it that's simple enough that even a Cro-Magnon FBI agent should be able to understand it."

"You don't understand—"

"*You* don't understand. It's time for you to do your job, to investigate Morris, his daughter, and The Sons of Paine. They've tried to kill me at least four times. Start there."

"That's a job for internal affairs or the state police, not the FBI."

"It's your job, and if you don't do it, I'm going to tattoo your name alongside the bullet wound on my ass and moon every television network in America." I hang up the phone.

I'm breathing hard and shaking a little. I sit on a bench outside the library, breathing deeply, trying to calm down. Within a few minutes, the anger ebbs, and I feel hollowed out, like my rage was something that lived inside me and has crawled out, leaving a shell clinging to this bench like the husk of a cicada.

What now? I'm not sure what to do with myself. I'm exhausted, hungry, dirty, and sore. I want to go home. I call Mom.

She doesn't answer. For a moment, I'm so crushed that I nearly burst into tears. Then I'm scared—did Tapper shoot her after all? Maybe she's not answering because I have a new phone, a new number. She's probably waiting for me to call, not answering any other numbers. I call back and leave a message with my new number.

At the bike rack I get another surprise. My stolen bike has been stolen again. I hope its original owners found it.

I drag my legs down to the YMCA on Westfield Boulevard. I've never been inside, but I've biked past it a few times. I tell the lady at the front desk that my name is Jake Pinarello from Portland, Oregon. She asks for ID, and I tell her that it was stolen along with all my money. Is there any chance of getting a shower?

I must look truly pitiful, because she takes me under her wing. She gives me a key to the showers, a clean shirt and sweatpants from the lost and found, and a bag of snacks—a hard granola bar, fruit rollup, and a bag of Cheetos.

A half hour later, I'm clean and a little less hungry, but the Y is closing. What do I do now? Maybe Tapper will actually investigate and arrest Morris. Maybe I'll step in manure dropped by a flock of winged pigs. More than anything else, I'm tired. Tired of being on my own, tired of not knowing what to do, tired of having no one I can trust. I think about Laurissa—where is she and what is she doing?

There's a message on my phone; someone must have called while I was in the shower. I pick it up and nearly collapse in relief when I hear Mom's voice. She wants to come get me. She says she won't take me to the psych ward, but I'm not sure I believe her. At least now I know she's okay.

I wander outside and find a spot at the back of the YMCA where it faces the Monon Trail. The building's brick wall presses uncomfortably against my back. But I fall asleep almost instantly.

67

Betsy

When I return to my accounting class, there are two security guards waiting. The professor has called them to help me, as if they could. I tell them that my bruises are from falling, which they clearly don't believe. Eventually, they give up.

I zombie through the rest of class, barely hearing a word of the lecture. I know I should just leave, but I feel safer here, surrounded by people. Jake is nowhere in sight when my class ends. Nor do I see him on the ride home. I'm not scared of him, but I don't care to talk anymore.

Jake was right about my father, about me. We killed 157 people to get at one congressman. My father lied when he said he wouldn't hit me and lied when he said he didn't know where my mother went. He's been lying to me all my life. I

357

can't bring any of the people on that flight back, but if I can survive long enough to tell the truth about why the plane crashed, I'm going to do it. Even if it means I'll spend the rest of my life in prison.

Father hasn't come home, which is a relief. I have no idea where he went. Is there anything else I can do to get ready? I'm going to have to escape soon, maybe tonight. Jake apparently knows almost everything, and since he knows, sooner or later everyone will. Or maybe Father will get to him first.

I think about what Jake told me about the FBI. He's right—they could protect me, if they wanted to. And maybe they'd investigate my story. It'd be better if I brought them something—solid evidence that would put my father in prison forever. I return to his room, open the window, and set my backpack beside it. Then I boot up his computer.

The last time I snooped around, I only looked at The Sons of Paine bank account. This time I go through his computer files. They're a jackpot: detailed plans for crashing Flight 117; schematics for the custom tanker trucks; lists of sources for bulk methane. I take a jump drive out of my backpack and start downloading everything. There's enough info here to put my father in prison forever. Maybe enough to keep me safe from him.

Then I happen on something even worse, something that makes my whole body feel cold despite the warm night air flowing through the window. I check his search history, confirming what I learned from his files. Now I know why Father left. I know exactly where he's going. I need to tell someone, report it. I need to make sure that he's caught, that he'll never beat me again. The Indianapolis police are out—he'd hear about it almost instantly. I need to call someone in the FBI or FAA, someone who will take me seriously. I don't have any contacts in the FBI, but Jake said he did.

I call Jake.

68

Jake

My ringing phone wakes me. I fumble blearily for it and glance at the time as I answer—it's almost midnight.

Betsy's voice comes on the line. "You've got to help me, Jake."

"Huh?"

"I've got to take my own advice, disappear."

"Disappear? Why?"

"It's the only chance I have to get out of this. Maybe to survive."

"Wait, your dad's after you now?" I stand up and start pacing alongside the brick wall of the YMCA.

"Maybe. Probably."

"Where is he now?"

"He left earlier today."

I remember the white Crown Vic pulling out of their garage. "You don't know where he is?"

She answers slowly, as if she's not completely certain what she wants to say. "Yes. . . Sort of."

"I don't understand."

"He didn't tell me where he was going. But he didn't clear the search history on his computer. . . ."

"What was in his search history?"

"Hundreds of searches on mapping sites and satellite image sites. Google Maps, Google Earth, and some others."

"And this has you freaked out because?" I ask, but I think I already know the answer.

"He was searching for wooded roads outside Raleigh-Durham International Airport in North Carolina. They're going to do it again. They're going to crash another plane."

69

Jake

"Who's they? Your dad and a bunch of the people from The Sons of Paine? Why do they all wear Muslim clothes? Why did you? When is he going to do it? Who else did you tell?"

"I need your contact at the FBI," Betsy says.

"Tapper? You don't want to get involved with him. Dude's not just nuts, he's walnuts." But then it occurs to me that *I* want Betsy to talk to him. She's one of the few people who can tell him the whole story, get him to leave me alone. Leave my family alone. I give her the "Tom Cruise" number.

Betsy hangs up, and I keep pacing back and forth behind the Y. What should I do? My brain still feels foggy from sleep. I've barely gone twenty feet when Betsy calls me back. "The number's no good," she says.

I give it to her again, hang up, and try it myself. An electronic voice answers, "The number you have called is no longer in service. Eighty-seven four-B." Tapper is covering his tracks.

Betsy calls again. "I need a good number for your contact. Now, tonight. If I can stop this thing, I'll be a hero. There's no way they'll prosecute me."

And your dad will be flattened by the wheels of the bus you threw him under, I think. What changed—why has Betsy gone from mostly-willing assassin to wannabe hero? "How much time do we have?" I ask.

"I don't know. There won't be many flights overnight. I figure they'll get set up at night and hit one of the morning flights."

I tell Betsy I'll try to get in contact with Tapper and hang up. I try the FBI office in Indianapolis. A machine answers, giving their office hours and telling me, "If this is an emergency, please hang up and dial 911." So I do that. I'm less than thirty seconds into my story about plane crashes, methane releases, and the Bermuda Triangle when the 911 operator interrupts me. She wants to know exactly where I am. She says she's going to send help in the same tone of voice you use with a toddler in the throes of a temper tantrum. Or a lunatic. I know exactly what kind of "help" she's going to send. I hang up.

I clench the phone in my fist. I want to stomp on it a few times, but that won't help, so I have to settle for trying to squeeze it to death. I'm wandering south, and I've veered onto the Monon Trail. I bike along this trail occasionally, so I'm familiar with it. I've never been on the trail at night, though, and I've never seen it this deserted. During the day, this section is usually thronged with joggers, skaters, and bikers.

I need to get to North Carolina. Maybe I can warn the

police there. Although now that I think about it, why choose Indianapolis and Raleigh-Durham for crashes? Because The Sons of Paine have connections on the police forces there?

I text Laurissa.

My phone rings, but it's my mother. Now that I know she's safe, I don't really want to talk to her. I'm still afraid she'll try to drag me to the psych ward.

A minute or two later, Laurissa calls.

"I need help," I say.

"What's going on? Where are you?" Laurissa asks.

"On the Monon Trail. Heading south. Almost to Broad Ripple."

"It's late! That's not safe."

"No place is safe right now." My phone vibrates, and I take it away from my ear long enough to glance at the screen: Betsy's trying to call me.

"There was a rape on that part of the trail a few years ago."

I'm on the footbridge over the White River now. The trail is dark and silent, although I can faintly hear the low bass thumping from one of Broad Ripple's nightclubs to the south. "Nobody's around," I say.

"What's going on?" she asks again.

"I need to get to Raleigh-Durham, North Carolina. Fast," I say.

"Okaaay. That's not what I expected you to say. Why?"

I give her an incredibly abbreviated version of the plane crash story and what I learned about The Sons of Paine. While I'm talking, Betsy tries to call again. And my mother leaves another message. When I finish, Laurissa says, "I'll take you. We can try to get help on the way."

"How? You don't have a car."

"I'll get Charlotte to pick me up. I can climb over the back wall and meet her on the road behind our house."

"You can do that?"

"You're talking to the girl who rappelled out of a hospital window carrying your sorry ass. Hell yes, I can do it. The motion sensors will go off, but I'll be gone before anyone can catch me."

"Okay. I'll be at the Broad Ripple McDonald's."

Betsy calls seconds after I hang up. "Did you get the number?" she asks.

"No. Tapper is covering his tracks," I say.

"I tried the FAA and the local FBI office. Nobody staffs the phones at night. I'm going to try the national hotline next."

"Okay. We're going to Raleigh. We'll try to get help on the way."

"Who's we?" Betsy asks.

"Me and the real Laurissa."

"You've got to take me," Betsy says.

"What? Why would I want you—someone who's tried to kill me repeatedly—in the same car with me? And more to the point, what makes you think Laurissa will let you into *her* car?"

"I don't have anything against Laurissa."

I hold the phone away from my face and just stare at it for a moment. The disconnect is mind boggling.

I hear Betsy's voice faintly, "You there?"

"Are you kidding me? You impersonated my girlfriend to kill me! And your group is so racist they want a holy war to wipe out all Muslims and black people."

"They're not my group. Not anymore."

"Just like that?"

"Do you want to stop The Sons of Paine or argue about them? I know where they'll park the tanker trucks. Well, not exactly, but I know all the locations Father was searching."

"So tell us over the phone."

"No. I need to be there. Need to be part of it. That way, maybe I can cut a deal, get placed in the witness protection program or something."

I hate the idea of bringing her with us. But she could corroborate my story, maybe convince someone that the threat is real. I stride four or five steps down the trail before I answer. "Get to the McDonald's in Broad Ripple as fast as you can."

I reach it in less than five minutes. It's a twenty-four-hour location—lots of drunk partiers from the nearby bars come and go. The smell of grease is nearly intoxicating—the snacks I got at the Y were a godsend, but not much of a dinner. If I had any money, I'd buy one of everything on the menu and wolf it all down. I sit on the curb and wait.

Laurissa beats Betsy to the McDonald's. She's driving her blue Prius. I rush to the passenger side and slide in.

"You look terrible," Laurissa says. "Like you've been starving yourself."

"You look great," I say, and she does. There's a flat spot in her hair from the pillow, she's not wearing any makeup, and it looks like she threw on an old T-shirt and jeans, but she's the best thing I've laid eyes on in days. I reach across the console and give her a hug. "Where's Charlotte?"

"I dropped her off at her house. It's only two blocks from mine. Do we have time to get you some food?" she asks.

"Yeah," I say, "we're waiting for Betsy anyway."

"What? Why?"

"I'm not sure it's a good idea either. But she knows where they'll set up the tanker trucks. Or at least a few places where they might."

"Can we trust her?"

"I don't know. Probably not. But we need her to stop her father."

"It doesn't feel right."

"I know, but—"

"But I trust you." Laurissa reaches across the console and squeezes my hand. I grip hers, swallowing back sudden tears. "We'll keep an eye on her together," Laurissa says.

The squawk box blares, "Welcome to McDonald's, may I take your order?"

"What do you want to eat?" Laurissa asks.

I restrain myself and only order two extra-value meals. She gets a large Diet Coke, nothing else. "I don't think we should confront a group of armed terrorists on our own, Laurissa says."

"I don't think we'll have to," I reply. "We'll work on getting help on the way."

Laurissa hands me a bag and a large coffee. The words, "Caution, I'm Hot" are stamped into the lid, and an idea occurs to me. If we do have to confront Morris and his hench-men, I think I know how to do it.

Betsy rides up on her red Schwinn. I roll down my window and invite her in. I wonder if I'm doing the right thing. I've just welcomed Fake Laurissa/Betsy into the car for a road trip to try to stop her father.

70

Jake

Betsy ditches her bike, right in the middle of the parking lot, and hops into the back. Laurissa has the car rolling before Betsy can close her door.

"So this is your wet-dream girl," Laurissa says, glancing in the rearview mirror.

"More like my assassin," I say.

"I'm the worst assassin in the history of assassins," Betsy says.

"I, for one, am glad you suck at your job," Laurissa says.

"Whatever," Betsy says.

"What happened to your face?" Laurissa asks.

"Nothing," Betsy says.

"Someone's fist happened to your face," Laurissa says. "One of your victims fought back?"

369

"No, and it's none of your business," Betsy says.

Her bruises look worse than the last time I saw her, but I can't tell if any of them are fresh. "Are you okay?" I ask.

"I'm fine," Betsy practically growls. "I'm going to call the FBI hotline. You should call, too. Maybe they'll take us more seriously if we both report it."

"Okay, I'm going to try something else, first." I call the Indianapolis FBI office and work my way through to Agent Soufan's voicemail. I leave a message with my new cell number and ask him to call me ASAP. I tell him that the terrorists are going to strike again. Maybe that will convince him to call back. Then I go through the whole process again, trying to reach Tapper. But all I get is his work voicemail.

Then I call the FBI hotline and reach a female operator who sounds exhausted. When I mention terrorism and planes, she perks up.

I tell the whole story in detail, and then the operator asks me to repeat it, interrupting with dozens of specific questions. Then she takes my information—everything from my age, occupation, and ethnic background to my mother's maiden name and place of birth. I can hear snatches of a similar conversation from Betsy in the back seat. I ask the operator for Soufan's and Tapper's cell phone numbers, but she won't give them to me. By the time the FBI operator lets me go, we're in Ohio. Betsy is still on the phone with the same FBI hotline. From the bits of the conversation I've overheard, they've connected her with an agent who specializes in police corruption, and she's telling the whole story again.

"That sounded promising," Laurissa says.

"I don't think they buy that it's urgent," I say. "They

wouldn't have kept me on the phone for two hours if they believed that there'd be a crash in the morning. Maybe Soufan will call me back. I need to get a hold of Tapper."

"Because you've got some leverage on him?"

"Yeah, I think so. I don't know if anyone would believe me if I blew the whistle on him. But if he gets nervous that someone might take my story seriously, maybe I could use that."

Laurissa fishes her phone out of her pocket and dials a saved number while driving one-handed.

"Who are you calling?" I ask, but whoever it is has already picked up.

"It's me, Dad," Laurissa says into the phone. "Yes, I know what time it is . . . no, I'm not in bed, I'm somewhere in Ohio . . . yes, I know . . . I got Charlotte to return it . . . yes, that's why the alarm went off . . . yes, I'm driving. . . ."

Laurissa hands the phone to me. "He wants me to pull over, because he read some research on how dangerous it is to talk on the phone while you're driving. He's become a total Nazgûl about it. You'd better speak to him."

I'm surprised by how hot the phone is. I hold it in my lap. "What do I say?" I ask.

"We need Tapper's cell number. Dad can get it. Ask him to call Donnelly."

"Donnelly?"

"One of our senators? You know who our senators are, right?"

"Oh. Right," I say, although in truth, I had no idea.

I pick up the phone. "Um, sir—"

"You tell my daughter that she's to turn that car around this instant," Mr. Davis's voice is a booming bass, like rumbling thunder.

I start to relay the message to Laurissa, but she says, "I heard him. Not going to happen."

"Sorry, sir. I've got to get to Raleigh."

"I'll sell her car back to the dealership," Mr. Davis says.

Laurissa replies calmly, "That's fair, he can sell it back when I get home."

I relay the message to her father, who's momentarily silent. "Raleigh? Why there?"

"There's going to be another plane crash. If there hasn't been one already."

"Hold on." There's a long silence. I hear a television in the background. "CNN is interviewing someone who got sick on a cruise ship. A complete time-filler. So there's been no plane crash."

"That's good. Laurissa thinks you can put me in touch with an FBI agent. Tapper, he works out of the Indianapolis office."

"I don't know anyone in the FBI. And don't you want the FAA?"

"If I can talk to Tapper, I can make him listen. Maybe even make him help us."

"I want my daughter home safe."

"It wasn't my idea for her to come along, sir."

"She's always been a bit headstrong," Mr. Davis says.

"I heard that, Dad," Laurissa yells.

"Why should I believe any of this? You gave me your word that you wouldn't speak to Laurissa again. Why shouldn't I report the Prius stolen and set the cops on you?"

I'm not sure what would convince him. I could go through the whole story with him, but that would take time we might not have. I want help. Fast. "Your daughter believes me," I say.

"She thinks you can get Tapper's number through your senator. And hundreds of people will die if we don't stop The Sons."

Mr. Davis is silent for a long time. Finally, he says, "I'll wake up Donnelly. Might take a while to connect with Tapper this late at night. I doubt Donnelly has any kind of direct access to FBI personnel records."

"Thank you," I say.

"And then I'm going to call the police."

"But—"

"I'll tell them about the threat of a plane crash, not set them after you."

"Oh, okay." Maybe Laurissa's dad would have better luck than us convincing someone that the threat is real.

"You tell Laurissa to be careful. Tell her I love her. And that I might be able to keep her mother from killing her."

I relay the message, and Laurissa replies, "I love you, too, Dad," which is incredibly awkward to say to him, but I do it anyway. Betsy is still answering questions in the back seat.

I hang up the phone and set it in the cupholder. Something about the whole conversation triggers a wave of depression. I sink back in my seat and rest my head against the door. "Your dad really cares about you," I say.

"Yeah," Laurissa says, glancing my way. She reaches over, snags my hand, and holds it for a moment.

I think about what might happen when we arrive. Could we find the terrorists on our own? If we can't get help from the authorities in time, we need to prepare.

"Can I borrow your phone?" I ask Laurissa.

"Of course."

I use her data connection to search along our route for a

big outdoor or sporting goods store. I find a Bass Pro Shop in Raleigh about ten minutes from the Raleigh-Durham Airport. We should be there by about nine thirty in the morning. I tell Laurissa about the stop and program it into her phone.

My phone has three voicemails on it. Two of them are from my mother. I text her that I'm okay and not to worry. The third message is from a number I don't recognize. Instead of spending time listening to the voicemail, I dial the number.

"Tamer speaking." The voice sounds familiar, but I don't know anyone named Tamer.

"This is Jake Solley, who am I speaking to?"

"Agent Soufan."

"Thanks for returning my call." I give him the abbreviated version of everything I've learned about Morris, The Sons of Paine, methane, and Tapper's threats.

When I'm done, he says, "And this police officer's daughter, Betsy, she can corroborate what you've told me?"

"Yes. At least the stuff about the plane crash and her father. Tapper was very careful not to threaten me when there were witnesses." I give him Betsy's number.

"So that crazy-sounding stuff about Tapper and the drone you told me before? That was true?"

"Yeah."

"Look, Jake, if everything you've told me is true, maybe I owe you an apology."

"I don't care about that. Just figure out how to stop Betsy's dad."

"If I can prove what you're telling me about Tapper, I will hang him out on the line like yesterday's laundry."

Finally. Why couldn't he have helped three days ago when

I really needed it? "I need Tapper's cell number."

"Let me deal with him. But the more immediate problem is the plane crash. I need to get a team on that. Now. I'll be in touch." Soufan hangs up.

I call him back to ask for Tapper's number again, but the call goes straight to voicemail. I hang up and call the police in Raleigh. A bored-sounding night clerk takes a report. I'm certain he doesn't believe me. He spends more time asking for details about me than listening to my information about the threat.

Betsy finally gets off the phone, and I give her the number for the Raleigh police. Maybe she'll have better luck convincing them to take this seriously. She's got a message on her phone from Soufan and decides to call him back first.

I call the FAA safety hotline. They tell me to call the FBI and only agree to take a report when I assure them that I already talked to the FBI. I have no doubt that Betsy and I have stirred up a hornet's nest of federal and local investigators. I also have no doubt that they'll respond too late.

When Betsy gets off the phone, we go over the information she got from her father's computer. There are hundreds of places he checked on Google Maps, but only six places he viewed more than once. I program all six spots into Laurissa's phone.

"Did you try the National Transportation Safety Board?" Betsy asks.

"No," I say. "Don't they just investigate after the plane has crashed?"

"They've got a twenty-four-hour hotline," Betsy says. "I'm going to give them a try."

"We've got to stop for gas soon," Laurissa says.

"I thought these Priuses never ran out," I say. Behind me,

Betsy has reached someone and is starting to tell the whole story again.

"They have itty-bitty tanks and they sip the gas slowly, but if we don't stop in the next half hour, we *will* stop shortly thereafter whether we want to or not," Laurissa says.

"Can we get something to eat?"

"Sure. I'll pump the gas, and you go pick out anything you want. Junk food sounds good about now. Get me some Junior Mints. And Pringles. Barbecue Pringles. And a fountain Sprite, if they have it."

We stop at a gas station in Wheeling. I crane my neck around to look into the back seat. Betsy is still on her phone. I mouth, "Want anything?"

Betsy mutters, "Hold on a sec," into her phone. Then she tells me, "See if they have a phone charger. I'm almost out of juice."

Laurissa swipes her black Amex at the pump. When the card clears, she lets out a huge sigh of relief. "I was afraid Dad would cut it off," she tells me. Then she hands the card to me. I load up inside: beef jerky, corn chips, trail mix, a six-pack of Mountain Dew, a whole box of Hostess CupCakes, Junior Mints, Barbecue Pringles, Sprite, three phone chargers and a USB splitter. The clerk doesn't bat an eye at the black Amex with Laurissa Davis on it. The station doesn't have any shopping bags, and I've picked out so much junk food that it takes me two trips to get it all to the car.

The National Transportation Safety Board wasn't much help to Betsy, so we've run out of places to call. I happily munch my way across the next fifty miles of interstate. When I've finished everything off, I'm not hungry for the first time in three days.

Despite the Mountain Dew, exhaustion settles into my

body like sudden-onset flu. I catch my head drifting forward several times and startle awake. Betsy is snoring gently in the back seat. "Do you mind if I take a nap?" I ask Laurissa.

"No, go ahead."

I lean the seat back as far as it will go and wedge my head into the corner between the seat and the door. Now that I've decided to go to sleep, I can't. "Thank you," I say.

"For what?"

"The ride. Believing me. Trusting me."

"You know, I think that's what love is. Not the tingling in your fingertips when you touch or the flush of pleasure from a kiss. It's the hard work of understanding whomever you love, especially when he's not perfect, when not everything goes the way you dreamed it would."

I'm sure she's right, but "yeah" seems like a totally lame response. Instead, I say, "I love you."

"Well, obviously I love you, or I wouldn't be taking my last road trip ever in the middle of the night searching for some terrorists who'll probably just kill us even if we do find them." Laurissa snorts and punches my shoulder, although the expression on her face is grim.

"I've got a plan," I say.

"If we survive this, at least I'll have some great material for college essays."

"You think anyone would believe you?"

"Probably not. I hardly believe it myself."

"Yeah."

"Go to sleep, Jake," she responds.

And, lulled by the motion of the car and her words, I find that I can.

71
Jake

When Laurissa shakes me awake, it's light outside, and the car is stopped in Bass Pro Shop's parking lot. I rub my eyes, stumble out of the car, and shake the sandy feeling from my limbs. Betsy is snoring in the back seat.

"Did your dad call back?" I ask Laurissa as she locks the car.

"Not yet."

"We should call him," I say.

"He'll call us as soon as he has something."

We tear through the Bass Pro Shop at light speed, buying two pairs of high-powered binoculars designed for hunting and a ridiculously expensive prepackaged kit of emergency gear meant to be stored in a boat. When we get back to the car, I open the kit and check it carefully, making sure it has everything I need.

We're only fifteen minutes from the airport. I program Laurissa's phone to give us directions to the closest of the six possible locations where Morris might set up.

On the way, I check my phone for messages. There are two from Mom and one from Agent Soufan. He's on his way to Raleigh, but his flight won't arrive until afternoon. If he believes everything I told him, why is he taking a plane? He leaves a number for the FBI office—he calls it a resident agency—in Raleigh and tells me to ask for Agent Bowers. By the time I'm done listening to his message, we've reached the first location on our list. It's a cemetery across I-540 from the airport. On Google Earth, it looks like there might be enough trees along one edge of the cemetery to shield a group of tanker trucks, but once we get there, it's clear that there's nowhere to hide.

I program the second waypoint.

"Maybe they've already gone?" Laurissa says. "They could have crashed one of the early morning flights and left by now."

I pull up CNN on her phone. "I don't think so. There's nothing on CNN's website about it."

"If there had been a plane crash, CNN would talk about nothing else for, like, months."

"I know, right? It's the crash news network."

Laurissa's phone rings. I start to hand it to her, but she tells me to answer it.

It's her father. "Where are you?" he asks. I tell him, and he says, "We're about three hours behind you."

"You're what?"

"We're all on our way to you."

"Who's we?"

"Dieter, Hans, my wife, and me."

I hear the wail of a police siren faintly over the phone. "Not again," Mr. Davis mutters. "You kids are going to owe me a couple thousand dollars for speeding tickets. Second time we've been pulled over tonight. You'd think if the cops saw a black Mercedes doing a hundred and ten, they'd realize we have important business and leave us alone."

"Did you get Tapper's number?" I ask.

The police sirens in the background swell until it's tough to hear Mr. Davis over them. "Oh yeah, the reason I called. I'll text the numbers to Laurissa's phone. I've got to go." Mr. Davis hangs up.

My cell phone rings. I figure it's Mr. Davis calling back, and I answer without checking the caller ID. Mom's voice comes on the line. "Jake, are you okay?"

"I'm fine, Mom." Surprisingly, this is true despite my various injuries. For the first time, I have a plan—I'm not being chased anymore; I'm doing the chasing.

"Thank God I finally got through to you."

"I'm really sorry, Mom. I've been busy."

"Where are you?"

"We're in Raleigh."

"If you turn around now, we can meet in two or three hours somewhere in West Virginia."

"There's no way you can make it to West Virginia in three hours."

"I'm halfway through Ohio," Mom says. "On my way to you. I called Mr. Davis, and he told me where you were going. Turn around now, Jake."

I grip the phone tighter. The plastic is damp and slippery.
"I can't do that, Mom."

"Let the professionals handle this. You're a teenager."

Laurissa's phone dings four times in quick succession. I
glance at it. There are four texts with new contacts labeled
Tapper Desk, Tapper Cell, Section Head Angelos (Tapper's
boss), and Senator Donnelly Cell."

"I'm sorry, Mom," I say. "I've got to get off the phone. I
need to call Tapper. Or maybe Tapper's boss."

"The only thing you have to do is come meet me."

"I will. Soon."

Laurissa has pulled up to an intersection. She's mouthing
"which way?" at me.

"I've got to go," I say into the phone. "Love you, Mom." I
hang up and check Laurissa's GPS. I tell Laurissa to turn right
and then dial the number for Tapper's official cell phone.

He answers almost immediately, "Special Agent Tapper."

"Tom Frigging Cruise here," I say. "The same bunch of
terrorists who crashed Flight 117 are planning to do it again
near Raleigh, probably today."

"Is that a threat?" Tapper asks. "Threatening to bomb an
airline is a felony under Title 49."

"It's not a threat, you idiot, it's a tip. Take down these GPS
coordinates." I put the phone on speaker and flip to the map
app, so I can read off the five sites we haven't checked yet.

"How do I know this information is accurate?" Tapper asks.

At the same time, Laurissa has reached another intersection. "Which way?" she asks.

"Turn left," I say. Laurissa makes the turn, taking us down
Bluegrass Road, the second of the six sites Betsy flagged.

"I've got to go," I say to Tapper. "Get me some help out here. I'm just dying to show the tattoo on my ass to CNN."

"I'll be on a plane to Raleigh in thirty minutes," Tapper says.

I hang up the phone. Obviously he doesn't believe me either. With any luck, the terrorists will crash Tapper's flight. And Soufan must be keeping Tapper in the dark—Soufan should already be on his plane.

I turn around, planning to shake Betsy awake, but she's already rubbing her eyes and stretching. She tries Soufan's cell, but the call goes to voicemail. I give her Tapper's cell and the number for the Raleigh FBI. Then I try the number Mr. Davis gave me for Tapper's boss. I get a recording and leave a message.

Bluegrass Road is perfect—a quiet road with only a few houses and big trees that overhang a generous shoulder. But there are no tanker trucks.

"Sign says 'No Outlet,'" Laurissa says.

"Yeah, it's just a big T-junction and a horse farm back here," I say.

"I don't think Father would pick a place like that," Betsy says, interrupting her conversation with Tapper. "They'd want several ways to get in and out of position—at least one escape route."

"Yeah, let's turn around," I say.

I wonder if we're too late. They could have driven in last night and been in position first thing this morning. They wouldn't wait—sixteen tanker trucks are going to be noticed, no matter how remote the road.

I flip to CNN on Laurissa's phone—they're still doing some ridiculous non-story about cruise ship passengers getting sick. I've never been on a cruise, but what do they expect when they jam five thousand people on a boat for a week or more? Some of them are going to get sick. Duh.

We drive through a couple of nearby neighborhoods: Barton's Creek Bluffs and Hawthorne Wood Valley. There are plenty of ways in and out of this area, and huge trees that over-hang the road, but way too many houses. Lots of cars and ser-vice worker trucks are out and about even in the late morning—landscapers, plumbers, electricians. I cross the third area off our list.

Next I direct Laurissa to a huge electrical substation just north of us. There are at least four roads into the area, but when we get to the first entrance, we find a problem I couldn't see on Google Earth—the road is blocked by an enormous chain-link fence and gate.

Laurissa pulls up to the gate, and all three of us get out of her car. The road is perfect—gravel, but heavily packed, built for big trucks to traverse. The trees on either side of the road have grown up to shade it. Once they had their trucks parked, nobody would be able to see them from the main road or overhead.

The gate is twelve feet tall and secured with a heavy chain and industrial-sized padlock. "How are we going to get through that?"

"Do we need to?" Laurissa asks.

"Yeah. It's a perfect spot. They can cut the lock off, drive through, and replace it with their own lock. Then nobody, not even electric company vehicles, can follow them easily."

We're silent for a moment. I'm thinking about how to get through the fence, wishing we'd stopped at a hardware store and bought a bolt cutter or hacksaw.

Laurissa has been gazing upward. "Look," she says. There's a plane overhead—already tiny, ten thousand feet or more above us. "Would a methane release work from this far below the plane? Cause a crash, I mean?"

"No way," Betsy says. "Sixteen tanker trucks hold a lot of methane, but it'd be a race between the wind and the surface tension in the methane bubble. Any kind of breeze would disperse the methane before it got that high."

"We're too far away from the airport," I say.

We rush back to the car. "It must be one of the two sites on the south side of the airport," I say. "We should have started there."

"I'm going to get on the interstate," Laurissa says. "It'll be faster."

It's past lunchtime, but I'm not hungry. My stomach is knotted in a small, dense ball that's only getting tighter as the day wears on.

As soon as we hit the interstate, Laurissa jockeys the car into the left lane and floors it. I wonder what the point of flooring a Prius is, but the car accelerates faster than I would have guessed, and pretty soon the speedometer is approaching a hundred mph. Slow down, I think—getting pulled over isn't going to help—but then it occurs to me that having a posse of cops tail us to wherever the terrorists are set up wouldn't be such a bad thing.

Out of the corner of my eye, I see a tanker truck in the oncoming lanes. It doesn't catch my interest at first—there are lots of tanker trucks servicing the airport. This is at least the third one I've noticed today. But as we zoom past it, I turn to keep an eye on it. There are no markings on the drivers' door, none at all, which strikes me as weird. The back of the truck doesn't have a ladder like most do. And at the top, there's a line in the metal—a spot where the truck can split open like a clamshell.

"That's it!" I yell. "Going the other way! That tanker truck, it's one of them."

We pass an exit sign, "Lumley Road, ¼ Mile," but Laurissa doesn't pull over into the exit lane. "Hold on!" she yells. She hits the emergency blinkers and slams on the brakes so hard that I'm thrown against my seatbelt. Then she turns left on the interstate, onto the grass median, narrowly threading the car between a metal guard rail and a steel post that holds cables meant to prevent exactly this kind of maneuver. The car jounces up and down over the grassy median, and I'm hurled against my door as Laurissa executes a way-too-fast U-turn. She rockets onto the left shoulder of the interstate. Horns blare and brakes screech as the northbound drivers swerve to avoid us.

"Wicked," Betsy says. I glance over my shoulder and see that she's grinning like she just lost a tickle war.

We're back up to nearly a hundred mph in what seems like no time at all. "Wow," I say, "you should have gotten a Porsche, like your brother."

"I know, right?" Laurissa says. "I'm a *much* better driver. May as well enjoy this Prius while I've got it."

"There it is." I point at the tanker truck on the exit ramp just ahead of us.

Laurissa darts through three lanes of traffic, cutting only inches in front of a white Ford Expedition that's easily eight times the size of her Prius. Even with her white-knuckle driving (well, my knuckles are white—she's not even sweating), the truck is out of sight by the time we make it down the ramp, but we know it was in the right-hand turn lane. Laurissa turns right on red into the middle of a dangerous wall of oncoming traffic. A sky full of Canada geese couldn't out-honk the cars around us.

"Where'd it go?" Laurissa asks. I can see a long way down the road, farther than the truck could possibly have gone. But there's no sign of it. We pass an Exxon gas station, but the truck's not there. It must have turned somewhere.

"Slow down." I say, straining my eyes, scanning both sides of the road ahead. Then I see it—a flash of stainless steel through the trees on my right. There's an unmarked driveway. "Just ahead. Right turn."

As we reach the driveway, I can see the back end of the truck passing through a chain-link gate held open by two men wearing Arab-style robes. Their robes are loose enough to hide anything. There's a rundown parking shack and a peeling sign that reads "PREFLIGHT PARKING." It's clearly out of business and has been for some time.

"That's them," Betsy says from the back seat.

Laurissa starts to turn and I yell, "No! Keep going." If we turn, we're going to be spotted.

Laurissa corrects, and we pass the entrance to the abandoned parking area. I lose sight of the truck and worry that I made the wrong call when I told Laurissa not to turn. There's an overgrown strip of trees between us and the parking lot—I can't see anything through them. We pass an old brick commercial building that looks mostly abandoned, then take the next right. There's a massive Estes trucking terminal on our left, a squat, dusty building planted in a rutted dirt field that sprouts nothing but dozens of semi-trailers.

On the right, there's a clean white building that gleams in comparison to the trucking terminal. The sign out front reads CAPITOL CABARET, which seems strange—why would there be a nightclub in the middle of what otherwise looks like an industrial park? The lot is freshly paved, scattered with medians decorated with grass and palm trees. There are only four cars in the lot, but they look right at home in the luxe surroundings: a Porsche, a couple of BMWs, and a Cadillac.

Past the cabaret, we come to the back fence of the abandoned parking area. There's no screening woods here, just an eight-foot, chain-link fence planted in cracked, weedy asphalt. And a porcelain toilet, of all things, sitting abandoned by the fence. Laurissa slows as we pass the back gate—it's chained and padlocked with a big rusty sign that reads, "PINCH AREA, KEEP HANDS CLEAR!!" The asphalt slopes past the gate, and down the hill I can just barely make out the top half of a row of decrepit roofs. They used to be covered parking structures, but big patches of the roofs are missing now. The whole place is abandoned and desolate except for one thing: Every single one of the parking structures is occupied by a gleaming, stainless-steel tanker truck.

72

Jake

"Turn in here and park," I say to Laurissa, pointing at the business just past the abandoned parking lot. Its sign, ASTEEL FLASH, YOUR EMS PARTNER, means nothing to me. It's a brick building with some kind of huge chemical tank alongside it. The parking lot is nearly full—Laurissa takes one of the last spaces—but nobody is around.

I put both our phones on vibrate and hand Laurissa her phone and a pair of binoculars. I hang the other pair around my neck and grab the boating survival kit from Bass Pro Shop. I hope I won't need it.

"Stay in the car," I tell Betsy.

"No, I'm coming with you," she says.

Laurissa is glaring at me, but there's really nothing I can

do to stop Betsy from coming with us. If she wanted to betray us, she could have done it with a phone call long before now.

"Make sure your phone is on silent," I tell Betsy.

There's a narrow strip of trees separating the Asteel parking lot from the abandoned PreFlight Parking facility. We creep along the edge of the woods, working our way closer to the tanker trucks. There's an ancient brick wall topped with a tall chain-link fence between us and the parking facility. It would be easy to climb, but I don't try it—there's no cover at all on the far side, just a cracked and weedy parking lot. We pass a grove of pine trees that smell as gorgeous as the parking lot is ugly. Someone from Asteel has put a picnic table out here, but it's long past lunchtime, and nobody's using the area.

I catch glimpses of the trucks as we get closer. They're in neat rows under the parking sheds, their cabs toward us, packed tightly, the front of each truck touching the rear bumper of the next. Twice while we slink along the fence, a plane roars overhead, so close that the noise rattles the pine needles. Each time we stop, aiming our binoculars at the trucks, but the tanks remain tightly closed.

We reach a point about a hundred yards from the lead truck, crouch behind the brick wall, and peek over it. We can see the rows of trucks clearly. Laurissa trains her binoculars at the windshields of the semis, scanning them in turn. "Morris," she whispers, "second semi from the right." I bring my binoculars up— he's sitting in the passenger seat, wearing a white turban. The driver is in a similar getup. I turn slightly, scanning the windshield of the semi next to his, and startle when I recognize the man in its passenger seat—it's the same guy who threatened to stab or strangle me in the truck cab more than two months ago.

"I want to look," Betsy whispers.

I pass Betsy my binoculars, and she locks on to Morris almost immediately. "Dad," she mutters, and the word is loaded with some undefinable mixture of hate, regret, and love.

I text our location to Tapper's and Soufan's cell phones with the message, "Come now. They're here!" I make sure the flash is off, take a picture of the trucks, and send that, too.

Another plane roars overhead. I wonder what The Sons of Paine are waiting for. They must have a spotter stationed at the airport to report plane locations, enabling them to time the methane release precisely. Betsy told us she'd filled that role for them in Indianapolis—I wonder who's doing it here?

Another tanker truck pulls through the gate at the far side of the parking area and slowly rolls into position under one of the more distant sheds. They're staggering the arrivals of the trucks to avoid arousing any suspicion. Are they all here yet? With the angle and the sheds, I can't see them all. There might be sixteen trucks.

Another twenty minutes pass. Our parents are still almost an hour away. Soufan is also an hour away, if he got on a flight when he said he would.

I hear the roar of a jet engine approaching the airport, growing steadily louder. Scanning the tops of the trucks with my binoculars, I see something that chills me to my core. The top of every tanker is sliding smoothly open like a clamshell, in a way no tanker truck ever should. Soufan is too late. It's up to us.

73
Jake

I grab the item from the top of the boating safety kit: a flare gun meant for signaling passing ships or aircraft. I stand clear of the brick wall and fence and aim the gun upward at an angle that, I hope, will send the flare arcing high over the fence and trucks. Betsy and Laurissa speak at once—Betsy whispers "no" and Laurissa releases a fierce "yes." There's no time for thought or debate—hundreds of people on the approaching plane will die if I don't act. I pull the trigger.

The flare rockets upward, such a bright pinkish-red that it sears a temporary streak into the back of my eyes. What kind of explosion might sixteen truckloads of compressed methane make? I turn to Laurissa and Betsy and scream, "Down!"

I dive, flattening myself alongside the brick wall. Before I can even look around for Laurissa and Betsy, a flash of light turns the world to an orange and red duotone. I have only a split second to register the heat on my back, so intense that I can smell my own hair burning, and then the shock wave hits. The noise is overwhelming, like the roar a jet engine might make in the instant before you got sucked inside and reduced to meat puree. The chain-link rips free from the brick wall with a terrible screech. Trees are cartwheeling above us, broken or ripped out of the ground, roots and all. As the tops of the trees spin past me, I notice that they're burning. Then something slams into me, and everything goes dark.

74

Jake

I fade in and out of consciousness. I see Laurissa being loaded onto a stretcher and carried to a waiting ambulance. She's wearing an oxygen mask—I realize that I am, too. The hair on the sides of her head has been burnt away, and a few strands of her normally curly hair are almost straight, sticking out from her forehead like a frayed flag in the wind. I don't see Betsy, but there's another ambulance already leaving the site. Maybe she's in it.

I wake several times as my ambulance jostles over bumps in the road. The ceiling is a shiny white strip, lined on either side with bins. A guy in a light blue uniform sits beside me, watching readouts on a screen connected to me by wires.

Later I'm in a room created by a curtain. The ceiling lights are so bright, they burn my eyes. At least five people in white coats surround me. There's an IV line attached to the inside of my elbow, but I have no memory of it being inserted. Someone injects a syringe of liquid into the line, and a moment later, I fall asleep again.

I wake in a hospital room almost identical to the one at Methodist Hospital, where I was when all this started. There's no tube in my throat this time, thank God, and I'm lying on my side, not my back. Mom is sitting beside the bed, holding my hand.

"Is Laurissa . . . ?"

"She's okay," Mom says quietly. "A few burns on her back and a couple of broken ribs. She's in a lot better shape than you are. Her room is three doors down. She dragged you out of the fire—saved your life."

"Again," I say. The back of my neck feels like it's on fire. I tell Mom.

"The nurse said you might need a little more painkiller." Mom picks up a box with a button that connects with my IV and pushes it. "It'll take a few minutes to kick in. You've got another concussion, too."

"That's not good." I remember something from health class about the dangers of multiple concussions—higher risk for brain damage.

"No," Mom says. "You've got to quit ramming your head into stuff."

"Good advice. Did the plane . . . ?"

"The pilot saw the explosion. The plane got bucked around a little, so he looped around and landed. Nobody was hurt."

"Good."

"The terrorists? Morris?"

"Nobody could have survived. They were still trying to get the fire under control when I got there. Jesus, Jake, I thought you must be dead. I couldn't even get close—the fire department had the whole area cordoned off. All I could see was smoke—there was so much smoke."

"But you found me."

"No, firefighters saw you at the edge of the blaze and rescued you. A police officer told us that three kids had been taken to WakeMed. Who's the third, by the way?"

"Betsy."

I fill in the parts of the story she doesn't know. It takes more than an hour. Mom asks a few questions, but mostly she just lets me talk. When I'm finished, I'm not sure what to say. There's a long silence that I break with an apology, "I'm sorry I scared you."

"I owe you an apology, too." Mom takes my hand and holds it.

"It's okay."

"I should have trusted you, believed you."

"I barely believe everything that happened myself."

"I'm just glad you're alive." Her grip on my hand is so tight it's almost painful.

"Have you seen Agent Soufan?" I ask.

"No," Mom says. "But Tapper was here. The nurse ran him off, put herself between him and your door and refused to budge. The standoff didn't end until someone called hospital security, and they threatened to cuff him."

"That's awesome. Wish I'd been awake to see that."

"I wish they had cuffed him. That man needs a jail cell around him like coffee needs a mug."

"Is my phone here? I need to call Soufan."

"You just need to rest, honey."

"I don't think this can wait," I say. "Please? I need to know if Soufan is going to deal with Tapper, like he promised. I won't be able to rest until I'm sure everything is going to be okay."

Mom hands me my phone. I pull up Soufan's contact and dial.

"Jake?" he answers. "How are you? I'll be at the hospital in an hour, maybe two. We need to get a preliminary statement from you right away."

"About Tapper?" I ask.

"We're going to focus on wrapping up the terrorism case, and then shift to Tapper."

"I thought you were going to hang him out like 'yesterday's laundry?'"

"I will, I swear it. I'm working on getting Angelos on board. He'll come around. Just give me some time."

What would Tapper do with that time? I'm not sure I can afford to wait.

"Then," Soufan goes on, "when you're feeling up to it, we'll take another statement at the FBI resident agency here in Raleigh. There'll be a grand jury hearing soon, too."

"I just want to go home."

"I know. The next few months are going to be kind of rough. But I'll be there with you, Jake. You'll get through this. Okay?"

"Okay," I say, although I'm feeling a little queasy.

"And look, when the media gets a hold of this story, they're going to pester you. Camp on your doorstep, that kind of thing. Don't say anything to any of them. If you need help dealing with them, call my cell. Anytime, night or day. I'll be there for you, Jake. I'll talk your mom through it, too."

"Okay." I feel like I might vomit. Would my life ever get back to normal? "When do you think this will all be over?"

"I'm not going to lie to you; there might be congressional hearings. But within a year or two, you'll be able to put it all behind you. And Tapper will never be able to threaten another suspect. That's worth something, Jake."

"Yeah. See you soon." I hang up.

I relay Soufan's end of the conversation to Mom. She sits down on the edge of the bed and pats my leg. I think about it for a while. Putting Tapper out of business is important. But haven't I done enough? Do I have to solve every problem? And the longer this goes on, the less likely Laurissa will be able to put her life back in order. To work things out with her parents. Surely there has to be another way.

"Do you think Tapper's still around?" I ask Mom.

"I hope not," Mom shudders. I feel the same way about Tapper, but I need to talk to him.

"Could you check? Try to find him? I've got to talk to him."

"What? No. I'm never letting that man within a thousand feet of you again."

"I don't think he's the kind of guy we can afford to ignore."

"I don't trust him."

"Then trust me. Please, Mom?"

She sighs and gets up from the bedside.

While Mom is gone, I fiddle with my cell phone for a minute and then stick it under the sheet beside my hip.

Mom returns in less than ten minutes, Tapper in tow.

"Found him in the cafeteria downstairs," she says.

"You ready to talk?" Tapper says, looking at me.

"Yeah."

"That's good. Give us some privacy," he says, looking at Mom and hooking his thumb at the door. Mom's face twists like she's going to literally growl at and possibly bite Tapper.

I speak up quickly, "No, stay," I say. "Isn't it illegal to question a seventeen-year-old without his parent present?"

"Not when there's a terrorist cell on the loose, it's not."

"They're not on the loose. They're dead."

"Who supported them? Who paid for all those crazy customized tanker trucks? Morris sure as hell couldn't afford it on a cop's salary."

"I have no clue. Ask Betsy."

"I will. But you and I need to start over," Tapper says. "At the beginning. When were you first—"

"No," I say. "We're not going through all your bullshit again. You've got two choices, Tapper. You can keep right on with your crazy cowboy act, in which case I'm going to get nurse Stalingrad back in here to throw you out."

"There's already a subpoena in the works—"

"And then I'll invite every reporter in the country in here, and I'll tell them everything, Tapper. I'll tell them about your little drone program, all your dirty little illegal threats, and how you tried to murder my girlfriend just to put pressure on me."

"Nobody will believe you."

"So what? It'll raise questions. They'll start looking at you. They'll find something. I'm sure I wasn't the first suspect you've bullied."

"You're not scaring me, Jake. If the American people knew

SURFACE TENSION   401

what I do, they'd thank me for it. I'd strain my neck under the weight of all the medals they'd hang on me."

"You're proud of it. Proud of trying to kill my girlfriend. Proud of torturing me, turning my life upside down."

"Damn right I am. I'd do it all again. I do what it takes. Someone has to."

"Even if it's completely illegal," I say.

"Whatever it takes," Tapper says.

I take my cell phone out from under the bed sheets and tap a few buttons. Tapper's voice plays back, small and tinny from the cell phone speakers. I turn the volume up, and we listen to the last few seconds of the conversation in silence. "Whatever it takes," Tapper's voice says, and I click off the recording. Tapper lunges toward me, and my mom grabs him from behind, wrapping her arms around him, like he's choking and she's giving him the Heimlich. She knocks the wind out of his lungs, and he doubles over, gasping and coughing.

I slide the cell phone out of sight under my butt. The phone's corner digs uncomfortably into my wound, and I scooch sideways a little. The call button for the nurse is on a cord beside me. I put my hand over it but don't push it yet.

"There's another option," I say as Mom releases Tapper, and he falls to his knees, still gasping. "Laurissa and I were never there. You keep us completely out of it. Give all the credit to Betsy. She tipped you off. Blame the explosion on a terrorist screw up—one of them lit a cigarette or something and blew the whole gang sky-high. That happens, right? Suicide bombers detonate too early, bump the button or whatever."

"And if I keep your name out of it, what do I get?" Tapper asks.

"Nobody ever finds out about your nasty little drone program. I'll tell Soufan I'm not going to testify. We leave it all as it stands. I got shot by some random guy celebrating on Rockville Road. Nobody finds out he was just your patsy."

"Jake, no," Mom says. "What if he does this to someone else? This guy belongs in prison, or at least fired from the FBI."

I turn toward Mom. "If we try to take him down, we'll be tied up in court cases, a media circus, maybe even congressional hearings, for years. I don't want that. I want to be safe. I want to be normal again. Maybe even ride my bike without worrying about a drone overhead."

"I get your cell phone, too. As part of the deal. Now." Tapper holds out his hand.

"No. I'm keeping my phone. And that recording. As insurance on your good behavior."

"And what insurance do I have of your good behavior? There are records of you and Miss Davis being taken from the crime scene. Those will have to disappear or be explained somehow."

"I'm totally confident you can make that happen," I say.

"But I do all that work, and then you screw me afterward?"

"You'll still have your drone program. If I come after you, I'm going to do it now and in the noisiest way possible, so that if you use your drones, everyone will know it was you. Better for both of us if we agree to forget about each other. Forever." I hold out my hand toward him, although I'd rather grab a rattlesnake. "Deal?"

There's a long pause while Tapper stares at my outstretched hand. Then finally he seizes it. "Done." Tapper drops my hand, pivots, and strides out of the hospital room and—I hope—out of my life forever.

As soon as he's gone, I mash the nurse's call button under my hand. "That was awesome," I tell Mom. "Thanks for grabbing him like that. I thought he was going to puke."

"I wish he had," Mom says. "I'd like to squeeze that guy so hard he pukes his heart and lungs out."

"Is that even possible?" I ask.

"I doubt it." Mom says.

The nurse comes in, and I ask her, "Is there any way . . . would it be possible to see Laurissa—Miss Davis, I mean? She's just a few doors down, right?"

The nurse looks me over critically. Maybe the desperation I feel seeps from my face, because after a minute, she relents. "Okay. Just for a few minutes. I'll be right back with a wheelchair."

One of the German bodyguards is standing outside Laurissa's room. He shakes his head and holds out a hand to stop us.

"Please?" I say. "Could I at least ask Mr. Davis for permission to see her?"

He opens the door and whispers something. A moment later Mr. Davis comes to the door. He looks haggard, as if he hasn't slept in days. I look past him to where Laurissa is snoozing on the bed, her head turned toward me. I've never wanted anything as much as I want to cross the eight feet between us, to hold her gently and kiss her. But Mr. Davis stands between us.

"No, Jake," he says before I can even ask.

"But—"

"I'm thankful that my daughter is safe. But there's already been an FBI agent coming around, wanting to talk to her. Because of you, she's going to be tied up in months of interrogations at a time when she should be enjoying her teenage years and working to get into a good college."

"I took care of that." I describe my deal with Tapper to Mr. Davis.

"That was good thinking," Mr. Davis says. "And I'll stand by my promise to give you the legal help you need to clear this up. But my decision stands. You're not to have any further contact with Laurissa."

"But—"

"I'm sorry, Jake." Mr. Davis closes the door.

I reach out and press my palm against it. It's cold and solid under my hand, made of thick oak. Despite the fact that Laurissa is only a few feet on the other side of this door, it feels like she's miles away.

75

Betsy

The first visitor to my hospital room is a balding, slightly overweight guy in a bad suit. "Special Agent Tapper," he says.

"You're Tapper?" I reply. "From the way Jake talks about you, I thought you'd be, well, scarier."

"So very sorry to disappoint you," he says.

"It's okay, I suppose."

He sits down uninvited in the chair by my bedside. "Start from the beginning. When did you first become aware that your father was involved in illegal activities?"

"I want a lawyer."

"You're not being questioned as a suspect here."

"Get me a lawyer, we'll work out a deal, and then I'll tell you everything."

◆ ◆ ◆

It takes almost two days to iron out the details. The court-appointed lawyer isn't bad—she gets me what I want. A new life, new name, and a new job far away from Indiana or North Carolina. I'll probably be sent to The Dalles, Oregon, I'm told. The Sons of Paine still exist. Swan is still out there somewhere, funding them. I must disappear to have any hope of a normal life. Although what exactly constitutes a normal life? Most seventeen-year-olds don't have two dead parents. Most didn't have a role in their father's death. Will anything ever be normal for me? I doubt it.

I also get immunity from prosecution for crimes I committed in relation to the case in return for telling the FBI everything I know about Swan and The Sons. I'll never be punished for my role in the Indianapolis plane crash. Or for trying to kill Jake. I'd like to see him. I'm not sure if I'd thank him or curse him for his part in killing my father. Either way, I'd apologize for trying to kill him. The FBI won't allow a meeting—Tapper says it's best to make a clean break. Best for whom, I wonder.

The day after my deal with the FBI is finalized, another agent visits my hospital room. He's short and dark-haired. He holds out a badge, but he's standing too far from the bed for me to read the name on it. I'm pretty sure I know who he is from Jake's descriptions. "You must be Agent Soufan," I say.

"That's me," he says. He doesn't approach the bed or extend his hand.

"I thought Tapper was the lead agent for the investigation?"

"He is. I've been transferred," Soufan says.

"Sorry."

"Don't be. I asked for the transfer."

We stare at each other uncomfortably for a moment.

"So you're one of them?" I say.

"One of what?"

"A Muslim." Despite all the time I've spent talking about them over the years, I've never actually met one.

"Yes," Soufan replies.

"So why do you do it?"

"Do what?"

"Work for the FBI. Isn't America the enemy?"

"I work for the FBI for the same reasons most agents do. To protect the country I love and her citizens. To do some good in the world. And earn a paycheck, meager though it sometimes seems."

"But we're all infidels, right? Isn't that why Muslims want to kill us?"

Soufan sighs and closes his eyes for a moment. "'Take not life, which Allah has made sacred, except by way of justice and law: Thus does He command you.' That's from the Quran."

"Then why do they kill Christians?"

"The extremists aren't good Muslims. Mohammed, peace be upon him, made a covenant with St. Catherine's monastery that's honored to this day. He protected the Christians around him."

"I never learned about that."

"Almost everything you've been taught about Islam is wrong, Betsy."

There's a long silence. "I guess my father lied to me about a lot of things."

"Yes," Soufan says. "But that's not why I'm here. I'd like you to testify honestly—"

"I plan to."

"You're going to tell the world about Jake and Laurissa's role in stopping The Sons?"

"They don't know anything about The Sons. And Tapper told me they don't want to be involved. What good would talking about them do?"

"If Jake did get involved, the whole truth might come out," Soufan says. "I might be able to take down Tapper."

"Look, Agent Soufan, I'm sorry about my role in this. Killing the congressman just because he was Muslim was wrong. And killing all those other people on Flight 117 was even worse. I've got to—"

"Help me make it right."

"It will never be right. But I'm helping Tapper take down the rest of The Sons. And I've told him I'll consult with the FBI's Counterterrorism Division."

"But Tapper walks free, despite what he did to Jake. Despite the fact that he tried to kill Laurissa."

"Yes. Because that's the way Jake and Laurissa want it. And I owe them a lot more than I owe you or Tapper."

Soufan stares at me for a moment, then swivels and marches out of the room without saying goodbye.

The bruises and cuts on my face are starting to heal. It's right, somehow, that the last physical sign of my father's presence in my life is a bruise. The burns along my neck and back will take much longer. My father's medical insurance is paying for my care. When that runs out, the FBI will start picking up the tab.

The questioning and testimony will take months, maybe years. I can—and will—endure it. When I'm finally finished, there will be a new life waiting for me in Oregon. A better life.

76
Jake

Agent Soufan stops by a few hours after Tapper leaves my hospital room. He's furious that I've decided not to testify. We argue until my mother throws him out of the room.

I try to see Betsy, but no one will tell me what room she's in. The FBI released a blurred photo of her face, and it's all over the news—she's been dubbed "The Terrorist's Daughter." The media can't seem to decide whether to crucify her for her father's crimes or consider her a victim and drip fake sympathy all over her. They're treating Beaner in a similar way, although it appears he was duped by his partner, Morris. He did install the SIMON program on my phone at Morris's request, but he thought it was just a program that would allow them to remotely access data from my phone and track me. Nothing about me or Laurissa has leaked, which is exactly the way I want it.

The Davises leave the hospital three days later. One of the nurses tells me that they've chartered a private jet and hired a full medical staff to accompany them home. Mr. Davis still won't let me see Laurissa.

Two days after that, I'm declared well enough to travel. Mom and I pass the site of the explosion on our way out of town, and I ask her to stop.

The abandoned parking facility is cordoned off, still swarming with police and National Transportation Safety Board investigators. From the side of the road where we've pulled over, I can see what's left of PreFlight Parking: nothing. It's just a gigantic blackened area with a crater in the center. The back of the cabaret was blown wide open. Asteel's brick building fared better, but it's still badly scorched.

I step out of the car and stare at the devastation for a minute. As I turn to get back in, I see a glint on the ground. I squat and pick up a small piece of stainless steel. The edges are melted, not ragged—it must be part of one of the tanker trucks. I tuck the scrap of metal into my pocket and rejoin Mom in the car. I lean the passenger seat back and sleep through most of the drive.

Mom takes me to my doctor when we get home. The skin grafts on the back of my neck are going to need months of follow-up care.

I call Laurissa's house almost every day. On the rare occasions when I reach Mr. Davis, he's kind, but adamant. I'm not to speak to Laurissa.

Nothing changes until the day Laurissa's school, Park

Tudor, starts again for their fall term. I get a text from one of her friend's phones and suddenly, we're back in touch. It feels like I've been sitting at the bottom of a swimming pool, staring at the sky for weeks, and now, finally, I've been allowed to surface and take a deep breath. I drop my Physics II class and pick up Geology instead. I'm utterly uninterested in Geology, but it allows my lunch break to overlap with Laurissa's across town at Park Tudor. We talk almost every day. I eat my lunch in the halls between classes. Laurissa tells me to quit calling her dad. She'll bring him around, she says, but it might take time. I'll wait as long as it takes.

About two weeks later, I'm sitting in my room at home reading a book that caught my eye at the library—*Little Brother*. I get up to raid the fridge. As I pass the living room doorway, I see Mom standing next to the mantel. She's hunched over slightly, resting her head next to the urn that holds Dad's ashes, so close that her hair has spilled in a pool around the urn, embracing it. She's taken the medal off the urn, and it's clutched in her hands, the red, white, and blue ribbon wrapped around both of her palms.

I step quietly into the room and put my arms around my mother. She lifts her head from the mantel—her eyes are dry, which surprises me—and then she kisses my forehead.

"Mom, you know . . . I was thinking, maybe, maybe it's time. Maybe we should bury Dad. You know, in a regular grave or whatever."

"I don't know," she says.

"I . . . we wouldn't forget him. Not ever. And I think he'd still be here with us, even if we buried his ashes."

Mom disentangles her hands from the medal and ribbon.

She hangs it up, not around the urn, where it has resided for the last eleven years, but on a corner of the framed photograph of Dad in his pilot's uniform that's centered on the wall above the mantel.

Mom turns and clutches me with her newly freed hands, and her body shakes as her tears begin to flow. I hug her fiercely, holding on as I start to cry, too, holding on until the tears on our cheeks mingle.

77
Jake

It takes about a month to make the arrangements. We gather at West Ridge Park Cemetery: my mother, me, Zach, and Laurissa. It's the first time I've been allowed to see her since our road trip to Raleigh. Hugging her feels like standing by a campfire on a frozen winter day. We don't talk—we've done that almost every day for more than a month—we just hold each other. Tears are streaming down my face when the embrace breaks. Laurissa is crying, too. I dry her tears, and then my own, and we turn to watch my father's burial.

We stand around a small grave. It's shallow, only about two feet deep, and square instead of rectangular. There's a little concrete box at the bottom of the hole that's just a bit bigger than the urn with Dad's ashes. An attendant who works for the cemetery lowers the urn into the concrete vault. I stand between Laurissa and Mom, my arms wrapped around both of them.

Zach is on the other side of the grave. I'm going to start training with him next week. I'm not sure if I want to go to Belgium anymore. I don't want to be that far from Laurissa or Mom. Laurissa wants me to go for it, to try to get an invitation to USA Cycling's training camp. She's planning to go to an East Coast college—Princeton or George Washington, she hopes. Belgium is only a six-hour flight away. Maybe I will go for it. If I decide to try, I have no doubt that I'll make it. Winning a few bike races will be cake compared to what I've been through.

It's a gorgeous sunny day—more like June than early October—so beautiful it seems impossible to be sad. And I'm not, really. None of us are crying now.

There's a hand-operated hoist on the far side of the grave. The attendant attaches the hoist to the concrete lid of the vault and turns a crank. The vault lid lifts smoothly from the ground, and the attendant swings it out over the open grave.

"Wait," Mom says. She reaches into her purse and retrieves the partly scorched piece of white metal that has rested on our mantel for the last eleven years. She drops it into the grave. I take my own piece of metal out of my pocket—the scrap of stainless steel I'd picked up in Raleigh—and drop it into the grave, too. It clanks against the aluminum Mom dropped, making an almost musical chime. Mom nods at the attendant, and he lowers the vault lid into place, closing the remnants of Dad's accident and mine into darkness.

I take a handful of dirt from the nearby tarp and let it slide through my fingers into the grave. "He'd be proud of you," Mom says.

I nod, and we turn away from the grave, squinting into bright sunshine. Mom takes my left arm, Laurissa takes my right, and Zach follows us as we walk back to the row of cars that will carry us away from this cemetery, into the rest of our lives.

78
Betsy

There are two pieces of mail addressed to me today, which is surprising. Angela Klindt doesn't usually get much mail. Betsy Morris didn't either, but back when I was Betsy, I didn't live on my own.

The envelope on top is from Columbia Gorge Community College. I rip it open—it's my report card. Straight A's. The FBI made Angela Klindt a year older than Betsy Morris, so I've missed my whole last year of high school and gone straight to college. I worked my butt off to earn those A's.

The second piece of mail is a brown paper package about the size and shape of a brick. There's no return address. I tear it open, and bundles of 100-dollar bills wrapped in paper bands spill out.

I recoil in shock. There must be fifty grand or more scattered across my cheap Formica kitchen counter. Who would send me a pile of cash? Why?

My shock at the mound of money is nothing compared to what I feel when I unfold the note. The letter is printed on thick white paper and addressed to "Miss Morris." I glance at the bottom. There's no signature, just a printed name: "Swan." The letter reads:

"Benedict Arnold never redeemed himself, but you can. Instructions will follow. For now, retain the cash for operational expenses and stay close to Special Agent Tapper. The closer, the better. Burn this letter and keep all communications between us secret.

"Your mother is alive. If you follow my instructions exactly, you may earn a reunion with her on a pleasant Caribbean beach. If you fail, you will both be killed."

Acknowledgements

Surface Tension was far harder to write than I anticipated and went through seventeen major rewrites over the course of five years. I couldn't have finished it without a ton of help.

Thank you to the teen writers at the Antioch Writers' Workshop (Emmaline Bennett, Megan Betts, Kirsten Dilger, Emma Dues, Bailey Gallion, Emily Gallion, Mollie Greenberg, and Emilie Gunn) for their feedback on a very early draft. I cut almost everything you read, but I appreciate your help figuring out which parts I should keep.

Thank you to Aubrey Wesson for consulting with me on chemical engineering questions.

Thank you to the YA Cannibals (Shannon Lee Alexander, Lisa Fipps, Rob Kent, Josh Prokopy, Jody Sparks, and Virginia Vought) for critiquing *Surface Tension* twice. I owe particular thanks to Shannon and Virginia for convincing me to give Betsy her own voice in the story.

I had an enormous amount of help with Laurissa's character—Adrienne Butler, Edi Campbell, Ayanna Coleman, Kathy Hicks-Brooks, and Kirsten Weaver all provided invaluable insights. A special thank you to Adrienne for spending several hours on the phone discussing Laurissa and race in America. I learned a lot from our conversations.

Thank you to Khalid Ahmad Siddiq and Deeba Zargarpur for their feedback on Agent Soufan.

Thank you to the people of the Raleigh-Durham area for your warm welcome during my research trip there.

Thank you to the Danville Public Library—particularly for tracking down a copy of the Reid Interrogation Manual for me. Thank you to the Indianapolis Public Library, especially the staff at the Wayne Branch who gave me a grand tour of their back room.

Many thanks to Kate Schafer Testerman for her keen editorial eye and professional stewardship of all the business aspects of bringing *Surface Tension* to readers.

Thank you to Matt Buchanan and Brian Wheat for your hard work to create the *Surface Tension* audiobook, and to Matt for last minute copyediting heroics.

Thank you to Ayanna Coleman and Rebecca Grose for all their hard work making sure *Surface Tension* reaches its audience and for putting up with my horrible email etiquette.

Thank you to everyone at Publisher's Group West for your enthusiasm for my books and efforts to get them in the hands of booksellers, librarians, and readers.

And a huge thank you to Peggy Tierney for championing all my work over the last eight years. If you enjoyed *Surface Tension*, it's probably due to her editorial vision. If you didn't, it's probably due to my bullheaded stubbornness in not following some of it.

Thank you to all the thousands of readers, librarians, and booksellers who have embraced my work. I couldn't do this without you, and I deeply appreciate your support.

Finally, and most importantly, thank you to my wife, first reader, and best friend, Margaret. You're the bedrock under everything I do.